PRAIRIE CAT

Isabella and Holten were standing alone.

"I'm sorry, Eli, really I am!"

"Tell that to the poor corporal back there."

"Are you saying that I was responsible for that soldier's death?"

"If ya had stayed put maybe nothin' would've happened."

After gathering the newest batch of frightened settlers and helping them to bury their dead, the troopers and the scout had huddled everyone together for one last drink of water before heading for Fort Sampson.

While the settlers were watering down, Holten and Isabella had wandered off and were talking in the sparse shade of a scraggly cottonwood. The scout had already tried to cool off the troopers, who felt that Isabella had cost the life of one of their men, and was now attempting to convince the pretty blonde that the prairie was different from Boston.

"But my book, Eli! I'm already out on the plains, so why can't I just do the best I can? I'm sorry about that poor soldier, but I don't think it was my fault. I'll stay out of the way next time, I promise."

The pretty writer crossed her ample bosom with a finger.

"There won't be a next time," said Holten. "You're headin' back to Fort Sampson with the troopers and that's final."

Isabella eyed Holten with suspicion. Somehow, he thought, she knew that he wasn't so sure of his own words. . . .

THE SPECTACULAR SHELTER SERIES
by Paul Ledd

#1: PRISONER OF REVENGE (1147, $2.25)
After seven years in prison for a crime he didn't commit, exconfederate soldier, Shelter Dorsett, was free and plotting his revenge on the "friends" who had used him in their scheme and left him the blame.

#2: HANGING MOON (1148, $2.25)
In search of a double-crossing death battalion sergeant, Shelter heads across the Arizona territory—with luscious Drusilla, who is pure gold. So is the cargo beneath the wagon's floorboards!

#3: CHAIN GANG KILL (1184, $2.25)
Shelter finds himself "wanted" by a member of the death battalion who double-crossed him seven years before *and* by a fiery wench. Bound by lust, Shelter aims to please; burning with vengeance, he seeks to kill!

#4: CHINA DOLL (1185, $2.25)
The closer the *Drake* sails to San Francisco, the closer Shelter is to the target of his revenge—until he discovers the woman hiding below deck whose captivating powers steer him off course.

#10: MASSACRE MOUNTAIN (972, $2.25)
A pistol-packin' lady suspects Shell is her enemy—and her gun isn't the only thing that goes off!

#11: RIO RAMPAGE (1141, $2.25)
Someone's put out a ten grand bounty on Shell's head. And it takes a wild ride down the raging rapids of the Rio Grande before Shell finds his man—and finds two songbirds in the bush as well!

#12: BLOOD MESA (1181, $2.25)
When Apaches close in around him, Shell thinks his vengeance trail is finally over. But he wakes up in the midst of a peaceful tribe so inclined toward sharing—that he sees no reason to decline the leader's daughter when she offers her bed!

Available wherever paperbacks are sold, or order direct from the Publisher. Send cover price plus 50¢ per copy for mailing and handling to Zebra Books, 475 Park Avenue South, New York, N.Y. 10016. DO NOT SEND CASH.

#8
THE SCOUT
PAWNEE RAMPAGE
BY
BUCK GENTRY

ZEBRA BOOKS
KENSINGTON PUBLISHING CORP.

ZEBRA BOOKS

are published by

KENSINGTON PUBLISHING CORP.
475 Park Avenue South
New York, N.Y. 10016

Copyright © 1983 by Buck Gentry

All rights reserved. No part of this book may be reproduced in any form or by any means without the prior written consent of the Publisher, excepting brief quotes used in reviews.

Printed in the United States of America

For Richard Curtis, with thanks....

Scouting is a congenial profession
leading to a terrible death.
—George Armstrong Custer

Commanding officers are expected to
continue a pursuit until capture.
—Standing Army order during
the Indian Wars of the 1870s

ONE

Eli Holten hunkered on his knees in the late afternoon shadows and kept his steely blue eyes fixed on the five skittish pronghorn antelope that were drinking at the shimmering prairie pool just fifty yards away.

Holten smiled. It was dinner on the hoof.

The tall, lean chief scout of the Army's 12th Cavalry slowly, almost imperceptibly raised his 1873 Winchester .44-40 repeater to his right shoulder and squinted through the blinding mid-summer sunshine. A big, proud buck stood squarely in Holten's sights. The scout figured a quick volley would drop the buck and several of the other antelope almost in their tracks. Holten blinked a trickle of perspiration out of his eyes, licked his parched lips, and aimed down the long, cold barrel.

The scout began to squeeze the trigger.

Suddenly a twig snapped loudly off to the scout's left. The five nervous antelope quickly raised their heads and bounded into the sun-baked prairie beyond, leaping out of Holten's range within a few seconds.

The scout lowered his rifle and glared at the two smiling frontiersmen who were standing in the quivering bushes a few yards away. The seasoned men were part of Holten's hunting expedition.

Fifty-year-old Coyote Jim Stephens and young Kansas Joe Adderly were experienced army scouts who should have known better than to spook a herd of watering pronghorns. The pair of buckskin-clad hunters smiled sheepishly and began to crash through the bushes toward where Holten was now standing in the shadows of a towering cottonwood tree.

"The army sent us out here to hunt up some game," said Holten dryly. "But I don't reckon we'll get much if you two keep stompin' through the brush like a couple of pregnant buffaloes!"

Old Coyote Jim cackled. "Hell, Holten," he said in a thin, reedy voice that seemed strained from years of yelling through wind storms and prairie dust, "seems like it was you who done spooked them antelope. Maybe it's 'cause you're a little nervous 'bout tomorrow, eh?"

Both of the approaching scouts laughed.

Kansas Joe slapped Holten on the shoulder. "A scout like you who done survived Indian wars, outlaw gunfights, and prairie dust storms," added the young hunter, "sure as hell shouldn't be so nervous about gettin' married!"

The two plainsmen laughed again.

Coyote Jim Stephens and Kansas Joe Adderly were longtime scouts with the Army's 12th Cavalry, having fought in most of the bloody Indian battles across the Dakota Territory during the past several years. Holten respected both of the weathered plainsmen as friends and as fellow frontiersmen, and his sudden anger was short-lived.

Coyote Jim was a wizened old timer with a lean, white-bearded face and long, scraggly white hair that poked out from beneath his time-worn coonskin cap. Buckskin-clad and hardened from his many years in the wild and woolly Dakota prairie, Coyote Jim got his nickname a few years ago by waiting out a raging blizzard in a den full of nervous coyotes. A sure shot with his Sharps .50 caliber rifle, the aging frontiersman was just about at the end of his colorful scouting days and was used mainly by the army on relatively harmless hunting expeditions.

Kansas Joe Adderly, on the other hand, was a short twenty-six-year-old half-breed scout who was considered to be one of the best trackers on the Dakota plains, but not much of a hunter or gunslinger. Joe's long black hair and high-cheekboned face betrayed his half-Sioux heritage, and his swarthy appearance and flashing brown eyes often scared away many white settlers who were looking for a little funnin' at the expense of a drunken half-breed.

Holten and his two scouting friends had been sent into the sun-baked, mid-summer prairie by the army to bag enough wild game to feed the soldiers and the many guests who were expected to crowd into the fort in the morning. For the next day was going to be a time to remember at old Fort Rawlins—it was the day the Sioux nation was finally going to end years of bloody warfare and sign a peace treaty with the United States Government.

For Holten the day was going to be doubly important.

Besides watching his former Sioux brothers, with whom he had spent six years of his life, sign the long awaited peace treaty, the scout was also changing his life. Eli Holten, who after twenty years had the look of the plains etched in his leathery face, was going to resign as an army scout.

And he was going to get married!

The pretty dark-haired girl was called Yellow Feather and she was from the Oglala Sioux tribe where Holten had spent some of the happiest days of his life. The nineteen-year-old Indian maiden had swept the veteran scout off his feet with her sensuous sex appeal, and to everyone's surprise—especially Holten's—the two suddenly decided to get married and settle down on the Dakota plains. The date of the wedding, during the peace treaty ceremony, was the idea of General Frank Corrington, the 12th Cavalry's wiry commanding officer.

Now, during the last minute hunting expedition on the scorching plains, Holten was still the target of numerous jibes from his fellow scouts. After all, scouts weren't supposed to get married. Kansas Joe insisted that the antelope had bounded away because of Holten's jittery, pre-wedding nerves.

"I ain't nervous about nothin'!" said Holten.

"'Cept some purty little Sioux squaw who's waitin' for ya back at Fort Rawlins, eh?" said Coyote Jim with a mischievous glint in his sparkling blue eyes.

Kansas Joe laughed and shook his head. "Never thought I'd see the day when ol' Eli Holten would be gettin' hitched! And doin' it real proper like with a big weddin' and all!"

"Ya might never see another day in your life, half-breed, after I skin ya alive for chasin' away all the game!" said Holten with mock anger in his voice. "Now let's do what in hell we was sent out here for."

Then a wide grin creased Holten's leathery face.

"Besides," he said with a smile, sudden images of Yellow Feather's luscious golden body flashing in front of his mind's eye, "I'm kinda anxious to get this over with and get back to the fort, boys, if ya catch my meanin'."

All three of the scouts roared with laughter.

"I'll head after them pronghorns," said Holten, padding through the knee-high buffalo grass. His Winchester .44-40 was gripped in his big right hand. "Why don't you boys see if ya can't rustle up a mess of prairie chickens for tomorrow's dinner table?"

"Still thinkin' 'bout tomorrow, eh?" said Coyote Jim.

"Get movin' before I plug ya with lead!"

The two army scouts laughed and headed for the plains.

After watching the two buckskin figures disappear into the bush-covered prairie in search of some plump grouse, Holten made sure he still had his Remington .44 pistol strapped to his belt and his fearsome ten-inch Bowie knife in its sheath on his hip. Looking over his shoulder the scout checked to see if his big, intelligent sorrel gelding was still tethered in the copse of pine trees behind him.

Then glancing quickly at the parched, sun-baked July prairie that only a few weeks ago had been dusted with layers of purple, red, and yellow flowers, the scout gripped his repeating rifle and headed after the fleeing antelope just ahead. After all, he wanted the guests at his wedding to be happy and well-fed.

The sudden thought of the impending wedding sent a strange chill of anxiety rippling along the scout's spine. He had fought toe to toe with some of the toughest killers on the Dakota plains, shot bloodthirsty Indians who were about to plunge glistening knives into his chest, and galloped full speed into a stampeding herd of wild buffalo. Yet the thought of getting married inexplicably made his stomach churn with cold, nauseating anxiety.

Then the scout pictured Yellow Feather's billowy breasts, curvaceous hips, and long, lovely legs that came together in a bushy black garden of sexual delights, and he knew he was making the right decision.

If ever a scout was going to settle down, a young Indian girl from one of the plains tribes was the type of woman he needed. And, thought Holten, they didn't come any prettier or sexier than Yellow Feather. He felt an erection growing in his buckskin pants.

The scout wiped the sweat from his brow with the sleeves of his buckskin jacket, smiled at his recollection, and started to concentrate once again on the task at hand. Holten spotted the skittish, brown-haired antelope at another shimmering pool of water near some trees just ahead, and this time he was determined to bag a few bucks. The moccasin-clad scout padded cautiously through the grass like an Indian hunter approaching a giant buffalo.

Then Holten saw two Indians just twenty feet away.

The shaven-headed Pawnee warriors were lying flat on their bellies on a nearby grassy ridge and were looking intently across the hazy late afternoon prairie at Fort

Rawlins in the distance.

The scout's pulse quickened. As a member of the Oglala Sioux, Holten had learned about the great animosity between the Pawnee and his old tribe. He had even killed his share of the near-bald braves who wore long, black ridges of hair down the center of their scalps. Now the sudden appearance of a couple of brightly-painted Pawnee spies caused the scout to straighten suddenly and arc his Winchester in the direction of the Indians.

Suddenly a crow cawed and a blue jay shrieked.

The startled Pawnee braves whirled toward Holten with the speed of a couple of frightened wildcats and, with survival instincts honed from years of savage warfare on the treacherous Dakota plains, the two painted, shaven-headed warriors quickly sent a couple of iron-tipped arrows whooshing in the direction of the wide-eyed scout.

Holten dived to his left with the quickness of a striking rattlesnake, landing hard on the dusty ground and momentarily jarring the Winchester from his hands. The whistling arrows whooshed harmlessly over his head. Then one of the hard-faced Pawnee warriors quickly unsheathed a glistening long-bladed hunting knife and lunged toward the scout. The other Indian spy bolted toward the plains.

Without time to bring his long-barrelled repeater into play, the scout quickly raised his feet and lashed out at the charging shaven-headed brave. His moccasin-clad feet smashed into the suddenly startled warrior's stomach causing the wide-eyed Pawnee brave to grunt with the impact and to tumble to the dusty prairie floor.

The scout shot to his feet, whipped out his fearsome long-bladed Bowie knife, and went into a knife-fighting crouch, his steely blue eyes glued on the glistening blade in the scowling Pawnee warrior's hand. His heart was beating against his ribs like an Indian tom-tom. The fallen warrior quickly regained his feet and, with his knife held flat in front of him, turned toward Holten in a crouch of his own.

The shaven-headed brave mumbled something in the guttural Pawnee tongue, one of the few plains Indian lingoes the scout didn't understand, and then fixed Holten in an icy glare.

"Yeah," said the scout, "the same to ya!"

Then as the blistering late afternoon sun began to dip behind the shadowy Black Hills to the west, the two knife-wielding combatants circled slowly in the dust like a couple of giant scorpions squaring off in a life or death struggle, the wide prairie as their special arena.

Both Holten and the dark-skinned brave jabbed and feinted with their glinting blades, waiting patiently for the right moment to strike. The handle of the scout's heavy knife was slippery in his sweaty palm as he studied the dark, shaven-headed brave in front of him. The war-paint-slashed face of the sinewy warrior was twisted with hatred.

Suddenly the hoofbeats of the other warrior's galloping war pony rose into the sweltering mid-summer air, and the remaining Pawnee brave flinched slightly at the sudden sound. The scout took advantage of the momentary lapse of concentration in his foe's defense to make a move.

With a sudden flick of his powerful wrist, Holten sent his glistening knife flying through the short distance between the two combatants and into the suddenly exposed chest of the startled Pawnee warrior. The wide-bladed Bowie knife buried itself to the hilt. The wide-eyed warrior screamed once with pain, clawed futilely at the blade that had slicked open his heart, and then slumped dead to the ground. All of a sudden the only sound drifting to the scout's sensitive ears was the barely audible drumming of the other brave's hoofbeats.

Holten stepped cautiously to where the fallen Pawnee spy lay twitching in a growing pool of glistening blood and quickly removed his knife from the dead brave's painted chest. Normally the scout's experienced frontier mind would be working feverishly in an attempt to figure out why in hell the two warriors were studying the fort so intently. Normally he'd probably high-tail it after the fleeing buck Indian.

But today wasn't a normal day in the life of Eli Holten. It was his last full day as the chief scout for the Army's 12th Cavalry, and he sure as hell wasn't going to risk ending his career with a Pawnee knife stuck in his gut—not on the day before his wedding!

The scout dismissed the incident as just two curious Pawnee bucks getting a close look at the soldiers' fort so they had something to talk about back at their campfire. The only thing that seemed strange was the appearance of Pawnee Indians so far north of their usual summer hunting grounds. Holten wiped the blood from his Bowie knife and continued his quest of the elusive pronghorn antelope. Let somebody else worry about the Pawnee, he thought.

After all, tomorrow's guests had to eat!

"Damn good lookin' antelope, Holten!" roared Coyote Jim Stephens as the three army hunters headed back to the nearby fort. Holten's big gelding was pulling a sturdy travois laden with the fat, dressed-out carcasses of a dozen pronghorns and the feathery trophies from his friends' grouse-hunting foray.

"Glad ya finally took your mind off that there Injun girl long enough to get us some meat!" crowed young Kansas Joe, a smile creasing his swarthy, high-cheekboned face.

Holten's friends roared with renewed laughter.

"Too bad you two didn't have much luck," chided Holten, gesturing to the small mound of freshly-killed prairie chickens on the travois.

"We just wanted to let ole Eli Holten have the glory on his last day as an army scout," said Coyote Jim, stroking his snowy white beard. "After all, tomorrow you'll be cleanin' out the tepee and keepin' house for your lady!"

"Eli Holten, turnin' into a squaw!" said Kansas Joe.

Again the two scouts cackled with laughter.

"Laugh all ya want, boys," said Holten. "I'll be thinkin' about ya during next winter's roarin' blizzards. While I'll be snugglin' up close to somethin' nice and warm, you'll be sleepin' somewhere with only your horse for company and your smelly old buckskins to keep ya warm!"

As the laughing trio made their way slowly toward bustling Fort Rawlins, Holten thought how glad he was to be marrying Yellow Feather; but at the same time the hardened scout knew how much he'd miss the camaraderie of his fellow plainsmen. One doesn't spend years at a job he loves, thought Holten, without some feelings of sadness when it all comes to an end.

Trotting close to the fort Holten noticed five dozen or so conical Sioux tepees already dotting the landscape around the army outpost. Tomorrow, he knew, the entire Sioux nation would be on hand for the treaty ceremony and the prairie would be clogged with hundreds of buffalo-hide tepees. The scout clucked to his horse and approached the square-shaped wooden fort.

Fort Rawlins, the headquarters of the Army's 12th Cavalry and the home of the garrison charged with the protection of the vast Dakota Territory and its white settlers, was a walled fort of the type built across the prairie before 1870. Its tall, rough-hewn log timbers rose twenty feet from the ground and encircled a compound consisting of a dusty parade ground in the middle, officers' quarters near the rear, enlisted men's barracks and a small general store off to the left, and a large mess hall centrally located for all to reach easily.

As Holten and his hunting expedition passed through the wide, wooden front gate, the normally peaceful army post was a beehive of activity in preparation for the historic peace treaty ceremony in the morning—and the scout's wedding, too.

As Holten entered the fortress a chorus of catcalls rose into the late afternoon air:

"There he is, the bridegroom!"

"He looks hen-pecked already, don't he boys?"

"Gettin' nervous, scout?"

The scout just smiled and led his expedition to the mess hall where Kansas Joe began to lug the bagged game into the fort's steamy kitchen. Ignoring the teasing all around him, Holten scanned the fort and felt a trickle of anxiety in his gut as he noticed that, according to the wishes of the visiting dignitaries from Washington, the treaty signing ceremony was going to be held outside the walls of the fort among the many Sioux tepees that dotted the landscape.

A treaty was fine, mused the scout, but something gnawed at his insides, a sort of sixth sense that had saved his life many times during his twenty years out on the prairie, and he shivered a little, despite the blistering July heat that was pounding the open fort like a blacksmith's hammer. But what the hell, thought Holten finally, I'm gettin' out of the scouting business. Let the others worry about the defense of the fort and the possible attacks by non-treaty-signing Indians with a hard-on against the army. The scout had other things on his mind right now—Yellow Feather, for instance.

After the last of the pronghorn antelope had been dragged into the mess hall, Holten turned the head of his snorting horse and trotted back through the fort's big wooden gate toward the cluster of tepees just ahead. The thought of his bride-to-be sent a twinge of desire rippling through his loins. The catcalls continued as he passed out of the fort.

"Wonder where Holten's goin', boy?"

"Ya ain't supposed to see the bride until the wedding day, scout!"

"Have fun, Holten!"

The scout smiled and pointed the prancing gelding toward a tall, bleached buffalo hide tepee among a cluster of five similar dwellings in front of the fort. Reining in his nickering mount after a minute or so, Holten slid his lean frame smoothly from the broad back of his gelding and tethered the horse beside a couple of skittish Sioux war ponies.

Then breathing deeply and squinting through the last vestiges of sunshine, the scout quickly scanned the nearby tepees and listened all around him to the babble of voices speaking Lakota. Somehow he felt strangely at ease and at peace with the world.

To Eli Holten the treacherous Dakota plains was the only real home he had ever known. Found wandering the prairie by the fierce Oglala Sioux when he was a fifteen-year-old runaway from Illinois, Holten was taken into the camps of Sitting Bull and Crazy Horse and raised for six years as an adopted son. He soon earned the nicknames Tall Bear, because of his size and He-Who-Never-Goes-Out-For-Nothing, because of his extraordinary hunting expertise. Holten learned to live and survive on the prairie like an Indian warrior.

Even after returning to white man's civilization the scout still considered the wide, undulating prairie his home. It was only natural, he thought, that he should be marrying a pretty Sioux maiden and be settling down on the wide open plains. After all, the prairie was his stomping grounds and the Indians were his people.

Now Holten sighed, turned toward Yellow Feather's tepee, and quickly pushed back the leather entrance flap. Stepping into the cool darkness of the tepee's shadowy interior, the scout blinked and scanned the fluffy buffalo robes on the ground, the circular stone fireplace that now lay dormant in the center of the conical lodge, and the beautiful long-haired girl who was standing at the rear of the dwelling with an expression of surprise etched on her pretty face.

"Tall Bear!" said Yellow Feather in Lakota, using the scout's Indian name. "I didn't expect you so soon! What will everybody say if they see you here?"

Holten smiled. "That I'm in love with the prettiest girl in the whole Sioux nation."

The scout and Yellow Feather went back several years together, and for Holten it was love at first sight. The luscious girl's sparkling beauty, sensuous lovemaking, and kind disposition had swept him off his feet. Holten wondered why it had taken him so long to propose marriage to her.

Yellow Feather strode briskly to where Holten was standing and touched his leathery face, her lustrous black hair falling over her slender shoulders.

"You are so kind to me, Tall Bear. I don't know how I could be so lucky to land you for my husband!"

"I'm the lucky one!" crowed the scout. "Let me look at ya!"

Then Holten gently pushed Yellow Feather away and began to study her beautiful features, a look of admiration spreading across his weathered, brown face. The scout's flashing blue eyes quickly roamed the smiling young squaw's shapely body from her firm round breasts, which were pushing against the buckskin shirt she was wearing, to the gentle slope of her hips and the roundness of her buttocks under her tight-fitting deerskin pants.

Yellow Feather smiled. "Stop it, Tall Bear!" she cried playfully. "You are embarassing me!"

"I'll do more than that if ya don't watch out!"

"Is that a promise?"

Holten caught the mischievous glint in Yellow Feather's flashing brown eyes and his groin quivered with sudden desire when their eyes locked. The scout turned and reached for a nearby deerskin water bag, his growing penis starting to press against his buckskin pants. Damn, he thought, what a beautiful woman!

The scout let the cool, thirst-slaking water trickle down his parched throat for a full ten seconds before he returned the water bag to its hook on the lodge poles. Like a coyote, he rarely drank while hunting, so his long body was thirsting for liquid refreshment after a long day on the scorching summer prairie.

Then Holten turned and stiffened when his steely blue eyes caught sight of the now naked Yellow Feather just a few feet away. The sumptuous maiden was standing in the shadows at the rear of the lodge, her billowy breasts, flat stomach, and glistening bush of pubic hair sending new waves of desire shooting through the scout's already aroused groin. She was a golden-skinned sex goddess waiting to be taken.

"You're supposed to wait until the wedding night," said Holten with a wry grin. He noticed the pleading look etched on Yellow Feather's pretty face.

"Please, Tall Bear! I need you now!"

"Have I ever denied you before?" he said playfully.

"I can't wait until tomorrow," breathed Yellow Feather in a throaty voice heavy with desire. "I need to feel the bigness of you inside of me right now!"

A broad grin cracked Holten's leathery face. "I always aim to please," he said, starting to haul off his sweat-clogged buckskin clothes.

"Let me help!" cried Yellow Feather.

Then, with the sumptuous Indian maiden frantically hauling off his clothes, her big breasts jouncing in the process, it was only a matter of seconds before Holten was standing stark naked in the middle of the tall, conical lodge, his enormous erection pointing toward the wide-eyed, awestruck young woman. Yellow Feather's flashing brown eyes flitted from Holten's matted chest, across his lean stomach, and fixed on his incredibly long and veined penis.

"It's so huge!" she shrieked.

"You bring out the best in me," said the scout stepping forward. He reached out and cupped Yellow Feather's billowy breasts in his big, rough hands, her nipples hardening as he gently kneaded the supple flesh, and her entire body quivering with desire at his very touch.

"Ah, ay, ay!" cried Yellow Feather. "Take me, Tall Bear!"

And then he did, gently pulling the luscious Indian girl down onto the downy buffalo robes and smothering her quivering breasts with kisses, his tongue gently flicking her rosy red nipples and causing the squirming sex kitten to shriek with delight at his erotic touch, the very closeness of her warm flesh against his legs and groin causing Holten to suck in his breath.

At the same time, Yellow Feather grasped the scout's pulsating penis in her small hand and began to slowly, exquisitely rub the elongated shaft from its hardened base to its sensitive pink tip, causing Holten to writhe in ecstasy at her velvet touch. The fully aroused scout felt as though he was going to explode then and there.

"Enter me, Tall Bear! Do it now!"

Without a wasted motion the panting scout quickly mounted the writhing hellcat, covering her tiny frame like a blanket with his muscular body and allowing her to guide his hardened shaft to her already dripping vagina, her hand pausing for a moment as she slowly rubbed the tip of Holten's enormous veined cock in the delicate folds of silky flesh at the opening of her warm and slippery channel.

Both of the lovers gasped with delight.

Then the scout plunged his elongated penis deep into the writhing young Indian's innermost regions, his rock-hard shaft piercing her slippery channel and causing the wide-eyed young bride-to-be to moan with sexual ecstasy, his repeated thrusts bringing Yellow Feather to glorious orgasms over and over again until finally she arched her body and the scout exploded into her, his hot, milky passion for the woman he loved spurting from deep within him until finally, after a few glorious moments of complete sexual release, the two sated lovers collapsed onto the buffalo robes and lay gasping for air.

As Holten lay on top of his sumptuous bride-to-be, his heart pounding against his ribs and Yellow Feather's breasts flattened against his hairy chest, he heard the excited babble outside the tepee as more Indians arrived for the big ceremony in the morning. From over near the fort he could hear the sounds of hammers and saws as the army prepared a humble wooden grandstand for the actual signing of the treaty with the Sioux.

The scout's fully refreshed mind quickly drifted to the treaty-signing ceremony, at which he would be the official interpreter, and the wedding ceremony that would immediately follow. He smiled and glanced down at the pretty girl beneath him, happy with his decision to leave the scouting profession behind so he could settle into a life of leisure and happiness with one hell of a woman!

"What are you thinking, Tall Bear?" asked Yellow Feather. "You didn't like our lovemaking?"

Holten smiled and kissed her on the lips. "I liked it very much," he said, his heart suddenly full of more love and happiness than he ever thought possible. "And I love my little, bright-eyed squaw!"

"I think we will be happy together, Tall Bear."

Holten smiled. "I know we will," he said softly.

Then the scout lay his head against Yellow Feather's supple young breasts and closed his burning eyes, his mind at peace and his entire being more completely relaxed than at any time during the past twenty years.

TWO

The evil-eyed gunrunner and killer named Black Bob Callahan sat atop his nickering bay and peered through the gathering dusk for the signal in the wooded valley below. His narrowed brown eyes mirrored the anger that was flaring inside of him.

An army wagon train laden with two dozen crates of brand new Winchester repeating rifles was due along the trail at any moment now and Callahan was getting edgy. He turned in his creaking saddle and looked at the mounted, two-hundred-and-fifty-pound gunman named Slim Powell who was waiting beside him on an overburdened chestnut.

"Damn army's late!" snarled Black Bob.

Powell shrugged his massive shoulders. "Ya can't depend on them soldier boys for nothin'," he growled. The fat killer then spat on the dusty prairie ground cover. "Hell, there probably ain't no guns in that there wagon train, for all we know!"

"The guns are there," said Callahan. "Our informer done told me them Winchesters will be comin' through this here pass just before sunset."

"Yeah, but he's army, too!"

"Maybe so, Slim, but we need the bastard right now."

Slim Powell began to laugh, his whole massive body seeming to reverberate as the deep, roaring laughter escaped from his lips.

"What's so funny?"

"Hell!" boomed Powell. "After tomorrow's fireworks at the fort our soldier boy might even be the commanding officer of the whole goddamn garrison!"

The two evil outlaws chuckled.

"It do seem kinda funny," said Black Bob through his laughter, "that after all these years fightin' them goddamn soldiers we'll soon be teamin' up with one of 'em!"

"Maybe we oughta go straight!" said Slim Powell.

Black Bob cackled. "Well, after tomorrow's attack we won't have no choice. After all the trouble we're gonna start, ain't nobody gonna let us go straight!"

Black Bob Callahan was a veteran drifter with an evil reputation that reached all across the vast Dakota Territory. Born in Virginia of a poor white blacksmith and a Negro slave, Black Bob's most striking physical trait was his dark, almost blue-black skin tone that some cowboys said looked as though the tall, lean drifter had been standing next to a barrel of gunpowder when it exploded, tinting his lean, bony face a strange bluish color. Thus the nickname Black Bob was attached to the young troublemaker and it stuck with the southern half-breed all through his nefarious bandit career.

A Confederate raider during the War Between The States, Callahan drifted West, as did many former rebel soldiers after the War, and began a life of troublemaking across the vast Dakota Territory. Cattle rustling, holdups of all sorts, and gunslinging were Black Bob's evil specialties. He soon formed his own gang of killers and cut-throats and before long found his dark, evil face adorning a number of wanted posters in towns all over the region.

Tall and lanky with square shoulders and a narrow, chiseled face, Black Bob's flashing brown eyes burned with defiance in deep-set sockets and his broad, flat nose gave a hint of his Negro heritage. His flowing mane of light brown hair was the only physical trait he had inherited from his muscular blacksmith father.

Deadly with a short-barrelled Colt .45 Peacemaker, a glistening hunting knife, or his fancily decorated Winchester .44-40 repeating rifle, Black Bob Callahan was often in demand by various evil prairie characters who had mayhem on their minds. Black Bob and his gang were the ones to hire, it was widely known across the Dakota Territory, if you wanted a dirty job done with ruthless efficiency. Like the holdup of the army wagon train that now was late arriving in the valley below.

"Maybe the army got word of our plans," said Powell.

"Naw, them soldiers probably stopped off at some whorehouse along the way to wet their whistles. They're late all right, but I believe what the captain told us."

Roly-poly Slim Powell snorted. "Ya got a lot more confidence in the army than I do!" he growled, spitting once again. "Soldiers ain't given me nothin' but trouble all these long years!"

Slim Powell was a blubbery gunslinger who was almost as wide as he was tall. His pinkish, pig-like face always seemed to be glistening with sweat, and his tiny, wide-apart green eyes gave his fleshy countenance a dumb-looking appearance. Waddling rather than walking when on his feet, Powell's ample gut hung over his gun belt and his thick arms stuck out at the sides as though his massive bulk prevented him from lowering them any closer to his body. The fat gunslinger's scraggly black hair stuck out from underneath his ragged, wide-brimmed hat, and his near-toothless smile added to the overall grossness of his physical appearance.

But despite his seemingly restrictive obesity, Slim Powell was a ruthless, efficient killer with an impressive roster of victims to prove it. He would shoot without hesitation anybody he considered to be his enemy, except, of course, Black Bob Callahan to whom the fat man was totally loyal. It had been Callahan who saved the roly-poly gunman's life during a raging Civil War battle, and now Slim Powell was a devoted member of the dark-skinned killer's evil gang.

Helping the gang to earn its deadly reputation through his many evil acts, the two-hundred-and-fifty-pound Powell had an almost insatiable sexual appetite and was especially fond of raping any of the gang's female victims, from age eight to eighty and Indian or white. Slim Powell was the consummate Dakota badman, a true connoisseur of wickedness whose very name sent shivers of fear down the spines of the local settlers.

Preferring to use the classic seven-and-a-half-inch long-barrelled Colt .45 Peacemaker, the massive killer was also adept with the two deadly daggers he kept in his boots and the Remington over-and-under .41 caliber derringer buried among the layers of blubber under his shirt. Most of the folks in the tiny Dakota towns where the gang ran wild, that is the folks who didn't run for cover the moment they spotted the over-sized bandit, never turned their backs on the waddling, heavily-armed, porcine killer for fear of getting a slug between their shoulder blades.

"There's the wagon train!" cried Black Bob Callahan.

The dark-skinned gang leader peered through the hazy evening air at the three cumbersome army wagons and their slow-riding escort of six dusty troopers that were starting to enter the wide, wooded valley below.

"It looks easy!" said Slim Powell, shifting his massive bulk atop his nickering horse. "Ain't gonna take long to wipe them bastards out!"

"Let's hope so," said Callahan.

Suddenly Black Bob heard the drumming of hoofbeats from down near the valley's edge. He shifted his predatory gaze away from the wagons and watched one of his top killers, called Big Nosed John Harper, gallop over to their position on the shadowy ridge. The hard-riding killer reined in his snorting mount in a shower of alkaline dust, the bandit's big, dreamy blue eyes full of excitement at the imminent arrival of the wagons full of guns.

"Everything ready down there?" asked Black Bob, his narrowed brown eyes searching the lean, hawk-nosed face of the mounted outlaw before him.

Big Nosed John nodded quickly. "We got the boys spread out just like ya told us, boss. Six of 'em on one side of the valley and six on the other. And nobody ain't gonna do nothin' 'til I give 'em the word!"

John Harper's most prominent physical feature, as might be expected, was his very large, beak-like nose that he seemed to stroke lovingly whenever he was nervous. A short, medium-built killer whose favorite weapon was his captured, three-and-a-half-foot-long army saber, Big Nosed John was the epitome of the scruffy Dakota drifter; stubble-faced, unkempt brown hair, and an unpleasant body aroma that would do any skunk proud.

But despite Harper's clownish appearance, he was a deadly killer who was equally proficient with a Colt .45 Peacemaker or a long-bladed Bowie knife. Also a veteran of the Confederate Army, Big Nosed John had been riding with Black Bob and his gang for over five years. His reputation around the plains was only slightly less evil than that of big Slim Powell.

"And what about our army friend, Captain Ben Zachary?" asked Black Bob with a wry smile.

"The soldier and his two dude friends are waitin' across the valley under some cottonwoods. Them easterners are ridin' in a goddamn stagecoach for Chrissakes!"

Slim Powell roared with laughter, his jowly pink face quivering as he moved. "What kinda horseshit pardners did ya fix us up with this time, eh Callahan? A couple of dudes from back East and a shaky army captain!"

Black Bob shrugged. "Hell, who gives a shit? Them gun-dealing dudes are loaded with loot, and they're payin' us real good. I got me a feelin' that if we pull off this job to their likin', then we might got us a good thing here!"

"If nothin' goes wrong," snapped Slim Powell.

"Ain't nothin' gonna happen," replied Black Bob. He looked down at the slow-moving wagon train that had started to enter their trap and a slight smile creased his dark-skinned face. No, thought the gang leader, this plan is almost fool-proof.

It had all started several weeks ago when tall, black-haired Captain Zachary of the Army's 12th Cavalry had contacted Callahan. Not trusting the moustached army boy, Black Bob had brought along several of his gang members to the captain's midnight rendezvous in the middle of the prairie.

According to the unhappy army officer, an upcoming peace treaty with the entire Sioux nation would bring a lasting peace to the Dakota Territory, and at the same time make life dull for those army officers, like Zachary, who felt that the murdering Sioux bastards should be wiped off the face of the earth. And it would also curtail the lucrative gun sales to the army by several big rifle manufacturers back East.

"So big deal," Callahan had said.

"Well," Captain Zachary had replied, "I have a couple of gun dealing friends, big executives from one of the East's top gun distributing companies, who also feel that the new treaty will be bad for their business."

"And what do they want with me?" asked Black Bob.

Captain Ben Zachary paused before answering. He was a tall, lean officer with bushy eyebrows and long, black sideburns. His thick patch of wiry black hair was cut short under his wide-brimmed officers' hat. A neatly trimmed black moustache gave his handsome face a business-like appearance, and his precise military bearing and neatly pressed blue uniform exuded a certain air of self-confidence and control.

But deep down inside the frustrated captain was

angered that he hadn't been promoted as fast as he would have liked during his ten long years in the dusty West. He needed some glorious military action to propel him into the spotlight and earn him the promotion he felt he richly deserved. The upcoming peace treaty with the Sioux would all but preclude that possibility.

Thus, his interest was piqued when he was approached by certain members of the gun manufacturers' association who had an ingenious plan that would turn the Dakota Territory into a rampaging bloodbath—and would present an opportunity for an ambitious, upwardly mobile army officer to show his stuff. So when asked by Black Bob what he was supposed to do, Captain Zachary looked at the dark-skinned outlaw leader and told him what the eastern gun sellers wanted him to do.

"They want you and your boys to start an Indian War," said the tall army officer calmly.

Black Bob blinked for a moment and then laughed, his deep set brown eyes alive with merriment. "And for this your friends are willin' to pay us?"

"Handsomely," replied Captain Zachary.

"What's the plan?"

"It's simple," said the traitorous army officer, and then Zachary began to explain the nefarious plot to the outlaws and outlined the gang's role in the plan.

Just before the day when the peace treaty was going to be signed with the Sioux, a small army wagon train carrying two dozen crates of repeating rifles was due to arrive at Fort Sampson on the southern edge of the Dakota Territory. With Captain Zachary's guidance and information as to the exact route and time, the gang was supposed to attack the wagon train and steal all of the guns.

Then, in a specially arranged meeting with a bloodthirsty Pawnee renegade chief named Mole On Face, with whom Captain Zachary had come to an agreement in a secret parley, the rifles would be turned over to the Indians for use in a special raid on Fort Rawlins.

On the day of the peace treaty ceremony!

"Give guns to Injuns?" asked Black Bob incredulously.

Captain Zachary shrugged. "With the Sioux signing that peace treaty, the only tribe around with a hard-on for both the army and the Sioux is the Pawnee."

"And your friends think that with a new war there will be a bigger demand for their rifles, eh?"

The neatly dressed officer nodded. "And by attacking both the fort and the Sioux during the peace treaty ceremony," Zachary said with an excited glint in his heavy-lidded brown eyes, "the Pawnee will ensure a long, tough war against two of their long-time enemies. And ensure more gun orders from the army brass in Washington."

"And all we have to do is rob the wagon train?"

"Sure," Captain Zachary said while stroking his black moustache thoughtfully. "But don't forget, Callahan, that once the Indian War starts, there'll be plenty of opportunity for you and your boys to raid some of the surrounding ranches and towns. The army'll be too busy to bother you. Hell, if the Pawnee do what they're supposed to do, the army might even take weeks to get itself together again!"

"What if the Pawnee don't live up to their part of the deal? What then?"

"I'll take care of the Pawnee," Captain Zachary had said finally. "You just get us those Winchester repeaters by raiding the army wagon train."

So now, in a tree-lined valley near Fort Sampson, Black Bob and his gang were about to keep their part of the bargain. The dark-skinned outlaw leader glanced quickly down at the approaching army wagons and then looked over at Big Nosed John Harper.

"Ya better get back down there and make sure the boys don't screw up," said Callahan. "We gotta meet with them goddamn Pawnee Injuns in about an hour and hand over half of them there rifles."

"Only half?" asked Slim Powell in a deep voice.

Black Bob nodded. "Our army friend thinks if we give 'em all the guns right away they'll high-tail it into the prairie some place and we'll never see 'em again."

"We'll get the guns, boss," said Big Nosed John. Then the lean, hawk-nosed killer dug his spurs into his horse's gleaming flanks and galloped down into the valley below.

"Well," said Black Bob, his deep-set brown eyes fixed on the slow-moving, horse-drawn covered wagons directly below his position, "let's give them army escorts somethin' to worry about!"

Slim Powell laughed harshly. "Like takin' candy from a baby!" he said, his tiny green eyes alive with excitement and his blubbery face creased in a wide grin.

The attack lasted only twenty minutes.

It wasn't really a contest.

Black Bob's hardened killers stormed out of the surrounding trees and fired a hail of hot lead at the suddenly startled army guards, knocking half of them out of their saddles before they even knew what had happened.

The three wide-eyed civilian drivers tried valiantly to turn their rigs around and head for the relative safety of some nearby trees, but a swift slash of Big Nosed John's gleaming saber decapitated one of the drivers while the other two were shot from their seats by well-placed blasts from Slim Powell's accurate six-shooter. All of the screaming soldiers were shot full of lead, but two of the guards, spewing blood as they ran, somehow made it to the cover of the surrounding cottonwood trees and eluded their pursuers. A quick search by the gang produced nothing.

"Where in hell did they go?"

"I dunno!" snapped Black Bob. "But y'all better find those army boys soon!"

"Hell," chimed in big Slim Powell as he lowered his massive bulk from his horse and waddled over to examine the wagons full of rifles. "Them soldiers were bleedin' so bad they're probably dead by now!"

So the search for the dying soldiers was called off and Black Bob and his boys checked the captured arms with all the spontaneous enthusiasm of small children opening their presents on Christmas morning. One of the wagons, they discovered, was full of fresh dynamite—perfect for creating havoc around the plains.

"We better get these here rifles off the trail," said Black Bob Callahan after a few minutes. "Drive the wagons toward the prairie and the goddamn Pawnee. I gotta meet with our army boy and his eastern dude friends."

"Really an impressive raid, Mr. Callahan," said the old, white-haired easterner. "I don't think the soldiers got off more than a few shots."

"Good job, sir," added the other dude, a heavy-set middle-aged blond man with a fancy knob-headed walking cane. "Perhaps we can do more business with you and your boys in the future."

Black Bob was standing awkwardly beside the two dudes' special mud wagon stagecoach and waiting for Captain Ben Zachary, who was listening in the background, to lead the way to the prairie rendezvous with the renegade Pawnee warriors. Callahan could only take so much of the easterner's bullshit.

"I'm sure Mr. Callahan appreciates your compliments gentlemen," said army officer Zachary as he stepped over to the specially rented stagecoach. The tall, ambitious captain stroked his bushy black moustache, straightened his neatly pressed blue uniform, and smiled at Black Bob.

"Yuh . . . yuh sure I do," muttered Callahan. "Any time y'all need another job, then me and my boys'll be glad to help ya out, ya know."

"Let's just take care of this job first," said the old white-haired dude. Black Bob watched the plump little gun dealer remove his wire-rimmed spectacles and clean them with his handkerchief.

The white-haired, bespectacled old man was Horace Van Nostrand, a highly successful and very rich gun dealer from New York City. The wealthy dude's neatly tailored three-piece suit and his highly polished boots seemed more appropriate for the big city than for the sun-baked, dusty Dakota plains. Callahan watched the little old man replace his glasses on the bony bridge of his nose, blink his narrow gray eyes as though to focus them, and smile benignly at the dark-skinned outlaw gang leader.

The second easterner cleared his throat. "Mr. Van Nostrand's right," said the fat, blond dude. "You and your boys handled the wagon train admirably, Mr. Callahan, but it will be the attack at the fort tomorrow that'll tell if we're going to have us an Indian War out here or not."

Black Bob shifted his gaze to the heavy-set dude who was sitting in the back of the stagecoach beside the old man. Elliott Brownstone, scion of one of New York's wealthiest families, was fat, unctuous, and very much a prairie greenhorn. About fifteen years younger than Van Nostrand, the rotund eastern gun merchant had curly blond hair that was graying at the temples. His large blue eyes seemed to mirror the apprehension he felt while travelling through the land of wild Indians and ruthless outlaws.

Brownstone's massive frame seemed to be pushing his tight-fitting clothes to the limit and his curled-brim English bowler hat appeared several sizes too small. Black Bob noticed that the wide-eyed, fat gun dealer liked to wield his shiny mahogany cane as though it were a sword. The uncoordinated dude nearly struck Callahan in the face once by accident while he was emphasizing a word with the cane.

"Well," began Black Bob, "I appreciate y'all comin' out

here from back East to take part in this here plan. I can tell ya that me and my boys will do our part to raise hell around the Dakota prairie."

Van Nostrand adjusted his glasses and smiled. "I was assured that you would do just that, Mr. Callahan. In fact, this whole venture is kind of an exciting change of pace for Mr. Brownstone and myself. And, of course, we hope it will all lead to more rifle orders from the army."

"And that means," said the fat Mr. Brownstone as he tried to pull his small derby hat further onto his head, "that the Indians must really make the army believe that there is a need for more guns!"

"Which reminds me," said Captain Zachary. "Callahan and I got us a date with some anxious Pawnee warriors. I think it would be better, Mr. Van Nostrand, if you and Mr. Brownstone return to Fort Sampson until the shooting starts tomorrow. Things could become rather . . . hectic."

"Yes, of course Captain," said Van Nostrand. "We've had enough excitement for one day anyway. It was a pleasure meeting such a professional as yourself, Mr. Callahan."

"Ah . . . yuh, right," said Black Bob nodding.

"Until later then, gentlemen," said the bespectacled old gun merchant. "Good luck, and may your attack on Fort Rawlins work as you expect it to."

The stagecoach driver, hired by Zachary, slapped the reins onto the butts of the high-stepping team of six skittish horses and the creaking private stage rolled out of the valley and disappeared into the gathering dusk. Black Bob shook his head slowly and looked up at Zachary.

"Never will understand dudes," he said.

"Don't need to understand them, Callahan. Just get along with them, make them happy, and then learn how to spend all the money they pay you."

The two men laughed heartily.

"Let's go meet the Pawnee," said Captain Zachary.

Like many Pawnee warriors, Chief Mole On Face was named for a prominent physical trait or characteristic. The muscular renegade leader of over one hundred bloodthirsty braves was short and broad-faced with a one-inch wide circular brown mole on his left cheek that darkened whenever the chief grew angry or was upset. As vain as he was violent, the shaven-headed leader of the renegade band decorated his red-painted chest with four hands painted in white, symbolizing the number of men he had killed recently in hand-to-hand combat.

Even Mole On Face's practical close combat weapons reflected the muscular chief's vanity: a shiny, factory-made dagger designed especially for stabbing and an ivory-handled, short-barrelled Colt .45 Peacemaker, with both the leather holster and the scabbard decorated profusely with highly polished silver ringlets and fastened with heavy silver buckles, most of the silver hammered from American and Mexican coins.

Mole On Face's flashing brown eyes burned with hatred for his longtime enemies, the army and the Sioux, and Black Bob Callahan flinched a little when his steely gaze met the half-crazed chief's icy stare. Callahan looked away quickly and was glad they were almost finished handing out a dozen crates of the brand new Winchester repeaters.

"That's the last of them," said Captain Ben Zachary, tossing aside the last of the empty wooden boxes that had US ARMY stamped on the sides. "One hundred and forty-four repeaters. Now let me check with Mole On Face to see if he understands everything that's supposed to happen in the morning."

"You understand that there sign language?" asked Black Bob, thoughtfully stroking his dark-skinned face.

Zachary nodded. "I sure as hell can't make heads nor

tails of all that Pawnee jibberish they speak!"

While Zachary was communicating with the Pawnee chief, Black Bob touched big Slim Powell on the shoulder and nodded at the hundred or so warriors who were enthusiastically poring over their new weapons in the clearing before them. Big Nosed John and the rest of Callahan's gang remained mounted near the captured army wagons at the edge of the clearing.

"Them soldiers at Fort Rawlins are gonna catch hell tomorrow, eh Slim?" snarled Black Bob.

The fat killer laughed harshly. "Especially since they think that the treaty they're signin' will end all the Injun trouble on the prairie!"

The two killers laughed heartily.

Finally Captain Ben Zachary strode over to them.

"Well," said the dapper army officer. "The Pawnee are ready. They'll attack Fort Rawlins sometime during mid-morning. I told Mole On Face that's when the treaty signing should be taking place. I'd like to have them hit the fort before the treaty can be signed."

"That there peace won't last long anyhow!" said Callahan.

The captain smiled. "The Pawnee are looking forward to scalping a few of their old Sioux enemies, too. It should prove to be an interesting morning."

"You gonna be there?"

"I have no choice, Callahan. Once the dust settles and the army counts up its losses, I expect to be named commander of the 12th Cavalry. I told Mole On Face to be sure and kill the bearded General Corrington."

Black Bob cackled. "Hell, with our own buddy in charge of the army," he said, slapping Zachary on the back, "the whole Territory better watch out! We're gonna raise some kind of hell!"

The three conspirators laughed even harder.

THREE

"Tall Bear!" cried Yellow Feather in Lakota, her brown eyes saucering. "What are you doin' here? If my father catches you in my tepee the morning of the wedding he may call the whole thing off!"

"I couldn't wait any longer to see ya," replied Holten with a boyish grin creasing his brown, leathery face. The scout closed the leather entrance flap of Yellow Feather's large tepee and gave his shapely bride-to-be a quick head-to-toe once-over with his piercing blue eyes.

Following their furious lovemaking session the afternoon before, Holten finally had crept away unnoticed from Yellow Feather's conical lodge and slipped into the enlisted men's barracks to pass a lonely night contemplating his future and remembering his past. Only an occasional late night catcall from the bedded-down troopers broke the lonesome monotony of Holten's last night as a single man. Sleep had come with difficulty as the scout tossed and turned on his bunk, vivid flashes of memory from his days as a scout flooding his brain: The successful campaign against Deer Creek Jack and his outlaw gang.... The crushing of a renegade Sioux uprising.... The elimination of the Lone Wolf Pourier gang.... The halting of King Kilpatrick's reign of bandit terror.... And lots more, including parlays with hostile Indian chiefs, week-long hunting expeditions, and dangerous treks across fifty miles of treacherous prairie as a courier.

Now the scout was giving up the adventurous life to settle down as a prairie homesteader with a sumptuous Sioux Indian girl who had stolen his heart. His thoughts about his future had kept him wide awake. But Holten finally drifted off to sleep sometime in the wee hours of the morning with sensuous images of Yellow Feather flashing in front of his mind's eye, and wondering, too, how much he'd miss all the action that scouting provided.

Then, when a glorious early morning sun had begun to brighten the shadowy prairie, the scout had padded quietly to his bride-to-be's tepee and slipped into the lodge, catching Yellow Feather brushing her long hair.

"Did you miss me last night?" she asked.

The scout laughed. "What do you think?"

"It won't be long now."

Holten stepped over to where Yellow Feather was stroking her long, lustrous black hair and gently grabbed her slender shoulders with his big hands. He looked down into the luscious nineteen-year-old's sparkling brown eyes and felt a warm rush of happiness spread through his chest.

"I love you very much," he said softly in Lakota.

Yellow Feather smiled and then reached up and touched the scout's leathery face. "I know, Tall Bear. And I will try to make you very happy."

"You already make me happy."

"We will have many children and all the boys will be army scouts like their father. And the girls will have big blue eyes and flowing brown hair!"

Holten laughed. "Whoa, there! One thing at a time!"

"Oh, Tall Bear!" said Yellow Feather as she wrapped her slender arms around Holten's waist and gave him a big, loving hug. "This is the happiest day of my life!"

The scout smiled broadly, kissed his bubbling bride-to-be on her forehead, and pushed her gently away from his body. Holten gave the smiling young woman a final head-to-toe glance and then turned on his heel toward the tepee's leather flap. Until now, the scout had thought he was incapable of feeling so much love for another person.

"Where are you going?" asked Yellow Feather.

"The treaty ceremony will be starting soon. I must be there to help interpret the papers for both Black Spotted Horse and the white chiefs from Washington."

Yellow Feather frowned and her pretty face was contorted with displeasure. "Why can't we just have the wedding ceremony?"

The scout smiled. "It won't be long now," he said.

Then Holten turned, pushed through the lodge's leather flap, and stood in the tepee-dotted area in front of Fort Rawlins. There the brilliant early morning sunshine smacked him on his weathered face. Checking to make sure nobody had spotted him leaving the lodge, Holten then strode briskly to the fort, his heart full of love and his spirits soaring.

After all, it was going to be a big day.

Fort Rawlins was bustling with activity as the hour for the historic signing rapidly approached. Pitched all around the parched prairie that surrounded the rough-hewn log fortress were dozens of conical Sioux tepees, their bleached buffalo hide outer coverings brightly decorated with colorful designs. Plumes of white cooking smoke drifted lazily from the small smoke holes at the top of some of the tall lodges. Inside the fort the entire 12th Cavalry, marching on foot rather than subjecting their nickering horses to the blazing summer heat, was preparing to move from the dusty interior parade grounds to the hastily constructed wooden grandstand in front of the army outpost. Even Coyote Jim and Kansas Joe had shaved and were standing nearby waiting for things to happen.

And on the canvas-covered grandstand, sitting stiffly in

hard-backed wooden chairs and sweating profusely as they waited for the Sioux delegation to arrive, were two bemedalled generals from Washington, General Frank Corrington of the 12th Cavalry, Captain Ben Zachary who was the 12th's second in command, and Eli Holten, who was going to act as the interpreter for the entire proceeding.

"Got word this morning," said General Frank Corrington, "that the regular wagon train carrying two dozen crates of new Winchesters was held up last evening."

There was a collective gasp on the grandstand.

"Looks like you'll need this peace treaty," commented General Maxwell, one of the two high government officials representing the President at the ceremony.

"It wasn't the Indians this time."

"Oh?" said General Maxwell. "Then who was it?"

"A prairie drifter named Black Bob Callahan and his gang of bandits," said General Corrington, spitting out the names of the desperados as though they were poison on his tongue.

Captain Ben Zachary stiffened. "How . . . how did you hear about the identification of the bandits, General?" asked the captain.

"A couple of the army guards escaped badly wounded, but they lived long enough last night to tell everything they knew to the officers at Fort Sampson."

"Maybe we need a treaty with the bandits," said Eli Holten with a grin on his brown, leathery face.

The other officers laughed.

Then General Frank Corrington turned toward his chief scout and grasped him by the shoulders, his soft green eyes full of respect and admiration.

"Things won't be the same around here without ya, Mr. Holten," said Corrington changing the subject. The wiry general spat tobacco juice onto the dusty ground. "Hell, now I don't know who I'll give all the dirty jobs to!"

The scout chuckled. "I'm sure you'll find somebody."

"Ya," replied Corrington, "but nobody who'll accept the jobs without any shit the way you always did. Ya did everything we ever asked of ya, Holten, and for that I want to say thanks and good luck to you and your new bride."

Holten nodded and looked quickly at his commanding officer, a man whom he'd gotten along with as well as anybody out on the plains. Tobacco-chewing General Frank Corrington was a Civil War hero and a ten year veteran of the Indian Wars. The general stood ramrod straight and was almost as thin, his lean frame hardened from years on campaign against various ruthless enemies. His narrow, hawk-like face sported a short, iron-gray beard that was streaked with a thin, amber-colored stain from tobacco spittle that never quite reached its target. The scout sighed, knowing that although he couldn't wait to settle down with Yellow Feather, he was going to miss being around the wiry, tobacco-chewing officer with the gentle disposition.

A voice shattered the scout's thoughts.

"Mr. Holten, do you think you can keep your mind off your wedding long enough to help us get this peace treaty signed?" asked General Maxwell, a short dumpy man who was one of the government's representatives from Washington.

All of the men on the grandstand laughed.

Holten just smiled. "I hope so," he replied.

"The Sioux are kinda late aren't they?" said Captain Ben Zachary suddenly from his seat at the end of the small grandstand. The tall, lean officer stroked his bushy black moustache and looked at the sun rising in the sky. "I thought the ceremony was supposed to be underway by now."

"You know the Injuns," said white-haired General McCormick, the other bemedalled officer from Washington. "They'll take their own sweet time gettin' here, you can count on that."

Holten saw Captain Zachary squirm in his seat. "Well, we ain't got all day," said the neatly dressed captain in a voice edged with irritation.

"Take it easy, Captain," said General Corrington, spitting on the ground once again. "We've waited this long to finally end the goddamn Indian wars, so we sure as hell can wait a few minutes more."

"Maybe Captain Zachary's got himself a hot date with one of them Indian squaws," remarked stubby General Maxwell. "Perhaps we can have a double wedding ceremony, with the captain joining the scout here."

Again the army brass laughed. Zachary smiled uneasily.

Soon the hundred or so neatly dressed army troopers marched out of the fort and took up a parade rest position in three neat rows off to the left of the grandstand. They carried only sidearms as a gesture of peace, their Springfield single-shot carbines having been left in neat stacks inside the fort.

Finally, just before noon, Holten saw Chief Black Spotted Horse, wearing the spectacular eagle feather headdress that signified his lofty position as the chief of all the Sioux tribes, and behind him, a group of twenty or so hard-faced sub-chiefs picking their way through the many tepees. The small Sioux delegation walked proudly, with their heads erect and their backs straight, their stoic brown faces conspicuous for the lack of white war paint, until, finally, they stopped in front of the grandstand. Black Spotted Horse raised his right hand in the traditional Sioux salute. The chief's many feathers blew in the gentle warm breeze that was drifting over the sun-baked prairie.

"How," said the chief in a deep voice.

The delegation of army officers on the grandstand rose smoothly from their seats and also raised their right hands, their chorus of "Hows" echoing through the tepees around the fort and carrying into the near-empty log fortress behind them.

"It is nice to see my friend Tall Bear again on such a momentous occasion for both of our peoples," said Black Spotted Horse in Lakota.

The scout nodded. "Thank you, great Chief. Peace has been a long time in coming. Now I must translate our remarks to the white chiefs behind me."

A smile creased the dark face of Holten's longtime Sioux friend. "That is one of the reasons we agreed to the treaty now. We know that with Tall Bear interpreting the words of the white chiefs, we will not be led astray by fancy talk."

Holten smiled and studied the feathered chief.

Chief Black Spotted Horse of the Oglala Sioux was a tall, handsome warrior with a big, hawk-like nose and flashing brown eyes. A master hunter and a fearless fighter, Holten knew that the intelligent leader of the once warlike Oglala now realized that the only peace his people were going to get would come from some sort of treaty with the whites.

Black Spotted Horse's appearance at Fort Rawlins right now, with hundreds of hard-faced but peaceful warriors behind him, marked an important moment in his colorful tribe's history. The Sioux casualties in battles with the white soldiers over the past few years had been tremendous, and the peace treaty would end the fighting forever.

Holten translated what he and the chief had been talking about for the benefit of the army men on the grandstand, and then turned once again to address Black Spotted Horse.

"You know General Corrington," said Holten in Lakota, gesturing toward the tobacco-chewing commanding officer of the 12th Cavalry. "And I'm sure you've seen Captain Zachary around the plains over the years. But these other two gentlemen, General Maxwell and General McCormick, are here on behalf of the great white chief in

Washington. They will present gifts to Black Spotted Horse and his sub-chiefs. And they will preside over the signing of the peace treaty."

Black Spotted Horse nodded his feathered head. "Tell the great white soldiers that I am honored to represent my people on this historic occasion here today."

Holten translated, then looked at General Maxwell.

"Mr. Holten," said the short, dumpy officer wiping some perspiration from his wrinkled brow with a soiled handkerchief. "Tell the chief that we'd like to start the ceremony by inviting him up on the grandstand with us, and for him to have his warriors perform their dance. What is it called . . . ?"

"The dance of the chiefs," said the scout.

Maxwell nodded. "Yes, yes, the dance of the chiefs. Tell Chief Black Spotted Horse and let's get this thing underway. This goddamn heat is excruciating!"

Holten translated the little general's message and then all of the principal leaders, including Black Spotted Horse, took their seats on the covered grandstand and prepared to watch the Oglala sub-chiefs perform the ritual dance of celebration, called the dance of the chiefs.

While the Indians were setting up their dancing drums, the scout glanced through the hazy heat at the assembled Sioux braves, squaws, and children and then looked at the patient, although uncomfortable, army troopers, who were standing at parade rest position in the direct glare of the broiling sun. Settling back into his chair, his buckskin clothes already soaked with perspiration, Holten couldn't remember another time when all of the soldiers and such a large gathering of Sioux had stood so close together for so long without fighting.

Then the scout spotted Yellow Feather.

His smiling bride-to-be was peeking out from her nearby tepee, her long lustrous hair glistening in the sunlight and her flashing brown eyes sparkling with merriment. Holten was suddenly filled with another warm rush of happiness, and he reluctantly turned his attention to the ceremonies in front of him, hoping to hell they wouldn't take too long. His job as interpreter was his last official assignment for the army before he was to be married.

TUM, tum, tum, tum. TUM, tum, tum, tum.

Soon the rhythmic beat of the Indian drums was echoing off the front of the rough-hewn log army fortress, and about twenty muscular Oglala sub chiefs, dressed only in skimpy white loin cloths, were dancing in a large circle before the grandstand, a spirited dance with lots of high kicking and waving of long buffalo lances. After several minutes the music stopped abruptly and the dancers jammed the handles of their brightly painted hunting lances into the hard-packed ground, signalling the end of the traditional dance that the Sioux performed before all major ceremonies. From the shaded grandstand where he was sitting, Chief Black Spotted Horse raised his long right arm and dismissed the sweating sub-chiefs.

"The Sioux are ready to begin," said Holten to the generals who were sitting next to him.

Little General Maxwell nodded, cleared his throat, and rose in front of his hard-backed chair. Then the army's head representative from Washington spoke for about five minutes, with Holten interrupting the perspiring general at every paragraph or so to translate the stubby officer's words into the Sioux tongue. The general told the Indians how glad the President of the United States, U. S. Grant, was to finally see a peace treaty signed between the Sioux nation and their white brothers in the Dakota Territory. Then Maxwell, with the scout translating, explained what the treaty meant for the Sioux.

According to the document the little general was holding in his pudgy hands, the treaty pledged that a forty-thousand-square-mile reservation be set aside solely for the use of the Sioux Indians in the Dakota Territory. In addition, the Sioux nation would receive government clothing, food rations, and one cow per family. Finally, the general held up a box full of medals and peace certificates that were to be given to the chiefs of the tribe as a token of the understanding between the two peoples.

Translating into Lakota, the scout held up the glistening peace medal that was to be presented to Chief Black Spotted Horse on behalf of President Grant and explained that the circular, two-inch bronze medal bore Grant's likeness on one side and a simple message of brotherhood on the other side. Holten also explained that the medal, and the peace certificates that were going to be presented to all the sub-chiefs, permitted the tribe's leaders to come and go from the reservation whenever they wanted. After he had spoken, the scout smiled and held up the official-looking peace prizes.

The assembled warriors whooped their appreciation.

The generals applauded from the grandstand.

"Now let's have the chief put his mark on this piece of paper, Mr. Holten," said General Maxwell after the cheering had died down.

And with a few strokes of a long quill pen, the army and the Sioux were officially at peace with one another, after almost forty years of sporadic, bloody warfare. Holten held up the signed document and again the hundreds of Indians who were assembled in front of the fort whooped with pleasure at the completion of the historic agreement.

"Thank the chief for us, scout," said General McCormick. "And let me thank you on behalf of our leaders in Washington. It's a shame the army is losing you to . . . ah, domestic pursuits."

The assembled officers laughed.

"Well don't go away just yet, General," interjected Holten's commanding officer, Frank Corrington. "Now you're gonna see our best scout finally get hitched!"

"I almost forgot," said the white-haired McCormick returning to his seat. "The wedding is set for right now!"

"Can't ya tell by Holten's shaky knees?"

Again the officers roared with laughter.

Suddenly the buzz of the gathered Indians died down and the cluttered area in front of the walled army fortress grew as quiet as a church on Sunday morning. All eyes turned toward the cluster of tepees and the small group of Indians that was making its way toward the covered grandstand. Holten squinted through the brassy mid-morning sunshine and his heart fluttered with anticipation when he noticed Yellow Feather and her relatives walking toward him. The sumptuous young woman was dressed in a stunning white buckskin wedding dress decorated with long fringes, knee-length white leather moccasin boots, and a red and white beaded headband with two eagle feathers stuck in the back.

The small procession finally arrived at a spot near the scout and stopped to face the grandstand. As his pretty bride stood demurely in front of him, Holten's gaze locked with Yellow Feather's sparkling brown eyes and the scout felt himself melt a little inside, another warm rush of happiness spreading through his chest, reassuring him that he was making the right decision.

"She's a beautiful girl, Mr. Holten," said General Maxwell as he leaned over to speak with the scout. "You sure know how to pick 'em!"

Holten swallowed a few inexplicable tears of happiness that had been welling inside of him and just nodded at the general, the scout's mind a complete blank now as the moment he'd been waiting for had finally arrived. So long army, thought the scout, and hello happiness.

The scout watched Broken Bull, Yellow Feather's middle-aged father, who was all decked out in eagle feathers, grasp his daughter's delicate hand and step over to where Holten was standing. Then the scout smiled at his future father-in-law and reached out to accept Yellow Feather's little hand.

But suddenly Holten stiffened as his animal-like sixth sense, his survival instinct, gnawed at his insides as though to warn him of impending danger. His adrenaline began to course through his veins.

But it was too late.

Holten heard a whooshing sound followed by a sickening thud. It was the unmistakable sound of a streaking Indian arrow finding its mark.

General Maxwell gasped with pain.

At first Holten remained frozen on the grandstand, his pretty bride's soft hand grasping his own, his happy mind not yet comprehending what was taking place.

But suddenly the sultry summer air was alive with the whooshing of arrows and the accompanying cries of pain from the assembled celebrants all around him. Stubby General Horace Maxwell, President Grant's peace representative, tumbled from the reviewing stand with an Indian arrow buried deep in his chest, blood spurting from his wound.

Yellow Feather screamed at the sight.

Then things seemed to happen with blinding speed.

Besides the ominous whooshing of arrows, the mid-morning air suddenly was reverberating with the sound of rifle shots. . . . Several of the nearby Oglala subchiefs cried out with pain and fell on the dusty ground. . . . The Oglala camp suddenly became a chaotic jumble of fleeing Indians looking for cover or scrambling for their weapons. . . . The army troopers quickly broke ranks, many of them falling dead before they could even take a couple of steps. . . . And the arid stretch of prairie in front of the fort was suddenly crawling with attacking shaven-headed Pawnee warriors who were brandishing glistening new rifles and sturdy bows, bloodthirsty war cries escaping from their lips.

"Holy shit!" cried General Corrington.

"It's an attack!" cried a nearby soldier as he ran toward the fort and the Springfield carbines that were piled in neat little stacks on the parade grounds.

A well-placed shot slammed into the fleeing trooper's back and sent him sprawling to the ground, a gaping wound in his back.

Voices of panic rose into the air.

"I'm hit!"

"Oh my God, we're trapped!"

"Get back to the fort!"

"There must be two hundred of 'em comin' at us!"

The gravity of the situation quickly registered in the scout's experienced brain and he flew into action. The pervasive mood of happiness a few moments before suddenly had been shattered by the ferocity of the unexpected attack. Holten tore away his gaze from the painted Pawnee braves who were streaming into the clearing from the prairie beyond and turned his attention to Yellow Feather and her father.

"Holten, look out!" cried General Corrington.

Like shadowy phantoms riding out of the sky, a dozen galloping Pawnee warriors, their wild-eyed war ponies churning up the parched Dakota soil, charged the grandstand area with their glistening Winchester repeating rifles aimed at the scout and his friends.

"Get down!" yelled Holten in Lakota, quickly hauling Yellow Feather to the ground. A sudden hail of bullets zipped over their heads and kicked up the alkaline dust all around their feet.

"Are ya all right, Mr. Holten?" gasped General Corrington from where he was lying on the ground. "And how about you, General McCormick?"

"I'm all right, General," shouted the white-haired visiting general from Washington. Bullets and arrows were zipping over their heads, and the area was alive with

50

screams of pain and terror.

"I'm okay, too," replied the scout.

Then he felt the warm stickiness on his fingers.

Holten's heart leapt to his throat when he saw that his hands were covered with glistening blood. He quickly checked his body for any signs of a wound, and then sucked in his breath with horror when the awful truth hit him like a right cross to the jaw.

Yellow Feather had been shot several times.

The scout quickly grabbed the beautiful young squaw by her slender shoulders and turned her around so he could look into her face. His hands suddenly touched a couple of gaping bullet wounds in Yellow Feather's back that were spurting blood onto the ground.

"No!" cried Holten.

Then the scout looked at Yellow Feather's face.

Or what was left of it.

With foul-tasting bile rising in the back of his throat Eli Holten glanced with widened eyes at the gaping, fist-sized bullet wound on the left side of his bride's head. Yellow Feather's once pretty face was covered with splatters of bone, blood, and slimy white brain matter. A horrified look of pain was frozen on the dead girl's face, a terrible death mask that reflected the bloody violence that had suddenly erupted just moments before the scout was to take the sumptuous young woman as his life-long partner.

Nausea was boiling inside of the scout.

Gone was the one woman whom Eli Holten felt he could settle down with. Gone was the prospect of a life full of marital bliss and familial happiness. Gone was the opportunity to give himself totally to another human being as never before in his life. Gone was a beautiful person.

The scout was overwhelmed with a sense of loss.

FOUR

"Oh my God!" cried General McCormick.

"Jesus!" breathed Frank Corrington.

The scout was frozen on his knees beside the mutilated body of his beautiful young bride, his nausea subsiding and his experienced frontiersman's brain starting to function once again. Yellow Feather was gone and the scout's grief was enormous, but now it was time to try and save everyone else. With bullets zipping past his ears, the grief-stricken Holten shot to his feet and started to get his bearings in order to mount some sort of counterattack.

He'd avenge Yellow Feather's death later on.

"We have to get to the fort!" yelled Holten.

"The fort is being burned!" said General Corrington.

With his heart pounding madly against his ribs like an Indian war club, the scout went into a crouch and cast a wary glance toward the now smoking army outpost. He noticed hungry tongues of yellow flames lapping at the rough-hewn logs and he saw that the headquarters of the Army's 12th Cavalry was being stormed by rifle-toting Pawnee warriors. The stench of gunpowder permeated the sultry summer air all around the scout.

"The treaty didn't last very long, did it Mr. Holten?" yelled General McCormick above the din, his pale blue eyes fixed on the bloodied body of General Maxwell on the ground.

"These Indians ain't Sioux," said Holten.

"Pawnee!" added General Corrington, looking at the

frightened general from Washington. "They've been enemies of the Sioux for centuries!"

"We better start fighting back before it's too late, don't ya think?" shouted General McCormick. Both Corrington and McCormick drew their .44 pistols in readiness for a sudden fight with charging warriors.

Hauling his army issue Remington .44 revolver out of its leather holster, the scout quickly scanned the action all around him; the suddenly vulnerable Oglala Sioux were trying valiantly to head for their tepees and recover their weapons; dozens of painted Pawnee warriors were galloping among the conical Sioux lodges and shooting at almost anything that was moving; the once neatly formed units of army troopers were scurrying unsuccessfully for the safety of the burning fort; and the interior of the nearly unprotected fortress was crawling with torch-bearing Pawnee braves who had mayhem on their minds. Bloodthirsty war cries, screams of the wounded, and the horrible nickering of panicky horses mixed with the sharp cracks of rifle fire to produce a deafening uproar.

Holten was about to lead the two generals on a mad dash toward the fort, and toward their horses in the livery stable, when he suddenly spotted Captain Ben Zachary standing near a cluster of Sioux tepees. The tall, black-haired officer was holding his service revolver in one hand and directing some of the fleeing troopers with the other.

The scout saw a flash of movement out of the corner of his eyes and noticed a wave of a dozen or so galloping, rifle-toting Pawnee warriors charging toward the suddenly vulnerable captain's defenseless position. Holten was about to shout a warning when suddenly a curious thing happened right before his eyes.

The rampaging warrior galloped at full speed right past the pistol-toting captain as though the moustached officer was actually directing them toward the fort. After the Indians had raced past in a cloud of dust, Holten saw the captain turn sharply toward the beleaguered grandstand and their eyes met in a long, questioning gaze.

"Now's our chance, Holten!" yelled Corrington.

The general's frantic voice hauled the scout out of his stunned inaction and back to the problem at hand. Tearing his gaze away from the pistol-toting captain, the scout looked down one final time at the mutilated corpse of his dead Indian bride and then whirled toward the fort.

"Let's go!" he cried. "Keep your guns ready!"

Holten heard the scrape of running feet.

"Look out!" shouted General McCormick.

Suddenly four painted Pawnee warriors leaped onto the covered grandstand, their war paint-slashed faces twisted with hate and their hands clutching fearsome Indian war hatchets. Holten turned and saw one of the braves slash a gash in General Corrington's suddenly exposed left shoulder, the commanding officer's blood spurting from the deep wound.

"I'm hit!" cried Corrington. "Goddamn it, I'm hit!"

Holten whirled with the reflexes of a startled cougar and quickly squeezed off a couple of rounds with his .44, the hot slugs slamming into the broad, dark faces of two of the attacking warriors and turning their flesh into bloody pulp.

General McCormick's .44 pistol roared and another of the shaven-headed warriors felt the bite of a bullet. The dead Pawnee buck went sprawling onto the body-strewn ground. Suddenly the final brave raised his tomahawk and leaped at the white-haired general. Holten saw the fear rise quickly in McCormick's ashen face.

"No!" pleaded the bemedalled general.

But he was too late.

The muscular brave lashed downward with the glistening, iron-headed hatchet and sunk the razor-sharp blade deep into the wide-eyed general's forehead, nearly slicing the white-haired officer's head in two like a ripe melon.

McCormick's legs buckled and he slumped dead to the ground.

Before the warrior could create any more havoc, the scout squeezed the trigger of his Remington .44 and sent a speeding slug slamming into the suddenly startled brave's dark, painted face. The dead warrior leapt backwards with the impact of the bullet and landed on the grandstand.

General Corrington moaned with pain.

Holten knelt quickly and saw that his commanding officer had a nasty gash in his arm that was bleeding profusely. The scout realized right away that the wiry, tobacco-chewing general needed medical attention soon or he was going to bleed to death.

"Let's head for the fort!" said Holten.

"Goddamn Pawnee!" cried the ashen-faced general.

While the Pawnee continued to slaughter both the Sioux and the soldiers all around him, the scout grabbed the bleeding general under the arms and started to drag the wounded officer toward the interior of the fortress. The smoke from the fort's burning log walls stung Holten's eyes and several times, as he was heading for the big wooden gate, bullets from the Pawnee's new Winchester repeaters zipped within inches of his head.

Then, just as the struggling scout and his badly wounded commanding officer reached the smoky interior of the cluttered army outpost, the brutal Pawnee attack ended as suddenly as it had begun.

"The horses!" cried Holten.

"Leave me here," said the general. "I'll be okay."

After laying General Corrington gently against the wall of the smoking enlisted men's barracks, Holten dashed toward the livery stable and helped several frantic troopers rescue the panicky horses, including the scout's nickering gelding. Hauling his saddle out of the burning stables, Holten led his big, frightened horse to safety and returned to help the general.

Gazing at the death and destruction all around him, the scout listened to the chorus of moans that was filling the air on what was supposed to have been the happiest day of his life. Swallowing his grief at the sudden thought of Yellow Feather, the scout knelt on the ground and tried desperately to save General Frank Corrington's life.

"I tell ya," said old Coyote Jim Stephens, "those was brand new Winchester rifles that them Injuns was shootin' out there today!"

Captain Ben Zachary shook his head. "I don't believe it," he said, brushing the soot and prairie dust off his blue dress uniform. "Who in hell could have given the Indians guns that were stolen down near Fort Sampson? Why that's some fifty miles away!"

"Maybe Adderly knows somethin'," said Coyote Jim nodding toward the approaching scout.

"Here's one of them guns," said Kansas Joe Adderly as he strode briskly to where Holten and the others were standing. The stubby half-breed was clutching a captured Pawnee rifle.

The two buckskin-clad scouts and Captain Ben Zachary were among the army's twenty-five survivors of the Pawnee raid. The two generals from Washington, over one hundred troopers, and a dozen army wives were all slain in the late-morning onslaught. The Oglala Sioux had even greater losses. Now Holten and the survivors were trying to pick up the pieces of their shattered lives.

"See!" cried Coyote Jim pointing at the gun in Kansas Joe's hands. "Why it even has US ARMY stamped right there on its butt!"

"Must've come from that wagon train robbery yesterday afternoon," croaked General Frank Corrington in a weak voice full of pain.

The bandaged commanding officer was lying against the outside wall of the barracks, which was the only building in Fort Rawlins that hadn't been burned to the ground.

Holten hefted the still oily repeating rifle and sighted down its long, cold barrel. If it was from the wagon train holdup then, regardless of the peace treaty with the Sioux, Holten knew the prairie was in for a long, tough war with the rampaging Pawnee. The scout took a deep breath and quickly scanned the devastation left in the wake of the savage, unprovoked Pawnee attack.

As soon as the howling, war-painted Pawnee warriors had high-tailed it away from the burning army fortress and disappeared into the scorching, sun-baked prairie, Holten had rushed around the fort's environs looking for survivors. His frantic search located only a couple of dozen military people still alive; not many more of the Sioux had survived the savage attack. After the raid the air was redolent with thick smoke from the burned-out log fort and the acrid stench of spent gunpowder from the Pawnee rifles.

Finally Holten had returned to the grandstand with a heavy heart and covered Yellow Feather's bloodied body with a blanket from the barracks. Now the scout, trying not to let his overwhelming personal grief cloud his ability to think logically, was hoping to learn who was behind the attack and how the Pawnee could be stopped. While Holten was contemplating his next move, the healthy soldiers tended to the moaning wounded—including General Corrington—who were lying on the ground near the smoky fort.

"Well," said Coyote Jim, stroking his white beard, "we done heard it was the Black Bob Callahan gang that pulled off that there wagon train holdup yesterday. I reckon that's the fellas we should be lookin' for."

Kansas Joe shook his head. "Yeah, but we still got a shitload of Pawnee braves out there who are armed to the teeth with brand new Winchester repeaters. I figure we gotta get some help from Fort Sampson and head out after 'em!"

"Don't pressure Mr. Holten too much, boys," said General Corrington in a weak voice. The wiry officer grimaced with pain. "Remember, he lost a bride today."

A sudden respectful silence filled the air.

"That's right," said Coyote Jim softly. "Sorry, Holten."

"Me, too, scout," said the half-breed.

Holten nodded slowly. "Thanks, boys," he said, hoping the real pain he was feeling inside wasn't showing on his face. "But as soon as we get the ones responsible for this . . . this massacre, then I figure I'll get me revenge."

"You can take some time off, Holten, if ya like," said General Corrington.

The scout shook his head. "Thanks just the same, General, but I think I got me an idea about how them Pawnee braves latched onto them Winchesters."

Silence settled over the fort. All eyes were on Holten.

Then the scout turned to face Captain Ben Zachary who was standing nearby. "Ain't that right, Captain?" said Holten, his steely blue eyes fixed on Zachary's suddenly pale face.

The captain stroked his bushy moustache. "Why . . . why I don't know what you mean, scout. Are you accusing me of dealing with the Pawnee?"

"Mr. Holten!" snapped General Corrington, wincing with pain. "Captain Zachary's a veteran of the Indian Wars with an honorable battle record!"

"With all due respect, sir, I'd like Captain Zachary to explain why on two separate occasions during the fighting I saw Pawnee warriors gallop right past him when all they had to do was reach out and kill him!"

Again a deathly silence filled the air.

Captain Ben Zachary shifted his weight. "Why that's a bunch of shit!" he snapped, stroking his bushy moustache and glancing quickly from Holten to the general.

"And were you not near Fort Sampson last night, Captain?" asked the scout. "After the Pawnee attack this morning, I found out from the quartermaster what time you came in last night. I suppose you were just visitin' some friends fifty miles away, eh? Or were ya in cahoots with the gang that robbed the rifles? Did ya give 'em the time and place the wagons were supposed to arrive?"

Zachary licked his lips and beads of sweat began to appear on his forehead. "I can explain everything," he blurted out. "I have a reason for everything. . . ."

"I bet ya do!" said Holten, taking a step toward Zachary.

"Stay away, scout!"

"What was your part of the deal, Captain?" asked Holten in a cold voice as he took another menacing step toward the now trembling officer. The scout suddenly saw Yellow Feather's mutilated head in his mind, his hands covered with her warm, sticky blood.

"Did the Pawnee promise ya they'd make ya an honorary chief or somethin'?" asked Holten. "Or did Black Bob Callahan pay ya off with a pile of gold?"

Captain Zachary began to back away. "Get back!" he cried, his lean face now glistening with sweat. "I don't have to answer to you, scout!"

"No, but ya gotta answer to all them dead people!"

"And to me, Captain!" snapped General Corrington.

Holten kept walking. Zachary kept backing up.

"Stop, Captain!" ordered Corrington.

Finally, the wide-eyed captain turned and bolted toward the tethered army horses that were grazing near the remains of the burned-out Sioux tepees. Holten saw the fleeing officer draw his .44 caliber revolver and fire a shot behind him as he was running.

"Look out!" cried Coyote Jim.

Zachary shot wildly. Holten and the others ducked.

By the time Holten and the scouts could regain their feet, Captain Ben Zachary was astride a frisky army horse and was galloping like hell toward the open plains. The scout yelled at some nearby Oglala warriors.

"Kill that soldier!" shouted Holten in Lakota.

Suddenly a half dozen sturdy ash bows twanged and six whistling arrows hurtled through the air. Captain Zachary cried out in pain as all of the feathered shafts slammed into his body, making him look like a human pin cushion with arrows stuck in his back, chest, and legs. The screaming traitor fell from his mount and landed with a thud in a cloud of alkaline dust, dead before he hit the ground.

"Well," said Coyote Jim, stroking his snowy white beard, "at least we know how them gunrunners knew about the wagon train."

"Never did like that bastard," said Kansas Joe.

Holten turned and strode toward the spot where he had laid Yellow Feather's body. "Yeah," he called over his shoulder, "but the captain's death ain't goin' to bring back the dead."

Then the grief-stricken scout lifted his dead bride's mutilated body in his muscular arms and strode purposefully toward a grassy knoll behind the remains of the fort. There, working under the blistering early afternoon sun, Holten prepared a traditional Sioux burial platform for his butchered lover.

After an hour of cutting down trees, fastening them together with thin strips of rawhide, and placing Yellow Feather's body on top of the six-foot-high platform, the scout sang several mournful Indian elegies while stretching his long arms toward the heavens. Rivulets of hot tears streamed down his cheeks all during the songs. Holten remained seated on the grassy hill long after he had finished singing the dirges, his mind recalling the soft and gentle girl whose life had suddenly been snuffed out in a wave of needless violence. Finally, the scout, his buckskin clothes still stained with Yellow Feather's blood, bowed his head and was alone with his grief.

* * *

"My heart is heavy with sadness for you, Tall Bear," said Chief Black Spotted Horse in Lakota. "The Pawnee will pay dearly for their evil ways."

"Thank you great chief," replied Holten somberly. "Many lives were lost needlessly today."

"How many Oglala braves died in the fighting?"

The chief looked pained. "Over fifty men, women, and children," said the badly wounded leader of the Sioux. A sudden spasm of pain caused him to wince.

Holten shook his head and sighed deeply. The scout had finished his heart-breaking burial ceremony up on the grassy knoll, cleared his eyes of the last tears for Yellow Feather, and had then decided to check on the casualties among his former Sioux brothers. The moaning and mourning among the burned-out tepees had told Holten all he needed to know. The scout entered Black Spotted Horse's large, conical tepee, which was one of the few lodges still standing, to check on the condition of the chief. Holten had heard that his closest Indian friend had been badly wounded.

Holten had found Black Spotted Horse lying in pretty bad shape with several bullet wounds in his chest, arms, and legs. The ashen-faced warrior's strength had all but disappeared and the hawk-nosed brave looked near death.

Now Black Spotted Horse coughed harshly a few times and motioned for the scout to come closer. Holten knelt beside the handsome warrior and watched the chief reach under some nearby buffalo robes. Black Spotted Horse extracted a small deerskin bag that was fastened together with rawhide.

It was the chief's sacred medicine bundle.

"Here, Tall Bear," croaked the badly wounded chief, extending the package to the scout. "Take this parcel of Big Medicine with you when you track down the killers of your bride. It will bring you good luck."

"I cannot accept this," said Holten solemnly. "It is

Black Spotted Horse's sacred medicine bundle. I know how much it means to the great chief."

From his days with the Oglala, the scout knew that a warrior's most precious possession was his personal, dream-inspired medicine bundle. The deerskin bag full of religious talismans and herbs was traditionally brought out of storage on the eve of a great battle, to ward off harm to its owner. Rarely did a brave loan his bundle to anyone else.

"You will need it, Tall Bear," said Black Spotted Horse as strongly as his many wounds would allow. "Until I can use this bundle, please take it as your own."

Holten hesitated, then accepted the sacred bag.

"Thank you, great chief," said Holten softly, handling the worn deerskin bag and its special contents carefully as though to jostle them would disturb the magic spirits. The scout then opened the bundle and peered into the bag.

Included in Black Spotted Horse's medicine bundle were the following items: a wooden bowl, a stone pestle for grinding herbs, a wooden ring containing several kinds of special prairie herbs, a small turtle shell bowl full of birch bark and a wild radish, a small leather pouch of sacred war paint, an eagle-bone whistle to call the braves to battle, and the skin of a jack rabbit stuffed with ten different kinds of wild herbs. That ought to do the trick, thought the scout as he carefully closed the bag.

"Now go and find the ones responsible for this terrible massacre," said Black Spotted Horse. Holten watched the wounded chief close his eyes and try to sleep.

Images of Yellow Feather's mutilated face flashed in the scout's brain, and Holten felt a sudden twinge of anger mixed with hatred ripple through his gut. He clenched his teeth and swallowed his anger.

"I will, great Chief," said Holten softly.

The scout rose smoothly, and when he stepped from the chief's tall tepee the afternoon sun struck him like a hammer. Holten squinted toward the still-smoking, burned-out hulk that had once been Fort Rawlins and saw the remaining two dozen troopers of the 12th Cavalry getting ready to leave for Fort Sampson to the south. The scout strode briskly to where the badly wounded General Corrington was lying in the back of a specially rigged buckboard, the wiry commanding officer's bloodied left shoulder heavily bandaged.

"I trust you understand what we discussed earlier, Mr. Holten," said General Corrington, his bearded face looking up at the approaching scout. "Until a new commanding officer can be sent up here to replace me, I'm leaving you in charge of the 12th Cavalry. I don't know how long I'll be laid up with this goddamn shoulder wound!"

Holten nodded. "I understand, sir."

"I hope ya can hit the trail as soon as possible and find them damn Pawnee bastards!" snapped the general. "By the time you find 'em, I hope to get a column together and have Coyote Jim, Kansas Joe, and the soldiers meet you where the Benzman Trail runs across the Gray River."

"Right, sir," said Holten, itching to get started.

General Corrington filled his cheeks with a fresh chaw of tobacco, stroked his iron-gray beard, and looked up at the scout.

"Damn shame about your squaw, scout," he said softly.

Holten just nodded. His anger was rising again.

Then General Corrington signalled to a nearby, baby-faced corporal and the entire procession began to move toward the shimmering, sun-baked plains just ahead. Holten stood watching the disappearing column for a few minutes and then turned toward his gelding. With a final, sorrowful glance toward the burial platform on the grassy knoll behind him, the scout dug his heels into his big horse's flanks and galloped toward the prairie.

He had some scores to settle.

Riding like the wind across the blistering plains, while

at the same time following the easy-to-read Pawnee pony tracks on the alkaline dust beneath him, Holten was burning with anger. Once the shock of Yellow Feather's violent death had worn off, the scout's overwhelming grief had begun to recede. Now Holten had only one thing on his mind: find the ones responsible for the young bride's death and make them pay the price.

Especially Black Bob Callahan and the Pawnee chief.

The scout galloped ahead.

As Holten urged his big mount through leafy stands of towering cottonwoods and past brown clumps of summer-parched buffalo grass, all the facts about the surprise Pawnee attack were gradually falling into place.

Obviously some sort of conspiracy had taken place involving the traitorous Captain Zachary, the Pawnee warriors, and perhaps somebody else who knew about the ill-fated shipment of army repeating rifles. With Black Bob Callahan and his gang of prairie cut-throats having already been identified as the ones who had carried out the wagon train holdup, the scout knew his job was a little bit easier. All he had to do was visit the usual hangouts of the Callahan gang members and he'd probably find the ones who were responsible for the robbery.

As for the Pawnee, they were probably a band of Sioux-hating renegades up from the southern plains with looting, raping, and killing foremost in their minds. Finding their camps wouldn't be much of a problem for the prairie-wise scout, but how he'd handle them all by himself was another story. But first things first, Holten told himself. Knowing renegade Indians as well as he did, the scout figured the Pawnee warriors would soon tire of camp life and head out on their own, killing and looting at will across the entire Dakota Territory.

The thought sent a chill down Holten's spine.

Then the sounds drifted to his ears.

The scout reined in his snorting mount in front of a nearby rocky ridge, the nickering gelding stopping in a spray of dirt, and listened intently to the sounds of an apparent Indian attack on a group of prairie settlers.

Indians were howling and settlers were screaming.

"Damn Pawnee!" muttered Holten, his anger once again beginning to boil up within his tall, lean frame. "I'll make the bastards pay!"

With a smack of his hand on the gelding's ample butt, the scout took off at a gallop toward the bone-chilling sounds just over the upcoming ridge. He reached the rock-strewn crest of the ridge within a few minutes and pulled back on the reins. What he saw in the clearing below sent a wave of anxiety washing through his stomach.

Half a dozen brightly painted, shaven-headed Pawnee renegade warriors had obviously ambushed a defenseless wagon full of seven white settlers only a few minutes before and were now having some fun with their victims. With his anger beginning to boil over now, Holten peered through the hazy mid-afternoon heat and watched the evil-eyed braves as they began to fasten their captives onto the spokes of the big, wooden wagon wheels for a terrifying death ride that the scout had witnessed before.

Enough was enough, thought the revenge-seeking scout.

Hauling his Winchester .44-40 from its leather saddle sheath, Holten dug his heels into the gelding's glistening flanks and started to gallop toward the clearing below. The scout shouldered his rifle, picked his targets, and started to fire a hail of bullets at the unsuspecting Pawnee murderers below.

"This is for Yellow Feather, you bastards!"

A Pawnee brave near the wagon cried out with pain.

Another near the settlers slammed to the ground.

Still a third shaven-headed warrior bit the dust.

"Look!" cried a middle-aged settler woman. "Somebody's comin' to help us!"

"Please hurry, mister!"

"Help us, please!"

Suddenly confused and obviously frightened, the remaining Pawnee braves fled from the settlers and started to run for their ponies. Holten didn't give them a chance.

Riding into the dusty clearing with his Winchester aflame, the scout pumped a volley of hot lead into a wiry warrior, cut down another wide-eyed brave with a couple of slugs, and, even though the Winchester was now out of bullets, bore down on the final fleeing warrior, holding his rifle like a club.

The shaven-headed brave turned suddenly and held up his arms in some sort of futile gesture of surrender; his widened brown eyes reflected the fear he was feeling inside. But Holten didn't pause for a second, clubbing the motionless warrior on the side of the head with the butt of the Winchester while galloping past. Leaping from the wild-eyed gelding, the scout dashed back to where the dazed Pawnee was standing with his aching head in his hands.

"Dirty, bride-killin' bastard!" snarled Holten.

Then with a lightning quick slash of his fearsome ten-inch-long Bowie knife, the scout quickly sliced the startled brave's throat with one simple swipe, the wide-eyed warrior's blood spurting onto the ground as the mortally wounded Pawnee tumbled to the ground. Holten stood menacingly over the fallen renegade brave, his eyes wide with a sort of half-crazed, animal-like anger and his breath coming in uneven gasps, his blood-stained blade glinting in the sun.

"My God!" gasped a nearby settler woman.

Holten turned sharply and saw the unbelieving expressions of horror etched on the ashen faces of the cowering settlers in the clearing, a couple of them shaking their heads slowly at the scout's sudden display of anger and brutality.

Holten looked down at the dead Pawnee warrior.

His quest for revenge had begun with a flourish.

FIVE

Holten finally was under control.

The scout was not a violent man by nature but only resorted to brutality when provoked by the evil forces surrounding him on the vast Dakota plains.

Like the murderous Pawnees who had killed his bride.

Taking a few deep breaths, the scout managed to explain the dangerous prairie-wide situation to the grateful but still wary settlers back at the clearing. Giving the nervous greenhorn travellers instructions on how to reach Fort Sampson to the south, Holten bid them farewell and continued on the trail of the Pawnee chief.

And the Black Bob Callahan gang.

Surprised himself at his sudden show of brutality back on the trail, the scout gathered his thoughts and tried to remain under control. Too many over-anxious tenderfoot greenhorns had stumbled into the well-laid Indian traps over the years because of their pell-mell rush to get the job done, hunt down a killer, or track down some stolen horses.

Or get revenge for a loved one.

Urging the gelding along the blistering prairie trail, Holten promised himself to keep his boiling anger under better control during his next bloody encounter with the rampaging Pawnee. Hardly able to wait for the next meeting with the Indians, the sweat-soaked, revenge-seeking scout galloped across the war-ravaged Dakota plains.

He didn't have to wait long for his next encounter.

A shot rang across the prairie. Then another and another.

Holten quickly reined in his snorting sorrel. From his twenty years on the treacherous plains listening to various firearms and their distinctive reports, the scout knew the whining crack of a Winchester .44-40 when he heard it. The sudden shots came from just beyond a gentle wooded knoll up ahead, a spot where the famed Benzman Trail crossed an open stretch of parched prairie.

The scout dug his moccasin-clad heels into the ribs of his wild-eyed gelding and galloped like hell for the sounds of a pitched gun battle just ahead. Holten knew from experience that the first few days of a new Indian uprising were the bloodiest, as the worked-up braves got a lot of the killing quickly out of their systems.

Suddenly the shooting ceased.

The scout leaped from his galloping horse just before the top of the knoll and hunkered in the shade of a couple of leafy box elder trees. With his pulse quickening in anticipation, Holten squinted through the brassy sunshine at the desperate scene in the grassy trail below.

The shooting had stopped because the five painted Pawnee warriors who had been attacking a fleeing Deadwood-to-Fort Sampson stagecoach had finally overwhelmed their cumbersome quarry. Holten studied the victimized stagecoach and the shaven-headed Indians who were approaching it. The scout quickly scanned the three bloodied bodies lying on the buffalo grass, the jabbering Pawnee braves poring over the rickety old stage, and the shrieking young blonde woman who was being hauled roughly from the bouncing coach's interior.

Finally, after the pretty young woman was thrown unceremoniously to the ground with her petticoats flying in the breeze, Holten watched a couple of the renegade warriors begin to argue as to which of them would rape the wide-eyed white girl first. Although not understanding a word of Pawnee, the scout caught the gist of the heated conversation through the animated gestures of the suddenly enraged braves.

The argument was finally settled when one of the braves jammed a glistening hunting knife deep into the stomach of the other, repeating the stabbing a half dozen times until the stricken warrior fell dead to the ground.

The blonde woman shrieked at the violence.

"Oh, please!" Holten heard her yell. "Let me go!"

The victorious brave stepped quickly to where the blonde was cowering on the ground, grabbed her breasts through the material of her dress, and jerked the gasping young woman quickly to her feet.

"You're hurting me!" she cried.

Then the hard-faced, shaven-headed Pawnee warrior said something to the remaining renegades and all of the Indians roared with laughter. With blinding speed the victorious, knife-wielding brave reached out with his hand and tore off the helpless blonde's dress with a couple of hard downward tugs. Within seconds the shapely woman was standing stark naked in the sunshine, her firm round breasts quivering and her triangular bush of pubic hair perfectly visible even from where the scout was observing the scene.

"No!" cried the woman, covering her breasts.

Holten had seen enough. He went into action.

Figuring that enough women had probably been violated by the rampaging Pawnee to suit a dozen Indian wars, the scout quickly hauled his .44-40 from its saddle sheath and strode briskly back to the crest of the knoll. Leaning against the broad trunk of a leafy box elder tree, Holten aimed down the long, cold barrel of his rifle at the smiling Pawnee warrior who was now naked himself and beginning to mount the struggling blonde woman. The copper-skinned brave was holding his elongated shaft and straddling the naked blonde.

The Winchester barked. The warrior jumped backwards.

Holten shot again. Another brave jumped with the impact.

Suddenly the remaining two Pawnee warriors glanced up at the knoll from where the scout was shooting, their painted faces registering the sudden fear the scout knew they were feeling inside.

One of the warriors, a short muscular Indian with a wicked-looking hunting knife gripped in his hand, leaped over to where the naked blonde was sitting on the grass, raised the glinting blade over his head, and prepared to slash the wide-eyed woman into bloody shreds.

The blonde screamed.

Holten had other ideas.

The scout squeezed the trigger and sent a speeding bullet slamming into the knife-wielding warrior's broad, dark face, the slug exiting at the back of his shaven head in a sudden spray of blood and brain matter. The brave was lifted off his feet with the impact of the bullet and he sprawled dead next to the screaming blonde.

Holten quickly squeezed off another round and sent the final warrior slamming to the grassy plains with a gaping bullet wound in his body. A widening circle of crimson spread across the dead brave's chest. The scout's shots were echoed in the sultry afternoon air.

"Bride-killin' bastards!" murmured Holten.

The blonde was sitting open-mouthed on the trail.

Holten rose quickly, swung his tall, lean body onto the gelding, and rode down to inspect the carnage, as well as to inspect the frightened woman.

By the time the scout reached the empty stage and the body-strewn trail, the shapely blonde had already lugged her heavy luggage down from the top of the stage and was almost finished covering herself with a tight-fitting deerskin riding outfit. The blue-eyed beauty was fastening the last of the brass buttons of her blouse when Holten reined in the gelding and leaped to the trail.

Normally the scout would've been excited to find such a beautiful and vulnerable woman all alone on the plains. He probably would have begun manuevering the luscious lass into bed. But Yellow Feather's brutal death had changed all that. Now he was living for one purpose only.

"Howdy," said Holten, tipping his wide-brimmed hat.

"Is that all you can say after killing five Indians and seeing the bodies of these poor stagecoach drivers?" asked the pretty blonde as she finished dressing.

Holten shrugged. "Nothin' I can say, ma'am, will bring any of 'em back to life."

"Well, I was almost raped, too!"

The scout noticed that the young blonde's slender hands were shaking from her ordeal with the savage Pawnee and that beneath her cool exterior she was frightened to death.

Finally the blonde sighed and smiled. "You're right, of course," she said in a soft voice. "I'm sorry I was so curt with you. It's just that this was my first experience ever with Indians!"

"It's a tough time to be travellin' right now."

"I understand from some friends of mine who have lived in the West for a number of years that it's almost always a tough time to travel across the wild Dakota Territory."

Holten noticed that the lady spoke with a broad-vowelled eastern accent, and that her clothes were obviously high quality garments from expensive big city shops.

"Oh, excuse me!" said the blonde, extending a delicate hand toward the scout. "You saved my life and I haven't even introduced myself. I'm Isabella Cartwright. I'm a writer and I'm out West doing a book about western men and their various lifestyles."

Holten grasped her soft hand. "Eli Holten, ma'am,"

said the scout, removing his hat with his other hand. "Glad I was able to help ya."

Isabella Cartwright's big blue eyes widened. "You're Eli Holten? Why I was told you were the best example around of a real scout!"

The scout smiled and reluctantly released the blonde's hand. She was a real looker. "You probably heard right, ma'am," said Holten as he put on his hat. "I guess lots of folks, both good and bad, have heard about me and the other army scouts around these here parts."

"Call me Isabella," said the bubbly blonde.

"All right, Isabella," said the scout, giving the luscious-looking writer a quick head-to-toe inspection with his piercing blue eyes.

Isabella Cartwright was a tall, sinewy blonde journalist from a *propah* Boston, Massachusetts family. Her sparkling blue eyes danced with merriment and her full supple lips were quick to curve into a warm, seductive smile. Men often gazed longingly at her curvaceous body with its firm round breasts, gently curving hips, and long lovely legs. Isabella's honey blonde hair cascaded about her slender shoulders, framing an angelic face with a flawless peaches-and-cream complexion.

But there was another quality evident in the young writer's pretty face, a sort of reporter's determination that manifested itself in the tight lines around her mouth and in the way she fixed her incessant gaze on a person as though trying to discern her subject's innermost thoughts.

A novelist of some repute out East, Isabella Cartwright raised a few proper Bostonian eyebrows when she announced that she was planning to tour the wild, wild West in search of material for her latest book—a volume about men of the West and the way in which they live. Her trip had been relatively uneventful until the meeting with the Pawnee, and Holten's timely arrival to save her.

"Do you like what you see, Mr. Holten?" asked the

smiling blonde writer, catching Holten's long, lingering gaze at her sumptuous body.

Holten recovered quickly. "Call me Eli," he said.

Isabella giggled. "All-right, Eli."

"Ya seem to have recovered nicely from your tangle with them Pawnee braves," said the scout, glancing at the bleeding Indians on the ground.

"I bounce back quickly, Mr. Holten . . . er, Eli."

Holten smiled. "Out here on the plains, that's a good quality to have. I've been out here twenty years and I've seen lots of folks lose their cool—and then their lives."

"I'd like to talk to you about your life on the prairie, Eli," said Isabella Cartwright. "It would mean a great deal to me and my book."

The scout nodded, then scanned the terrain. "Fine, but let's get the hell out of this trail. There's an Indian uprising goin' on right now and I sure as hell don't want to be out in the open any longer than I have to."

Isabella touched Holten's buckskin-clad arm. "Thanks again, Eli, for saving my life. I want to see the West as it really is, but being raped by some wild Indians isn't exactly what I had in mind."

"I just did what I had to do," said the scout, swinging onto the gelding's wide back. "But for now, you'll have to ride up here with me. I'll drop ya off at Fort Sampson tonight. Ain't no way we can get that stagecoach back to the fort right now."

"What about my bags?"

"Gotta leave 'em behind."

"But all my dresses and things!"

"Well," said the scout wiping the sweat from his forehead with his sleeve. "It's either leave your stuff behind or stay here with it until help arrives or another Pawnee war party comes along."

Holten saw a shadow of fear creep across Isabella's pretty face, darkening her eyes. "In that case," said the blonde easterner, "take my hand and help me up. Things are so cut-and-dry out here in the West!"

The scout smiled, hauled the slender female writer up onto the nickering mount's ample back, and clucked to his gelding. At least he was able to save one beautiful woman today, thought Holten as they galloped away from the stagecoach and the bodies on the ground.

"Indians!" cried Isabella Cartwright.

The pretty, honey blonde writer from Massachusetts sucked in her breath and pointed a long, tapered finger at an approaching band of long-haired Indians atop snorting painted ponies.

Holten reined in the gelding. "It's all right," he said reassuringly. "Them Indians are friends of mine. It's the damn shaven-headed ones ya gotta watch for!"

"I hadn't seen a live Indian up close until today," remarked Isabella. "Now I seem to be running into them everywhere I go!"

Holten felt her trembling hands on his waist.

"You can relax," he said. "These are Oglala Sioux, my former tribe."

"That's right, I almost forgot!" exclaimed Isabella, her blue eyes saucering. "I was told that you spent some years with the Indians out on the prairie!"

"Six years," said the scout. He glanced out at the dusty swirls being kicked up by the galloping Oglala ponies that were approaching up ahead.

"You'll have to tell me all about it, Eli!"

"With all the problems we got on the plains right now," said the scout through clenched teeth, "I don't rightly know when we'll have the time."

Holten recognized the hard-faced Oglala braves right away as being from Black Spotted Horse's camp. The warriors reined in their snorting war ponies in front of the scout. Holten noticed that the broad, dark faces of all the warriors were now streaked with white war paint.

"How," said Holten, raising his right hand.

Four Bull, a young sub-chief, responded in kind.

"Chief Black Spotted Horse requests that Tall Bear come to Oglala camp for a pow-wow," said Four Bull in Lakota. "We have been sent to bring Tall Bear back—"

"Tall Bear cannot come right now."

"Our chief says it is urgent."

"You speak their language, too?" interjected Isabella Cartwright, her blue eyes as big as silver dollars. "They won't believe this back in Boston!"

Holten ignored the blonde writer's comments. "Does Black Spotted Horse know something more about the whereabouts of the Pawnee camp?"

Four Bull shrugged. "Our chief only told us to bring back Tall Bear. But I think our scouts have found out who is leading the Pawnee uprising."

The scout's eyebrows shot up. "Who is it?"

"Mole On Face," replied Four Bull.

Holten's face hardened at the mention of the wicked warrior's name. The half-crazed Pawnee war chief had been a thorn in the side of most of the plains tribes for well over a decade. The scout had fought against the red bastard on several bloody occasions.

Holten quickly digested the new information and came to a quick decision: he'd abandon his search for the Pawnee camp until after he had spoken with Black Spotted Horse. For now the scout would be satisfied with a look into the nearby hangouts of the Black Bob Callahan gang to see how many of the murdering gunrunners he could find. He relayed the information to Four Bull and the others.

"Our chief will not be happy, Tall Bear."

Holten smiled. "Just tell Black Spotted Horse that Tall Bear is hunting the killers of Yellow Feather and the evil white men who gave them their guns."

Four Bull nodded and then turned the head of his snorting painted war pony. Holten watched the galloping warriors disappear over a nearby ridge and into the prairie.

"What was that all about?" asked Isabella Cartwright.

"An invitation to a meeting I can't attend."

"Why not?"

"'Cause you and me are goin' to look for some bandits."

Isabella's jaw dropped. "Really?" she cried.

"Don't sound so excited," cautioned the scout. "I'm only takin' ya along because there ain't no place to leave ya for now."

"Oh, Eli, thank you!"

Holten clucked to his sorrel gelding and headed toward the surrounding trees at the edge of the prairie. Somewhere in the hills, he knew, were Black Bob Callahan and his gang of gunrunning killers.

"Don't thank me," said Holten, urging the big horse into a full gallop across the dusty, alkaline trail. "Just stay the hell outta the way!"

"This is exciting!" exclaimed Isabella, hanging on.

"We'll see," said the scout.

As they were galloping toward the hills, the sudden close proximity of a beautiful young woman seemed to accentuate Holten's awareness that Yellow Feather was gone forever, and that her killers were riding free somewhere out on the plains. Holten's anger began to boil once again.

He smacked the gelding and rode like hell.

SIX

"Buzzard's Gulch?" asked Isabella Cartwright.

"That's the name of the town," said the scout.

"Sounds gruesome!"

"There are some pretty gruesome characters there."

Holten and the pretty blonde writer were kneeling in some wavering buffalo grass on the outskirts of the tiny prairie town of Buzzard's Gulch, the favorite stomping grounds of Black Bob Callahan and his gang. The scout licked his parched lips and scanned the sleepy looking outpost a hundred yards away.

After his talk with Four Bull, Holten had decided to try and locate the Callahan gang. Buzzard's Gulch was only a few miles away from the grassy Benzman Trail, and a quick search for the dark-skinned leader of the gun-running gang seemed to be in order.

Swallowing his grief and his growing anger while they were riding, the scout had given Isabella a quick re-cap of the bloody events to date. He passed quickly over the massacre at the fort and the horrible death of Yellow Feather. Isabella was aghast at the slaughter.

"So now you're looking for the men who killed your bride?" the pretty blonde had asked, while the gelding was galloping toward Buzzard's Gulch.

"That's right," Holten had answered solemnly.

"Oh, Eli!" Isabella had said in sympathy.

They rode the rest of the way in silence.

Now they were reconnoitering.

"The place looks deserted," said Isabella, pushing a matted strand of honey blonde hair out of her eyes.

"On the prairie," said Holten, "looks can be deceivin'."

Isabella laughed. "Everything's cut-and-dry."

"Not always."

"What do you mean?"

"As ya can see, Buzzard's Gulch has only got a saloon, a stable, and a few other buildings," said the scout. "But inside them buildings may be a dozen gunslingers each with twenty or more kills to his credit."

"So?"

"Well, maybe there ain't nobody there, too."

Isabella frowned. "Then how does one go about finding anybody around here?"

"By goin' into town."

"But what if the bad men are there? I mean, Eli, isn't it dangerous? You could be walking into a trap or something, couldn't you?"

Holten stood and strode to the gelding. "That's what I mean when I say everything ain't so cut-and-dry all the time around here."

"I'll remember that for my book!"

"Chances are you're right, though," said Holten. "I kinda think Black Bob and the others ain't goin' to be sittin' around waitin' for me to find 'em. We're probably just wastin' our time here."

Suddenly a flash of movement in front of Buzzard's Gulch's tiny saloon caught the scout's eye. Holten stiffened, glanced toward the town and saw the short, well-built young woman who had just left the bar and was walking across the dusty street. The swivel-hipped woman with a six-gun strapped to her waist disappeared into a small, shingled building on the other side of the street.

"Look, a woman!" said Isabella Cartwright.

Holten snorted. "That ain't no woman!" he said. "That there is Lily Bordeaux, a half-breed cut-throat and

Black Bob Callahan's gal. She's killed at least a dozen men all by herself. But if anybody knows where in hell that gunrunnin' son of a bitch Callahan is hidin' out it's Lily."

"So we're going into the town?"

"I got half a mind to leave ya out here with my horse," said the scout. "You're liable to get your pretty little head shot off in Buzzard's Gulch."

"I'll stay out of the way, really I will!"

Holten saw the childish enthusiasm in Isabella Cartwright's sparkling blue eyes, and he knew that no matter how hard he tried, the tall, sumptuous blonde from Massachusetts was going to get her own sweet way. Besides, she'd probably be safer anyway if she was at his side all the time.

"Okay, but keep quiet and stay with me."

"I will, I will!"

With the luscious blonde writer sitting behind him on the gelding, Holten clucked to the big, snorting mount and headed into Buzzard's Gulch, the home of Black Bob Callahan and a haven for the Territory's most ruthless gunfighters.

Trotting toward the tiny prairie outpost, the sweat-clogged scout scanned the town with his steely blue eyes once again: one dusty street, a tiny saloon off to the right, a dilapidated livery stable across from the bar, and a multi-purpose general store/hotel/undertaker's building just beyond the saloon on the same side of the street. The tiny village seemed as empty as a ghost town as the scout and his pretty travelling companion trotted down the one shadowy street.

"It's kinda spooky here," said Isabella.

"Shhh," said Holten. "We're bein' watched."

Isabella stiffened behind the scout. "Where?"

"Two men in the saloon and Lily Bordeaux to our left."

"I can't see a thing!"

Suddenly the wooden slab door of the multi-purpose

building across from the saloon swung open with a bang. The scout's big sorrel gelding bucked at the sudden noise. Holten struggled to rein in his skittish horse.

Holten turned toward the sound and saw Lily Bordeaux, a smile on her crudely pretty face and a cigar stuck in her mouth, leaning against the door jamb. The curly-haired killer's gun hand was resting on the pearl-handled butt of her Shopkeeper's Colt .45 revolver.

"Been a long time, scout," grated Black Bob's girl friend through clenched teeth, her cigar remaining in her mouth and her flashing brown eyes glued on Holten.

"Not long enough, Lily," replied the scout.

Lily Bordeaux tossed back her head, removed her cigar with short, pudgy fingers, and laughed an evil kind of cackle. Holten saw the high cheekbones and flashing Indian eyes that were a giveaway to Lily's half-breed Sioux heritage.

"I suppose you and your lady friend there are payin' me and my friends a social call, eh Holten? Or would ya happen to be interested in the whereabouts of Callahan?"

Again Lily Bordeaux cackled.

Holten slipped smoothly from the saddle and saw a sudden flicker of fear wash across Lily Bordeaux's high-cheekboned face, clouding her eyes.

"Eli?" said Isabella, remaining on the gelding.

"Just stay there," replied Holten.

"Ya best keep movin' on, scout," grated the half-breed.

"That ain't no way to treat an old friend, Lily. Besides, maybe your friends over in the saloon will invite me in for a drink. Then we all can talk about Black Bob and his Pawnee friends, not to mention some stolen army rifles."

Holten kept his eyes fixed on Lily's gun hand.

His pulse quickened.

The half-breed's anger flared. "I don't know where in hell Callahan is! And if I did, ya know I wouldn't tell the likes of you!"

"I don't believe you're tellin' the truth, Lily."

The scout took a menacing step toward the half-breed.

Lily's right hand began to twitch.

"Don't make me shoot ya, Holten!"

"Where's Black Bob?" said the scout in a voice as cold and hard as a bullet. He was only five feet away from the curly-haired outlaw lass. "That son of a bitch gave some rifles to them Pawnee. And because of that, my woman was killed this mornin' at Fort Rawlins!"

"Stay away from me!" shrieked Lily Bordeaux.

"Where's Callahan?" asked Holten. "And what about fat Slim Powell and Big Nosed John Harper? Speak up, Lily, or I'll squeeze it outta ya!"

Suddenly the creaking doors from the dilapidated saloon across the street swung open and a couple of stubble-faced gun hands burst into the late afternoon sunshine, their eyes full of sullen hatred for the scout and their big hands full of lead-spitting six-shooters.

"Eli, look out!" screamed Isabella Cartwright.

At the same time, Lily Bordeaux's twitching gun hand reached for her six-shooter with the quick reflexes of an experienced gunfighter. With the lightning quick reaction of a striking rattlesnake, Holten unsheathed his fearsome Bowie knife and sent the glistening blade hurtling through the sultry afternoon air toward the scowling half-breed.

The knife sliced through Lily's right wrist, knocked the .45 from her little hand, and stuck in the wooden door jamb that was to the half-breed's right.

Lily's wrist was pinned to the door jamb.

She screamed in pain.

The scout whirled toward Isabella, reached up quickly, and slapped the big, wild-eyed gelding on its ample butt. The powerful mount whinnied and lurched, before taking off like a scared jackrabbit down the street.

"Get down in the saddle and hold on!" yelled Holten.

"Oh my God!" cried Isabella.

"Stay low!" repeated the scout.

Suddenly a bullet zipped past Holten's right ear and another slug whistled over his head. Whirling to face the saloon, the scout became fully aware of the charging killers who were coming at him from across the street.

Hauling his Remington .44 out of its leather holster, Holten dove to his left and rolled onto the dusty street, coming up firing at the stubble-faced gunmen who were almost on top of him.

The scout squeezed the trigger twice and sent a couple of speeding slugs slamming into the first charging cowboy's chest, the impact of the bullets sending the wide-eyed killer spinning to the ground.

A bullet nicked Holten's buckskin shirt.

With the reflexes of a frightened mountain lion, the scout rolled to his left once again and came up firing. A couple of bullets kicked up the dirt in the place where he had just been lying. Holten squeezed his trigger and sent a bullet slamming into the startled face of the remaining gunman. The killer was lifted off his feet with the impact of the slug, his stubbled face suddenly a grotesque mask of bloody flesh, and fell to the ground with a thud.

The shots echoed among the buildings.

Gunsmoke hung heavy in the air.

Holten lay still in the dusty street, his heart pounding a wild tune against his ribs, and surveyed the result of his work. He hadn't found Callahan, but at least he'd whittled down the size of the gang a little.

"Goddamn you, scout!" snarled Lily Bordeaux.

"Eli, look out!" yelled Isabella from down the street.

Suddenly Holten heard the scraping of feet directly behind him and he whirled toward the sound. Somehow Lily Bordeaux, tough gal that she was, had pulled herself free of the door jamb and was charging the scout, his own Bowie knife held high in the air and ready to slash downward.

Arcing his smoking .44 across his body and up into the charging half-breed's angry face, the scout quickly squeezed the trigger. The Remington revolver spat fire and sent a hot slug right between the curly-haired killer's flashing brown eyes. The back of Lily Bordeaux's head exploded as the heavy bullet exited in a spray of blood and bone. She fell dead against the door behind her.

Isabella came running down the street.

Holten whirled toward the sound.

"Don't shoot, Eli, it's me!" cried the blonde writer, her big blue eyes saucering as she quickly scanned the bloodied bodies sprawled on the street.

"I told ya things ain't always cut-and-dry."

"Oh my God!" breathed Isabella, her hand to her mouth.

The scout rose quickly from the street, dusted off his buckskins, and holstered his gun. He glanced at the fading sun in the western horizon.

"It's gettin' late," said Holten. "We best be headin' toward Fort Sampson. No chance of makin' the fort today, so we'll have to spend the night on the trail."

Suddenly Isabella Cartwright spotted Lily Bordeaux's mutilated head, with its blood and gore, and the scout saw the color drain from her pretty face. The luscious blonde's sparkling blue eyes rolled in her head.

"I think I'm going to be sick!" she said.

Then, as the scout reached out and held the shapely writer's slender waist, Isabella turned and vomited onto Buzzard's Gulch's only street.

"Welcome to the wild, wild West," said Holten.

Finding the dead outlaws' horses waiting in the Buzzard's Gulch livery stable, the scout selected the most docile animal for Isabella and plunked a saddle onto the gentle bay. Then, after half an hour of easy riding through the gathering dusk, with Holten genuinely surprised at the pretty blonde's riding ability, the scout chose a spot along the tree-lined trail to spend the night.

After a few minutes of quick preparation, Holten had taken care of the horses, built a small campfire, and used his bedroll and a pile of leaves to fashion a relatively comfortable mattress for Isabella. By nightfall their campsite was ready to inhabit.

"All the comforts of home," said Holten with a smile.

Isabella smiled weakly. "Thanks, Eli," she said, bowing her head. "I guess I kind of made a fool of myself back there in town, huh?"

"Hell, no!" said the scout. "Lookin' at somebody's head inside out like that sorta makes most folks a little queasy in the stomach, ya know?"

"Maybe I made a mistake leaving Boston."

"Give yourself a chance."

Holten stoked the fire and checked the coffee pot he'd just placed on the flames. He was certain not to look directly into the roaring blaze, knowing that if he did he would be blind for a moment upon looking away. That was a tenderfoot mistake that the scout couldn't afford to make.

Then Holten sat stiffly next to Isabella and gazed up at the vast canopy of twinkling stars overhead. Suddenly he felt a vast emptiness deep inside of him and he realized what was beginning to happen. It was hard to believe but just a few hours ago he had been standing on the ceremonial grandstand at the fort looking into Yellow Feather's glistening brown eyes. A sudden twinge of sadness rippled through Holten's gut and he squirmed with discomfort, his mind suddenly flashing vivid images of his dead bride's pretty face, gentle smile, and sparkling eyes. Damn! thought the scout, smacking his balled fist on the ground.

"What's the matter, Eli?" asked Isabella quickly.

The scout turned sharply and stared at the sinewy blonde with flashing eyes, his heart pounding and his ears ringing. Sudden beads of cold sweat were beginning to break out on his forehead. Suddenly Holten was trembling with anger, sadness, and the frustration of not being able to reach out and smash the evil bastards who were responsible for the brutal death of the one he loved.

"Eli, what is it?"

Finally the scout took a deep, shuddering breath and began to calm down, his overwhelming sense of grief suddenly transformed into an iron-willed sense of purpose: find and kill the ones responsible for Yellow Feather's death. Holten knew he'd never be able to spend another peaceful night the rest of his life until he got his revenge!

Holten smiled at Isabella. "Nothin's the matter," he said in a strange, hollow voice. "Just had a few things on my mind."

A long silence filled the gap between them.

"Were you thinking about . . . your dead bride?"

The scout just nodded slowly.

Isabella reached out and grasped the scout's hand.

They sat in silence like that for about an hour until finally the scout poured a couple of cups of bitter frontier coffee and sat talking and sipping the inky brew with his shapely travelling companion. Holten's heart-wrenching grief and his horrible torment had seemingly receded for good, and now he was chatting amicably.

"Oh, Eli," said Isabella. "Tell me your life story!"

Holten laughed. "Ya got all year to listen?"

"Yes!" exclaimed the pretty blonde. "I want to hear it!"

"Well," said the scout sipping some coffee, "maybe I can talk about some of the things that's happened to me from time to time out on the plains."

And for the next couple of hours, while the spellbound Isabella Cartwright listened intently with widened blue eyes, Holten recalled some of the more exciting parts of his life on the vast Dakota prairie. He found he enjoyed reliving old adventures, and he was glad that the hours of conversation took his mind off Yellow Feather and her assassins. Then the scout stretched, quickly checked the surrounding terrain for any signs of trouble, and rose smoothly to his feet.

"Time to turn in," he said. "Got us a long day of ridin' tomorrow. By this time tomorrow night, Isabella, you'll be sleepin' in a big, soft bed at Fort Sampson."

"But who'll tell me stories?" she asked, a mischievous glint in her sparkling blue eyes as she gave the scout a lingering head-to-toe look.

Holten chuckled and waved. "Good night, Isabella. I'll be sleepin' in the shadows. More privacy for ya that way, plus I'll be able to hear better should anybody try and sneak up on us during the night.

The scout turned toward the edge of the clearing.

Then, while a bulbuous summer moon cast a silvery glow on the prairie all around him, the fully dressed scout lay his head on his saddle and tried hard to fall asleep. But to his dismay, vivid images of Yellow Feather, screaming Pawnee warriors, and hard-faced gunrunners kept popping into his cluttered brain again and again, their mind-shattering jumble causing him to squirm on the ground and writhe with discomfort. Finally he sat bolt upright, his face glistening with sweat.

"Yellow Feather!" shrieked Holten.

It was then that the scout noticed Isabella Cartwright standing stark naked beside him, her round breasts quivering in the moonlight and her sumptuous body bathed in the silvery glow. A warm, come-hither look was etched on her pretty face and her long, golden tresses were cascading about her slender shoulders.

"Let me help you with your grief, Eli," she said.

"But . . . ?"

"Shhhh," hissed Isabella, kneeling beside the scout.

And with quick, deliberate movements the sinewy blonde writer from Boston began to peel off Holten's sweat-soaked, blood-stained buckskin clothing, while the scout just closed his eyes and tried to catch his breath. Yellow Feather was gone and Holten knew that, in her own erotic way, Isabella Cartwright was trying to ease his pain.

"There!" said Isabella when she had finished, her sparkling blue eyes quickly roaming the scout's hardened frame from his matted chest, across his flattened stomach, to his suddenly enormous penis that was sticking up in the air.

"So big, Eli!"

Then the sumptuous blonde writer reached out and wrapped her long, tapered fingers around the scout's pulsating penis. The scout jumped slightly at her gentle touch. Isabella began to massage him and he reacted with a groan of delight.

The cool night air wafted over Holten's naked body, causing him to shiver slightly. Then he looked up into the shapely blonde's desire-filled blue eyes and met her gaze, his loins suddenly yearning for the feel of her warm body.

"I need you, Eli!" gasped Isabella in a throaty voice that was choked with urgency. Desire leapt from her eyes. "And I think you need me. Please, let's do it now!"

And without further ado the sumptuous blonde knelt on the ground beside Holten's groin, her delicate fingers still stroking his elongated shaft, and leaned forward to envelop his penis with her full, supple lips. With experienced precision the fully aroused sex kitten from Boston grasped Holten's long cock with her left hand and quickly began to suck on his swollen manhood, slowly and exquisitely drawing out the passion from his innermost regions.

"Damn!" gasped the scout, his eyes closed.

The only sounds reaching the now writhing scout's ears were the liquid sucking noises of Isabella's soft lips on his huge, throbbing penis. Holten's loins were quivering with desire and he knew it wouldn't be long before he would explode with delight at her erotic touch.

Then as if on cue, Isabella Cartwright suddenly removed her supple lips and lay on her back, quickly guiding Holten's big hands to her sumptuous frame, her big breasts flattening against her chest and her long legs opening provocatively in the silvery moonglow. Her honey blonde hair was splayed on the ground beneath her and her sparkling blue eyes were glistening with desire.

"Take me, Eli!" she gasped.

"I always aim to please," said the scout, his big hands suddenly roaming across Isabella's luscious young body, from the billowy flesh of her breasts to the glistening pubic hair where her long legs came together.

Suddenly Holten entered a firm, long finger into the writhing blonde's slippery vagina, pushing it gently through her warm and wonderful channel and then retreating to her firm, sensitive clitoris, causing her to gasp. The long and lovely writer from the East suddenly opened her big blue eyes and rolled them in their sockets, her sensuous mouth twisting into an expression of total ecstasy.

Sensing Isabella was about to come in a wave of glorious orgasms, Holten swiftly mounted the writhing young woman and deftly entered her, plunging his hardened cock deep into the gasping young blonde's innermost regions, thrusting again and again and again, until finally Isabella shrieked with delight and arched her slender back against the scout's shuddering final thrusts, as he filled her to the brim with a hot, milky flood of pent-up passion from somewhere deep inside of him.

"Ay, ay, ay!" shrieked Isabella.

"Damn!" groaned Holten.

Then the two sated lovers collapsed on the shadowy ground, their pounding hearts seemingly beating as one and their passionate, hot breath escaping from their lips in uneven gasps. The only sounds drifting to the fully refreshed scout were the lonesome call of a nearby coyote and the incessant beating of his heart against his ribs.

They lay in silence for several long, glorious minutes, Holten on top of the sumptuous blonde and his softening penis still buried within her. The ugly thoughts of the brutal attack at Fort Rawlins that morning had all but been expunged from the scout's cluttered brain.

"Feel better, Eli?"

"Like a new man," replied the scout.

Isabella giggled. "I was just getting to know the old one!" she said with a smile. Then the luscious, big-breasted blonde kissed the scout on the lips.

"What's that for?" asked Holten.

"For being such a good subject for my book!"

The scout laughed and slowly stood up, gently removing his now flaccid penis from Isabella's still trembling body. The blue-eyed beauty beneath him gave his lean, naked body a quick once-over with her sparkling eyes.

"I could really learn to like you, Eli," she said.

Holten started to dress. "Don't do it," he said. Suddenly he paused with one leg in his buckskin pants. A serious look spread across his brown, leathery face and darkened his eyes. "There ain't much future gettin' close to a scout."

Just ask Yellow Feather, thought Holten.

"But I . . ."

"Ya better get dressed," said Holten evenly.

The sudden thought of his murdered bride sent a wave of renewed anger coursing through the scout's hardened frame. Holten clenched his teeth and finished dressing. He'd try and get some sleep, but he knew it would be difficult while thinking about Yellow Feather's killers running around free. Even a sexual romp with a beautiful blonde hadn't erased all the hurt, anger, and feelings of revenge that the scout was experiencing inside.

He silently escorted Isabella back to the fire.

SEVEN

The mid-summer morning broke clear and sunny across the Dakota plains, with a promise of scorching heat later on when the broiling sun was higher in the azure prairie sky. After a quick, meager breakfast of almost inedible army hard-tack and too-bitter frontier coffee, Holten and Isabella hit the trail once again.

Neither of them mentioned the lovemaking of the night before, but in a way the scout felt glad that the sumptuous blonde had been along. She had, indeed, lightened his heavy burden of grief. And he knew, too, that Isabella was genuinely attracted to him, although the last thing Holten needed now was another emotional attachment.

"Where are we going?" asked Isabella while they were galloping over the grassy plains. Her honey blonde hair was blowing in the breeze. "Are we heading for the fort right away?"

"Naw," said the scout. "We gotta meet up with a column of soldiers first. Then after we see if any of the nearby settlers need any help, the troopers will escort ya to Fort Sampson. You'll be more comfortable there."

Isabella was quiet for a few moments, and then she spoke once again. "I'd rather stay out here with you, Eli," she said over the rush of the wind. "I need some more anecdotes for my book."

"Too dangerous," said Holten simply.

"Well, besides," said the pretty blonde, "I've become attracted to you, Eli. I . . . I want to be with you, you know. Can I, please?"

"No," said the scout. She was a hell of a woman, but he couldn't risk another attachment. "I catch your meanin', but it's still too dangerous. Why there may even be a Pawnee war party lookin' at us right now!"

Holten saw a flicker of fear in her pretty face.

"Besides," added the scout, "there's the army patrol up ahead. They'll be glad to take ya back to civilization, and ya should be glad to go."

Holten turned his attention to the swirls of alkaline dust on the trail up ahead and the approaching mounted troopers. When the scout noticed the small size of the column from Fort Sampson, his heart skipped a beat. He counted only fifteen soldiers—not much of a force to try and stop a prairie-wide Indian uprising.

As the dust-clogged troopers drew closer, the scout squinted through the early morning brightness and saw that they were being led by Bodie James, a young, no-nonsense lieutenant whom he'd seen in action a few times when visiting Fort Sampson. Galloping on each side of the long-haired officer, their buckskin fringes blowing in the breeze, were Coyote Jim Stephens and Kansas Joe Adderly, Holten's old scouting buddies from back at Fort Rawlins.

"Column, halt!" snapped Lieutenant Bodie James.

The young lieutenant was a short, muscular cavalry officer with long brown hair that flowed from beneath his wide-brimmed army hat. James' flashing brown eyes quickly turned to the scout, his hand snapping a salute to the new acting commander of the Army's 12th Cavalry. The column's tired army mounts were snorting all around him.

"Fort Sampson detachment reporting, sir, as ordered!"

Holten saluted and gestured at the men. "Is this all the army can spare, Lieutenant? There's an Indian War goin' on out here!"

"The other soldiers are needed to defend Fort Sampson, Mr. Holten. General Corrington is afraid them Injuns will attack just like they did at Fort Rawlins."

The scout let out a deep breath. "Well, I guess this'll have to do then."

"We don't need more 'an this, Holten!" said old Coyote Jim as he edged his snorting mount over to where the scout and the lieutenant were talking.

"Hell, no!" added Kansas Joe. "Them Pawnee are askin' for trouble when they mess with us!"

Then the young half-breed suddenly noticed Isabella Cartwright sitting on her nickering horse behind Holten. The scout caught the half-breed's gaze and made brief introductions all around, explaining without details how Isabella had been attacked while riding the stage.

"Miss Cartwright's writin' a book about western men and the way they live," explained Holten. "She'll be goin' back to Fort Sampson with ya until this uprisin' blows over."

Lieutenant Bodie James snorted. "Miss Cartwright oughtta put Black Bob Callahan into her book," said the young, long-haired officer. "Them two survivors of the wagon train holdup swore at the fort that he was the one leadin' them gunrunners against the army!"

Holten stiffened at the mention of Black Bob's name.

"Has anybody found the bastard?" said the scout. Holten turned in his saddle and looked at Isabella. "Excuse the language, Miss Cartwright."

Isabella smiled seductively at the scout.

Bodie James shook his head. "Seems to have disappeared into thin air, rifles and all. Of course he gave a lot of them Winchesters to the Pawnee."

"Any other identifications made?" asked the scout.

"The same old gang that's always been ridin' with Callahan. Ugly Slim Powell, Big Nosed John Harper, and all the others we've come to know and love."

The soldiers laughed, mostly to relieve their tension.

"There was one report from some army sentries that Slim Powell was seen headin' for the Broken Wing whorehouse."

Holten nodded. "Knowin' that fat, sex-hungry killer that seems about right."

"Anyway," said Bodie James, removing his dusty hat and wiping his perspiring brow with the sleeve of his blue uniform, "Slim is the only one of the gang who has been spotted."

"What other good news do ya bring this mornin'?" asked Holten with a wry grin. "Next thing you're goin' to tell me is that the Pawnee are massin' to attack us over the next rise!"

Coyote Jim cleared his throat. "Well," drawled the white-haired old scout, "there's talk that a couple of eastern dudes who've been seen hangin' around Fort Sampson are somehow in cahoots with Callahan and the Pawnee."

The scout's eyebrows shot up. "Dudes?" he asked.

"Yeah," added Kansas Joe. "Seems like they're fancy-dressin' gun dealers who've been doin' business with drifters the likes of Black Bob and his boys. The army's supposed to be trackin' down some kinda identification back East." The half-breed glanced at Bodie James.

"Them dudes," said the lieutenant, "had been hangin' around the fort for almost a week before the raid on Fort Rawlins. Now nobody knows where in hell they went!"

An eerie silence enveloped the small group.

"Well," said the scout finally, "looks like we got only one thing to do right now, and that's to round up as many settlers as we can from the nearby ranches."

"There's been some killin' and rapin' already, Holten," said Coyote Jim. The wizened old frontiersman stroked his bushy white beard and glanced up at Holten. "Whole families have been found cut to pieces."

Isabella Cartwright sucked in her breath. "My God!" she gasped, her hand going to her mouth.

Holten sighed. "It was bound to happen."

"Always does, eh scout?" said Lieutenant James.

"Especially when ya got a crazy war chief like Mole On Face gettin' brand new guns from dirty scum like Black Bob Callahan!"

"What's your plan, Mr. Holten?" asked Bodie James.

"We'll head along the Benzman Trail and see if we can find any small groups who were unlucky enough to pick this week to start their trips. Then this afternoon I figure you and the troopers'll take Miss Cartwright, and any other folks we might run across, back to Fort Sampson."

"And you?"

Holten turned the head of his snorting mount. "I've got a date with big Slim Powell! And then I gotta try and find the main Pawnee camp."

After all, he had some scores to settle.

The column headed away at a furious gallop.

For the next few hours Holten led the small column of troopers, and Isabella Cartwright, across the parched, sun-baked Dakota prairie in search of unfortunate ranchers, farmers, and townsfolk who may have been brutalized by the savage, rampaging Pawnee renegades.

Following the picturesque, tree-lined Benzman Trail, which was the main wagon trail for settlers heading further west, the scout and his sweat-soaked party came across several small groups of frightened white settlers who had barely escaped the fury of the Indians. The fear burst forth from these horrified survivors in a spate of words that were edged with panic.

"Injuns done killed our neighbors!" they yelled.

"Scalped everybody and cut 'em into pieces!"

"It was horrible!"

"Help us, please!"

By noon the column had gathered over twenty straggling settlers who were carrying whatever meager possessions they had been able to scoop up in their arms before the screaming Pawnee had swooped down onto their ranches. The column of fifteen soldiers, two shaggy scouts, Isabella Cartwright, Holten, and the frightened settlers resembled a caravan of gypsies trudging across the brown, mid-summer prairie.

The scout was pleased with the way Isabella was handling herself. He knew the scorching prairie heat and stifling summer humidity were different from what the pretty, blue-eyed writer was used to in her native Boston. And all the talk from the homeless settlers of bloodied corpses, violated women, and butchered children was enough to dishearten anyone. Yet the sumptuous blonde didn't complain once, and Holten attributed her attitude to her dogged determination to gather material for the book she was writing.

Just after high noon the weary column crested a grassy rise on the way toward Fort Sampson, and immediately the sounds of a fierce gun battle filled the sultry summer air. A faint odor of burning wood tweaked the scout's sensitive nostrils. The scout's pulse quickened at what he saw on the narrow trail below.

Holten held up his hand and the column stopped in its tracks. Lieutenant Bodie James and the two buckskin-clad scouts trotted alongside Holten and reined in their nickering mounts. The scout's companions looked at the trail below.

"What is it, Mr. Holten?" asked Lieutenant James.

Holten nodded toward the trail beneath them. "Goddamn Pawnee war party," said the scout between teeth clenched with growing anger.

Holten let his steely blue eyes quickly scan the desperate scene below. His piercing gaze flitted from the two covered wagons stalled on the edge of the grassy trail, one of them engulfed with flames, to the small knot of wild-shooting settlers who were firing at a circling band of about twenty-five howling, shaven-headed Pawnee braves. Several dead settlers lay sprawled on the trail beside the wagons, while a half dozen or so screaming women and children were huddling for protection under the fully packed wagons.

"Every one of them Injuns is firin' a brand new Winchester repeater!" snapped Coyote Jim in his thin, reedy voice. The white-haired frontiersman pulled his worn coonskin cap further onto his head.

"Compliments of Black Bob Callahan," grated Holten.

"And look who's down there, Eli!" cried Kansas Joe. The short, swarthy half-breed was pointing at the battle below. "An old friend of yours is leadin' them Pawnee warriors. I see him on that white stallion!"

Holten squinted through the bright, early afternoon sunshine. Then his jaw hardened when he spotted a big, powerful looking warrior galloping like hell astride a gleaming white horse.

"Red Knife!" breathed the scout.

"They don't come no meaner 'an him!" said Kansas Joe.

The big, dark-skinned Pawnee brave was famous throughout the Dakota prairie for his horsemanship, his fighting skills, and his ruthless manner of dealing with enemies. The shaven-headed warrior was known as The Blade by the Oglala Sioux, because of his superior skill as a knife fighter. The bloodthirsty warrior once captured a family of Sioux and had practiced his knife swinging stroke by decapitating the captives one by one. Holten had tangled with the hard-faced killer on a couple of occasions, and knew that Red Knife, or The Blade, was the consummate plains Indian warrior.

Suddenly Isabella Cartwright came galloping up to the rise and reined in her mount near the scout. "What's the matter, Eli?" she asked, shading her peaches-and-cream complexion from the blistering mid-day sun.

"An Indian attack," said Holten. "We're goin' to help."

"Good, I've never seen a battle before!"

"Well," said the scout, "you're goin' to have to watch this one from back here. Lieutenant, assign one of your corporals to stay with Miss Cartwright up here on the hill."

"Yessir!" snapped Bodie James. Then the long-haired officer turned the head of his snorting horse and galloped back toward the waiting column of troopers.

"But I'll stay out of the way!" protested Isabella.

"I know," said the scout. "Up here on the rise."

"Oh, Eli!"

"Lieutenant!" shouted Holten. "Prepare to deploy your detachment! Keep a couple of men here to watch over the settlers, and Miss Cartwright here."

"Oh, poo!" said the pretty blonde, a look of annoyance spreading across her finely etched features and clouding her blue eyes.

"It's for your own good, Isabella," said the scout.

"We better hurry, Holten!" interjected Coyote Jim. The old frontiersman was hauling his powerful Sharps .50 caliber rifle from its saddle sheath. "Another one of them settlers just caught a bullet!"

"Like I said," remarked Holten, looking at the luscious blonde writer beside him. "Stay up here!"

"It's so boring!"

"But it's safe!"

Then with a wave of his long, buckskin-clad arm, Holten urged Lieutenant Bodie James, a dozen of the troopers, and his two scouting buddies down onto the trail below to do battle with part of the painted Pawnee renegade band that had brutally attacked Fort Rawlins the day before and had killed so many innocent people.

And who had helped to kill Yellow Feather.

The scout grit his teeth and headed for revenge.

When the charging cavalry troopers were about halfway

down the grassy slope that led to the trail, Holten noticed that the circling Pawnee braves suddenly reined in their war ponies and were glancing at the soldiers. The scout shouldered his Winchester .44-40 and began to pick his targets. On both sides of him the troopers were doing the same with their army issue Springfield single-shot carbines.

"Pick your targets and fire at will!" cried Holten.

Suddenly the early afternoon air was alive with the staccato cracks of a dozen fire-spitting rifles and several Pawnee warriors in front of the galloping scout screamed with pain as they were shot from their mounts.

"Look, it's the army!" shouted a settler near the wagons.

"Them Injuns are on the run!"

"Give it to 'em, boys!"

While keeping his balance atop the galloping gelding by hooking his long legs under the powerful mount's belly, Holten let loose with a volley of rapid-fire shots from his smoking repeater, levering and firing a number of times. His accurate slugs sent four startled Pawnee braves slamming to the ground, their gaping bullet wounds spurting blood onto the grassy trail.

Suddenly the scout held up his long arm and halted the galloping column of troopers about a hundred feet from the Pawnee warriors.

"Form a skirmish line!" yelled Holten. "Then pick your targets and give 'em hell!"

"Do we pursue the red bastards?" asked Bodie James.

"Not now, Lieutenant! Them settlers are our main concern for the time bein'."

Within a few minutes the kneeling, dust-covered soldiers had nearly decimated the fully surprised band of warriors. Only a handful of the shaven-headed killers remained atop their wild-eyed ponies.

Suddenly Coyote Jim pointed back at the hill.

"Holy shit!" he cried in his reedy voice. "Look over there, Holten! That there eastern gal is sure as shit gonna get her pretty little head blown off!"

Whirling toward the grassy slope where the settlers and Isabella Cartwright were supposed to be waiting, the scout's heart leapt to his throat when he spotted Isabella galloping like mad toward the battle line, her flowing blonde hair streaming behind her as she was riding. Hot on her tail was the young corporal who had been assigned to watch the spirited writer.

"Damn greenhorn!" muttered Holten.

Then without warning the Pawnee warriors who had been trapped by the sudden onslaught of the troopers used the sudden distraction, and subsequent lull in the firing, to make their escape. Led by the muscular brave Red Knife, the galloping Indians headed for the prairie.

"Christ!" snapped Kansas Joe. "The Injuns!"

A renewed volley of gunfire from the soldiers cut down a couple of the fleeing Pawnee braves, but half a dozen managed to gallop out of range of a clean shot within a few seconds. The warriors fled in a cloud of alkaline dust.

"Look!" shouted Bodie James, pointing toward the grassy slope where Isabella Cartwright was reining in her snorting horse. "Red Knife is after the woman!"

Feeling a sudden stab of anxiety in his gut, Holten looked on with a growing sense of horror as the ruthless Pawnee warrior, The Blade, suddenly turned away from the galloping horde of fleeing braves and headed for Isabella.

The scout watched the big Indian quickly raise his gleaming new Winchester and squeeze off a quick shot in the direction of the baby-faced corporal who was nearly upon Isabella. The startled young soldier's hands flew over his head with the impact of the slug from Red Knife's rifle and the bloodied corporal tumbled dead to the ground. The charging, shaven-headed brave continued galloping until he was alongside the now screaming blonde.

"Son of a bitch!" snapped Lieutenant James.

"Hold your fire!" ordered Holten. "Ya might hit the lady!"

Then while Holten and the helpless soldiers looked on with a feeling of frustration, Red Knife hooked a powerful arm around Isabella's slender waist and lifted her onto his nickering war pony. With a quick kick to the ribs of his horse, the scowling warrior started to gallop away.

"Eli, help me!" cried Isabella. "Oh God!"

"Stay here with the settlers!" said Holten, kicking his gelding into a sudden gallop. "I'll get that red bastard if it's the last thing I ever do!"

Urging his big, powerful horse into a full gallop as soon as he left the soldiers behind, the hard-riding scout was only ten yards behind the fleeing Pawnee warrior within seconds. Holten had returned his rifle to its saddle sheath and now he was ready for a hand-to-hand battle with one of the best fighters on the plains. The galloping scout quickly drew abreast of Red Knife's overburdened pony and saw the startled look in the big warrior's flashing eyes.

"Eli, help me!"

Knowing he had to stop the battle-hardened brave's wild-eyed pony before Red Knife decided to toss Isabella onto the ground, Holten dug his heels into the gelding's glistening flanks and edged his big horse in front of the nearby pony's head.

The startled pony stopped in its tracks and reared.

Isabella screamed and Red Knife fell.

While the scout was reining in his snorting horse in a cloud of dust, Red Knife and Isabella slammed to the grassy trail and rolled on the ground.

"Oh my God!" gasped Isabella Cartwright.

Red Knife was starting to regain his feet when Holten leaped from the gelding and smashed into the muscular brave. The two hardened prairie veterans rolled in the dust, came up with flashing knives in their hands, and went quickly into a crouch.

Holten smiled. "We meet again, Red Knife," said the scout in Lakota. He knew the shaven-headed warrior across from him spoke the Sioux tongue.

"It will be the last time!" snarled the Indian called The Blade. Then the famous knife fighter lashed out with his gleaming, foot-long hunting knife and nicked Holten's left sleeve.

"Red Knife is growing old and slow," said Holten.

"Eli, be careful!" cried Isabella.

"Get back and stay out of the way!" commanded the scout.

Red Knife laughed. "Tall Bear still likes the pretty young white girls, I see. And so soon after we killed his Oglala bride, too!"

The warrior's harsh words dug into the scout's flesh like the razor-sharp blade of a knife. Holten's steely blue eyes narrowed and he glared at Red Knife.

"You killed her?"

Red Knife laughed again. "I was not lucky enough to be close to her or surely I would have. It was Mole On Face who spotted you both on the platform with the fat white soldiers and the squaw-like Oglala braves."

"Mole On Face!" hissed the scout.

Suddenly the nearby drumming of hoofbeats from some approaching cavalry horses filled the air. Red Knife looked up quickly, and the careless move gave Holten a chance. Taking advantage of the shaven-headed warrior's sudden lack of concentration, the scout reared back and hurled his fearsome, gleaming Bowie knife at the suddenly startled brave.

But Red Knife was a master at knife-fighting.

Reacting with the lightning quick reflexes that had helped him earn the moniker, The Blade, the painted

Pawnee warrior darted to the side. Holten's flying blade nicked Red Knife's massive shoulder, barely broke the skin, and went skittering across the ground.

Red Knife roared with laughter. "Goodbye, Tall Bear!"

Then as the powerful brave drew back his glistening hunting knife to toss it at the scout, Holten beat him to the punch with a sudden, cat-like dive at his legs.

The two fighters tumbled to the ground.

Trying desperately to arc his long hunting knife up into Holten's buckskin-clad body while lying flat on his back, the suddenly startled Pawnee warrior brought the gleaming blade across his own painted frame with his powerful arm. The scout caught the muscular brave's wrist with both of his hands, quickly reversed the direction of the razor-sharp cutting edge, and put the force of all his own weight on top of the fallen Indian's knife hand.

The blade buried itself in Red Knife's chest.

The Indian known as The Blade for his knife-fighting prowess suddenly had been impaled with his own fearsome blade. The powerful warrior cried out in pain. Then Red Knife's flashing brown eyes widened with shock and his dark, painted face twisted into a contorted mask of pain. He died almost instantly while staring at the scout.

The galloping soldiers reined in their mounts.

"Looks like ya got things pretty much under control here, Mr. Holten," said Lieutenant Bodie James with a quick smile on his boyish face.

Holten stood and retrieved his knife.

"I'm afraid it's just the beginning," he said.

EIGHT

Isabella and Holten were standing alone.

"I'm sorry, Eli, really I am!"

"Tell that to the poor corporal back there."

"Are you saying that I was responsible for that soldier's death?"

"If ya had stayed put maybe nothin' would've happened."

After gathering the newest batch of frightened settlers and helping them to bury their dead, the troopers and the scout had huddled everyone together for one last drink of water before heading for Fort Sampson.

While the settlers were watering down, Holten and Isabella had wandered off and were talking in the sparse shade of a scraggly cottonwood. The scout had already tried to cool off the troopers, who felt that Isabella had cost the life of one of their men, and was now attempting to convince the pretty blonde that the prairie was different from Boston.

"But my book, Eli! I'm already out on the plains, so why can't I just do the best I can? I'm sorry about that poor soldier, but I don't think it was my fault. I'll stay out of the way next time, I promise."

The pretty writer crossed her ample bosom with a finger.

"There won't be a next time," said Holten. "You're headin' back to Fort Sampson with the troopers and that's final. I got me enough to worry about without babysittin' for ya."

Silence filled the gap between them.

"Even after last night?" asked Isabella, her long, tapered fingers snaking down the scout's body until they reached his crotch and grasped his balls through the material.

The scout flinched and felt a twinge in his loins.

He removed her hand gently. "Look, Isabella," he said in an even voice. "I'd love to have ya along under normal circumstances. But these ain't normal times. There's goin' to be a lot more blood spilled before this here Pawnee uprisin' is under control."

Holten heard the press of boot leather on dirt.

"We're 'bout ready to roll, Mr. Holten," said Lieutenant Bodie James. "Them settlers are pretty scared. I hope to hell we don't run into no more Pawnee along the way."

Holten shook his head. "I kinda figure Mole On Face and his braves are goin' to lay low for a while and enjoy the spoils of their raids. Ya oughtta have a clear trail all the way back to the fort."

Bodie James cleared his throat. "Are ya ready, Miss Cartwright?"

Isabella shot Holten a nasty look that would have made a snarling grizzly back down. "I don't think it's fair, do you Lieutenant? This is a free country!"

"Sure is a free country, ma'am," replied Bodie James. "And we're aimin' to keep it that way by takin' care of these here Pawnee Injuns around the prairie."

"Have a nice trip, Isabella," said Holten with a smile.

"Hmmmmpf!" snorted the blonde writer. Isabella Cartwright then turned on her heel and swivel-hipped away from the scout like an insulted matron from Boston's high society.

Holten chuckled. Bodie James shrugged his shoulders.

"Hell of a woman!" exclaimed the lieutenant.

"As high-strung as a frisky mare," said the scout, a

broad grin creasing his leathery face and his steely eyes fixed on Isabella's swaying buttocks.

"Where ya headin' now, Mr. Holten?"

"I think I'll visit a whorehouse," said the scout as he began to walk back to where his gelding was tethered to a sage brush plant.

"Slim Powell?"

Holten nodded. "Until I can parlay with Chief Black Spotted Horse and the Oglala, I'll be lookin' for Black Bob and his boys. Then if Black Spotted Horse knows the whereabouts of Mole On Face we can hit 'em together."

"What do ya want us to do?"

"Take everybody to the fort, and then meet me tomorrow at sunrise where the Gray River cuts across the Benzman Trail. By that time I'll know somethin' more."

Coyote Jim and Kansas Joe came up to the scout.

"Ya want us to trail along with ya, Holten?" asked Coyote Jim in his thin voice. "There's an awful lot of mean critters around the plains these days!"

"Thanks just the same, Jim," said Holten. "But you and Joe oughtta stick with the troopers just in case they need ya on the way back to the fort."

Then, while the merciless afternoon sun beat down on the column like a hammer, Lieutenant Bodie James and the two buckskin-clad scouts led the settlers and Isabella Cartwright onto the grassy trail that led to the relative safety of the army's Fort Sampson. Eli Holten watched the dusty column disappear over a nearby rock-strewn ridge and then dug his heels into the sides of his nickering sorrel. He pointed his intelligent mount toward one of the busiest little whorehouses in the whole Dakota Territory.

And toward a killer named Slim Powell.

The Broken Wing saloon and whorehouse was a tiny, shingled building nestled among towering pine trees off of the wide Benzman Trail. The foul-smelling bar catered mostly to the prairie's vast criminal element, although a fair number of travelling settlers from the nearby trail had been known to sample its wares.

The sleazy establishment got its name from its proprietor, Fast Eddie McCreary, a skinny, bald-headed man whose left arm was once bent backwards until it snapped by an irate customer who'd had a few too many drinks. The arm had healed improperly, and because of the distorted limb and the word-of-mouth publicity given to the arm twisting incident, McCreary had changed the name of the place to the Broken Wing.

Now thanks to the tip given him by Lieutenant Bodie James, the revenge-seeking scout was approaching the shadowy den of cutthroats and thieves with all the caution of an Indian hunter stalking a wounded buffalo. Holten was hoping like hell to find the massive two-hundred-and-fifty-pound Slim Powell with his pants down—literally.

Having ridden hard for a couple of hours, the scout tethered his tired gelding to a well-hidden pine tree and started to pad toward the whorehouse in the clearing up ahead. Holten's narrowed eyes quickly scanned the surrounding terrain for any signs of trouble, and his wiry muscles were tensed for action.

If Slim Powell had felt confident enough to let army sentries watch him ride boldly to the whorehouse, then the scout knew that meant the fat killer must have been pretty sure he'd get some help from his buddies when he arrived.

Holten's nerves were as tight as a fiddle.

Breaking away from the cover of the shadowy pine trees with all the quiet stealth of a lion on the prowl, the scout padded quietly to the wooden slab door of the Broken Wing whorehouse and pressed his buckskin-clad back against the rough-hewn front wall.

The scout's heart was beating like an Indian war drum.

Scanning the area around the tiny shack, Holten noticed only four horses grazing in a small rope corral.

The only sound was the gentle sighing of the cool, prairie breeze in the tops of the towering pines.

Then he heard the voices.

"Hey Eddie!" boomed a deep, reverberating voice. "Bring us some more whiskey and some of that there settler stuff we grabbed the other day. What's it called?"

"Caviar!" called a voice that Holten quickly recognized as that of Fast Eddie McCreary.

"Yeah, that's the stuff," boomed the deep voice. "And you're tellin' me it ain't nothin' more than salty fish eggs, huh Eddie?"

"That's right, Slim, fish eggs!"

A couple of whores giggled.

Holten stiffened. Slim Powell was in the shack.

Bracing himself for a sudden entrance into the Broken Wing saloon, the scout quickly drew his Remington .44 pistol and sucked in some air. Here's another one for Yellow Feather, thought Holten as he let out his breath. Then gripping the butt of his revolver as though it was Slim Powell's neck, the scout lowered his shoulder and smashed through the flimsy slab door.

Holten burst into the dimly lit whorehouse amidst the crashing sound of the door falling to the wood-planked floor. The scout quickly went into a crouch and scanned the tiny two-room saloon.

Fast Eddie McCreary whirled around from where he was standing near the opened doorway of the back room, a sudden expression of fear on his lean face and a platter full of food balanced in his hands.

"What the . . . ?" stammered the bald proprietor.

"Get away from the door, Eddie!" snapped Holten.

"Eli Holten!" cried Fast Eddie.

"I said stand back!"

The scout squeezed the trigger of the .44 and sent a hot slug into the whiskey bottle the bald whorehouse owner was carrying on the tray.

The whores in the back room screamed.

The bottle disintegrated.

Fast Eddie McCreary jumped away from the open doorway, his trembling hands held high over his head and his widened gray eyes fixed on the scout's smoking gun. Holten stepped to the door.

The bald proprietor's quick leap to the side suddenly revealed the crowded interior of the small back room: a big brass bed, two wide-eyed whores sitting on the bed with the sheets drawn up around their necks, and big Slim Powell reclining leisurely on the good down mattress, a wide grin on his fleshy face. The killer's hands were hidden under the sheets.

"Figured I'd be seein' ya before too long, scout!" boomed the two-hundred-and-fifty-pound killer. "I here tell that one of them Injuns that was killed at Fort Rawlins was your little squaw!"

Holten quickly studied the roly-poly gunman's pinkish, pig-like face that was glistening with sweat, the wide apart green eyes, and the rolls of blubber that were plainly evident under the crumpled sheets. The scout noticed that the big killer's hands remained hidden from view.

"Findin' ya was easy, Slim," said the scout, his .44 levelled at the fat killer's broad, hairy chest. "All I had to do was look in the nearest whorehouse!"

Slim Powell roared with a deep laughter that filled the tiny back room. "Too bad I wasn't there at the fort, Holten. I would've liked to have fucked your squaw. I here tell from some of the boys that she was a real good lay!"

Again the deep laughter filled the room.

Holten felt anger begin to boil inside of him.

"Although I oughtta fill ya full of lead right now, Slim," said the scout in a cold, even voice, "I'm goin' to take ya back to Fort Sampson where they'll hang ya nice and proper like."

Holten saw a sudden expression of anger cross the fat

killer's jowly face, clouding his beady green eyes. "You ain't takin' me no place, scout!" snarled Slim Powell. "This ain't some Injun camp where ya can come in and give orders! Besides, we're the law out on the prairie now that the army's outta action. Ya ain't gonna stop this war by gettin' just one of us, Holten!"

"I aim to get all of ya!"

"Ha!" cried Slim. "Like hell!"

The scout's steely blue eyes bore into Slim's. "Now I want ya to slowly remove your hands from under that there sheet. One wrong move, Slim, and I'll fill ya full of holes!"

Seconds seemed like hours.

Holten's pulse was racing, his trigger finger itching.

Suddenly Holten's sensitive ears picked up the faint drumming of hooves growing louder and closer. The other four in the whorehouse seemed to notice, too. Slim Powell's fleshy face creased into a wide smile.

"Looks like your game is up, scout!" boomed the massive killer. "That's Black Bob and the boys comin' back from raidin' some settlers. I betcha they'll be pleased as punch to find ya waitin' for 'em!"

"So this is your hideout, eh Slim?"

"Hell no!" boomed the blubbery bandit. Holten noticed that the fleshy killer's hands were beginning to slide from under the sheet. "We just come here to bother Fast Eddie and screw the latest pussy he's got in from Deadwood."

The scout had to make a decision.

"All right, Slim," he said. "If Black Bob wants to get me, he'll have to shoot through your fat hide to do it. Now get outta that there bed nice and slow."

The scout noticed a sudden change in the fat killer's beady green eyes. It was the same kind of half-crazed look that came into the flashing eyes of a cougar or a wolf just before it leaped at its prey.

Suddenly the mammoth gunman kicked out with his

heavy feet and sent the two screaming whores off the bouncing bed and into the scout's field of fire.

"You son of a bitch! Indian lover!" boomed Powell.

The naked whores crashed into the scout, their flailing arms and legs knocking him back into the shack's main room and onto the wood-planked floor. While regaining his balance in the middle of the floor, Holten watched big Slim Powell toss back the sheets, level a classic seven-and-a-half-inch Colt .45 Peacemaker at the scout's chest, and squeeze the trigger.

The fat gunrunner's big revolver roared in the small confines of the tiny back room, its barrel belching fire and smoke as it sent a hot bullet slamming into the naked back of one of the whores. The startled girl screamed and sprawled dead on the floor.

"Shit!" snarled Slim.

Not wasting a moment, the scout arced his Remington .44 pistol upward and squeezed off a couple of quick shots. The two bullets tore into Slim Powell's fleshy gut and exited through his back in a shower of blood that splattered the wall with glistening red splotches. The fat killer's gun went flying from his pudgy hand.

Approaching Slim Powell with the same amount of caution he'd use if he was stalking a wounded bull buffalo, the scout kept his hand ready and his eyes peeled. Suddenly the dying fat man reached into his nearby boots, extraced a long dagger, and made to toss it at Holten.

The scout squeezed the trigger and sent another hot slug slamming into Slim Powell's massive chest, the force of the speeding bullet smashing the roly-poly killer back against the blood-stained brass bed. Holten watched the dying gun-runner's beady green eyes roll toward the heavens.

The panting scout had little time to waste.

Turning quickly toward the front of the whorehouse, Holten suddenly realized that the second of the two naked whores was opening the door and preparing to escape.

"Wait a minute!" shouted the scout.

But it was too late to stop the frightened young girl. The naked whore dashed for the safety of the approaching gang of riders. Holten stepped briskly across the room and slammed the flimsy door.

Then Holten heard the metallic clicks behind him.

"Drop your gun, scout!" said Fast Eddie McCreary.

Holten felt a cold tremor of anxiety in his gut.

"I said drop it!"

The scout let his .44 clatter to the whorehouse's wooden floor, raised his arms a little, and turned around to look into the deadly twin bore of the smiling bald proprietor's American Arms double-barrelled shotgun.

"Take it nice and easy, scout!"

Holten heard the shrieking whore outside the building babbling to the gunmen, who were rushing toward the tiny shack. Her frantic speech was followed quickly by the patter of footsteps on the hard-packed ground and the clump of boots on the whorehouse floor as the men burst into the room.

Holten turned to his right and looked into the deep-set brown eyes and dark-skinned face of none other than Black Bob Callahan, leader of the gunrunners. All around the scout were other hard-faced members of the gang, including the infamous gunslinger Big Nosed John Harper, as well as a small band of shaven-headed, brightly painted Pawnee warriors.

"Well lookee here, boys!" exclaimed Callahan. "If it ain't Eli Holten himself!"

"Makin' it easy for us to kill ya, eh Holten?" remarked Big Nosed John.

"Look in the back room, Callahan," said Fast Eddie.

"The back room?"

"Look what this here scout did!"

Black Bob stepped quickly to the doorway that led to the

tiny back room, stopped in his tracks, and then turned to face the scout. Holten watched the anger rise in the dark-skinned killer's chiseled face. Several other members of the gunrunning gang peered into the room and came away shaking their shaggy heads.

"Jesus Christ, it's Slim!"

"What's left of him!"

Callahan turned and faced Fast Eddie. "Holten did that?"

The bald-headed whorehouse owner nodded quickly.

Then Black Bob stepped over to the scout and motioned for a couple of his boys to grab Holten's arms. Rearing back with a couple of balled fists, the dark-skinned gang leader then pummelled the scout with a dozen or so quick punches to his face, jaw, and stomach. Each hammer-like blow to the head brought stars to Holten's eyes and the gut-wrenching smashes to his stomach took the wind from his sails.

Finally the nearly unconscious scout was allowed to fall to the hard floor, his head ringing and his breath coming in uneven gasps. Bloody welts decorated his face and a rivulet of blood was seeping from his nose.

"And that's only the beginnin', Holten!" snarled Black Bob as he stood hovering over the fallen scout. "Bring the bastard over to the door, boys!"

After Holten was yanked to his feet and tossed against the front door jamb, he peered through the fuzzy curtain of pain in front of his eyes at the dozen or so sobbing settler women who were huddling together in the back of a buckboard. Sitting atop their nickering war ponies around the shocked white women were half a dozen scowling, shaven-headed Pawnee renegade warriors. Another buckboard, Holten noticed, was full of boxes marked DYNAMITE.

"This goddamn prairie ain't never gonna get over the hell we're gonna raise, scout!" roared Black Bob, his deep-set brown eyes flashing with excitement. "Between the Pawnee and my boys, the Dakota plains ain't got a chance!"

Holten didn't have to ask what was to become of the women. He'd seen Indian uprisings many times before. If the settler gals were lucky, they'd meet a quick death at the hands of a frustrated or drunken buck Indian. But most likely the girls would be passed around from brave to brave until the blabbering women were skinned alive and tied to a tree.

"I hope ya got paid real good by them eastern dudes, Callahan," said the scout in a weak voice. "Because it's the last job you'll ever pull around these parts."

"He knows about them dudes!" cried Big Nosed John.

"Shut up!" snapped Callahan. Then the dark-skinned gunrunner turned to Holten. "You ain't in no position to be givin' threats, scout! After what ya did to poor Slim back there, you're gonna wish ya never lived with them goddamn Sioux. I understand the Pawnee don't have much use for the Sioux!"

The gathered gunrunners laughed harshly.

"And for your information, scout," added the dark-skinned gunrunner, "we've been paid real good for them guns. And there's lots more where they came from!"

Suddenly Big Nosed John Harper drew his three-and-a-half-foot-long army saber from its scabbard. The foul-smelling, stubble-faced former Confederate raider raised the sword menacingly above Holten's head.

"Let me whittle this boy down to size, Callahan! Then you can have what's left of the Indian lovin' bastard!"

Black Bob chortled. "Wish I could stick around and join the fun," said Callahan. "But Lily's waitin' for me. We're gonna celebrate real good tonight!"

The gunrunners laughed. The scout's pulse quickened.

Holten was glad that Black Bob hadn't visited Buzzard's Gulch yet, or he'd probably take a knife to the scout right now and slice him to pieces for killing his gal.

"Yeah," agreed the unshaven Harper, returning his fearsome saber to its scabbard. "Think I'll just return to the hideout and get me some of that there settler whiskey we picked up today."

Fast Eddie McCreary lowered his shotgun and spoke in a high-pitched voice. "Well ya oughtta do somethin' to this here scout to make him pay for killin' Slim, not to mention for makin' a mess of my place!"

"You're right!" said Black Bob, nodding.

Then Holten watched Black Bob Callahan turn and speak to a hard-faced Pawnee warrior in sign language, the universal silent tongue of the plains, telling the shaven-headed brave to do whatever they wanted to the scout.

The hard-faced warrior grunted, picked up a nearby kerosene lamp, and slashed his fingers across his chest in a cutting motion to indicate Holten's impending torture.

Black Bob cackled. Holten's guts constricted.

"I reckon ya saw that, eh scout?" asked Callahan. "This ol' boy wants to burn a few Injun decorations in your hide. Sure sounds fine to me!"

The assembled gunrunners roared with laughter.

The scout just stared straight ahead, looking for a chance to make his break for freedom. He'd seen the horrible Pawnee torture where scowling braves took turns burning intricate patterns into their victim's skin. It was a slow, excruciating way to die.

"Well, scout," said Black Bob Callahan, his flashing brown eyes boring into the scout's bloodied face. "Ya killed one of my best friends and now you're gonna pay for it with your life."

"You'll pay for all them innocent lives you and them Pawnees are takin' across the prairie, Callahan! Somebody'll catch up with ya pretty soon!"

Black Bob cackled and turned to leave. "It ain't gonna be you, Holten!" called Callahan over his shoulder.

"You're about to become a decoration!"

Most of the laughing gunrunners left the shack with their boss and leaped into their saddles. But the scout noticed that a few of the gunmen remained behind and began to unload some of the stolen dynamite boxes. Holten was starting to watch what they were doing with the explosives when a big hand clamped down on his shoulder. With his pulse quickening, the scout turned and glanced into the scowling, painted face of a shaven-headed Pawnee warrior who was collecting Holten's weapons.

The brave shoved Holten outdoors.

While he was being pushed outside, the scout quickly noticed that the screaming settler women were being stripped naked by the Pawnee and led to the woods. There, Holten knew, they would be raped by the excited warriors who had ridden in with the gunrunners. The scout also watched a few of the gunrunners carefully wrapping dynamite sticks together, undoubtedly to use as bombs against any army force that might come after them.

After Holten reached a spot near some tall, shady pine trees fifty feet from the whorehouse, the scout's buckskin shirt was unceremoniously hauled from his lean body by the same hard-faced warrior who had taken his weapons.

Holten grit his teeth in anticipation of the Pawnee torture and he could almost feel the bite of the burning sticks pressing against his naked flesh. Then, as a couple of torch-carrying braves approached the scout to begin the gruesome torture ceremony, the sudden drumming of hoofbeats rose in the afternoon air.

The Pawnee stopped in their tracks.

Holten glanced anxiously at the approaching trail. His mouth fell open as he recognized the figure who was galloping into the Indian-cluttered clearing.

It was Isabella Cartwright, pushing her mount hard.

"Jesus!" muttered Holten.

Suddenly the gunrunners working with the dynamite and most of the sex-hungry Pawnee warriors were looking at the pretty blonde horsewoman who was reining in her snorting mount at the edge of the clearing.

"Look at that pretty pussy!" yelled an outlaw.

"She came to the right place!"

Isabella's golden hair was flowing behind her and her curvaceous figure was pressing provocatively against the same tight-fitting riding habit that Holten had seen her slip into back at the stagecoach.

"Eli!" shouted the sumptuous, innocent blonde.

Holten didn't wait any longer.

Using Isabella's sudden and very unexpected appearance as a diversion, Holten quickly jammed his right elbow into the gut of the hard-faced warrior who was carrying the scout's weapons. The startled brave gasped for breath. The scout followed his initial blow with a chop to the neck that sent the unconscious warrior slamming to the pine needle-covered ground.

Holten reached down for his weapons and plucked his .44 revolver out of the dust. Suddenly the two painted braves with the flaming torches turned away from Isabella and noticed the scout's sudden escape.

The wide-eyed warriors reached for their knives, but it was already too late. Holten squeezed off two quick shots and sent a couple of heavy slugs slamming into the brightly painted chests of the suddenly startled braves. The dead Indians fell backwards on the ground with the impact of the bullets, the flaming torches they were carrying falling along with them.

Suddenly all eyes were on the scout.

"Hey, he's gettin' away!"

"Stop the son of a bitch!"

Darting forward with the quickness of a striking rattlesnake, Holten grabbed the two flaming torches and tossed them end-over-end into the overburdened buckboard containing the dynamite. The fiery sticks landed in a shower of sparks among the wrapped sticks of dynamite and rapidly began to spread their flames.

"Holy shit!" cried a gunrunner.

"Get that fire outta that there wagon!"

Holten grabbed his Bowie knife from the dead warrior on the ground, gripped his Remington .44, and dashed toward the spot in the woods where he'd tethered his gelding. Behind him he heard the panic of the gunrunners and the screams of the fleeing Pawnee. Suddenly Isabella came galloping across the clearing and into the trees.

"Get down!" shouted the scout, grabbing her reins.

With a healthy tug Holten jerked Isabella's nickering mount to the ground, caught the falling blonde before she hit the hard-packed dirt, and covered both their heads just in the nick of time.

A deafening explosion shook the ground.

As soon as the flames ignited the boxes of dynamite, the entire clearing in front of the tiny prairie whorehouse was engulfed by a yellow fireball. The rocking explosion caused the ground beneath the scout to shake like a stagecoach racing over a rutted prairie trail.

Holten managed to glance back toward the flimsy shack and saw horses, buckboards, and screaming gunrunners flying through the smoke-clogged air. Fast Eddie's whorehouse was now just a pile of lumber.

Then the scout heard the drumming of hoofbeats.

Looking toward the trail that led to the prairie, Holten's heart skipped a beat when he noticed half a dozen of the painted Pawnee braves galloping like hell.

"Let's go!" shouted the scout.

"Where?" asked Isabella, her blue eyes saucering.

"Into the Pawnee camp!"

Isabella stopped in her tracks. "What?"

"Them warriors," said Holten, nodding toward the fleeing Pawnee braves, "are goin' to be our guides. Now come on and get your horse!"

NINE

The escape from the smoky and confused whorehouse clearing was easy for the scout and his sumptuous travelling companion. Now they were galloping along the sun-scorched, grassy trail, following the easy-to-read tracks of the frightened Pawnee warriors. The scout turned in his saddle and smiled at Isabella.

"How in hell did ya happen to make it to the whorehouse?" he asked, a wide grin cracking his brown, leathery face and his blue eyes twinkling with affection for the blonde.

"I couldn't stay with the soldiers and miss all the action, Eli," said Isabella Cartwright with a seductive smile on her supple lips. Her long, honey blonde hair was streaming behind her as she was riding. "After all, I have a book to complete!"

"How did ya find the place?"

The pretty blonde writer's eyes sparkled with mischief. "Old Coyote Jim's directions were easy to follow," she said with a wide smile.

"Why that traitor!" said Holten with mock anger.

"Of course it took a little female persuasion to get the old coot to let me get away from the soldiers," said Isabella. "He's very loyal to you, Eli."

The scout chuckled. "Obviously not loyal enough!"

"Well, aren't you glad I came when I did?"

The scout nodded. "Yes, ma'am!" he said.

"Then I can stay with you?"

"Turnin' ya over to the soldiers don't seem to be workin', does it?"

"Oh, Eli, thank you!"

"But remember, things are goin' to get rough. If ya want to ride with me, ya gotta make yourself useful. I'll need ya to watch the horse, for example. That's a real important job, 'cause if somebody like the Pawnee braves steal our mounts then it's a long walk back home."

"I'll do a good job, Eli!" said Isabella.

Holten nodded. "After what's happened so far, I kinda think ya will."

"Where are we goin' right now?" asked Isabella.

"Well, them Pawnee warriors were so scared of that there dynamite I kinda figure they'll lead us right to their camp. It may not be their main camp, but there's a good chance Mole On Face will be there."

"Isn't he the one who . . . ?"

"Yeah," said Holten. "He's the one who killed my bride."

They rode in silence for a few minutes, Holten keeping his experienced eyes glued to the trail below and Isabella trying hard to keep her mount under control. The very mention of Mole On Face's name had sent a sudden wave of anger coursing through the scout's hardened frame, and, as they approached the open prairie and the Pawnee encampment, his muscles were ready for action.

"What about your friends, the Sioux?" asked the blonde.

"If we don't find nothin' up ahead, then we'll pay 'em a visit. Black Spotted Horse and the Oglala lost their squaws at the fort, so I'm sure they've been as busy as I have tryin' to find the Pawnee camp."

The gelding and Isabella's snorting horse ate up the miles. As the gathering dusk began to transform the prairie trail into a gray, shadowy storybook land where all the various shapes and forms seemed to meld together, the fleeing Pawnee warriors up ahead slowed their pace and entered a wide, grassy valley that was lined with towering pines. The coolness of the darkening slopes and the sweet fragrance of the Black Hills pine trees were a relief for the scout and his pretty companion after a day of hard riding over the blistering alkaline plains.

Suddenly Holten stopped his horse in its tracks.

"What's the matter, Eli?"

"Shhh!"

"What is it?"

"I hear voices," said the scout. "Now be quiet!"

While his tired gelding snorted and pranced, Holten listened intently to the familiar sounds that were drifting to his experienced ears. Somewhere nearby, he knew, the Pawnee renegades were having themselves a wild, old time.

"I don't hear a thing!" whispered Isabella.

"I do," said Holten. "The Pawnee camp is just over the next rise. If ya listen closely you'll hear drums, laughter, and some screams."

"Screams?"

"White settlers and Oglala squaws being tortured."

The scout watched the color drain from Isabella's face. Patting his gelding affectionately on the neck, Holten dismounted smoothly and motioned for the pretty blonde to do the same. Then he began to lead the horses up the slope to the tree-lined rise that overlooked what he was sure was the Pawnee encampment.

"What are you going to do, Eli?"

"First we'll have a look from up on the hill. Then I'm goin' into the camp."

He saw Isabella's blue eyes grow as big as silver dollars. "How are you going to get into the Pawnee camp? I'm sure they'll have something to say about that!"

Holten shrugged. "I'll just walk in," he said.

Isabella shook her head slowly and followed the scout

up the darkening slope until finally they were standing near a couple of tall box elder trees.

"We better tether the horses here," said Holten.

After securing their nickering mounts, the two weary travelers padded cautiously up the bush-lined hill, hunkered in the shadows on top of the rise, and peered into the tree-lined Pawnee campsite below. Holten heard the sumptuous blonde suck in her breath.

"Oh my God!" she breathed.

The scout pulled her closer to him. "Ya better stay down," he said. "Looks like them warriors are really enjoyin' themselves, but ya never can tell when one of them bastards might just look up here."

Then Holten scanned the shadowy, fire-lit renegade camp below. His steely blue eyes took in the dozen or so makeshift buffalo hide lodges, the half dozen crackling campfires, and the small knots of half-drunk Pawnee warriors huddled around the smoky fires. Around one of the blazes several of the warriors were pounding a drum while some of their friends were circling the fire in the traditional high-stepping Indian dance style. Near another crackling campfire some other braves were gorging themselves on the greasy meat of a butchered army mule, while others were quaffing bottles of rot-gut whiskey obviously supplied by Black Bob and his boys.

"Is this the main Pawnee camp?" asked Isabella in a voice filled with awe at the strange, horrifying sights below.

Holten shook his head. "This is just a temporary camp like all raidin' bands use when travelin'. The Pawnee live in big mud lodges in their main camp."

"Where's that?"

"Hopefully the Oglala will know."

A blood-curdling scream pierced the evening air.

Holten glanced at one of the makeshift lodges and felt a sudden jab of anxiety in his gut at what he saw. A few laughing, half-drunk Pawnee renegades were entering one of the lodges with several naked, screaming white settler women in tow. The warriors were naked, too, and their fully aroused cocks were extended in readiness. The scout grit his teeth, knowing from experience that the doomed women and girls would be passed from brave to brave until all of the renegades had been fully satisfied.

"Oh God!" gasped Isabella. "They're going to be raped!"

Then Holten saw Mole On Face.

The short, muscular Pawnee war chief was distinctly recognizable even at this distance, his shaven-headed scalp glistening in the firelight and his painted chest highlighted by the flickering flames all around him. The laughing leader of the renegades, and the killer of Yellow Feather, was dragging an Oglala squaw through the dirt by her long, black hair. The scout's heart sank when he recognized the woman as Green Moss, Black Spotted Horse's squaw.

"Murderin' son of a bitch!" murmured Holten.

"What Eli?"

"That's him," said the scout, nodding. "Mole On Face."

And while Holten and Isabella were watching, the laughing war chief waved to the celebrating warriors at the campfires and then disappeared into one of the nearby buffalo hide dwellings, with Green Moss behind him.

It was obvious to Holten what was going to happen.

The scout flew into action.

"Listen to me well," said Holten, turning toward Isabella. He could see the anxiety in the blonde writer's big blue eyes. "I'm goin' down to the camp and go after Mole On Face."

Isabella's jaw dropped. "But you'll be killed!"

"Not if ya do what I say," said Holten.

The pretty blonde nodded. "Okay, Eli, I'll help."

"After I'm in the camp, I'm goin' to try and kill Mole On Face. In any event, it'll be pretty tough down there. If I work things right, whether I kill the red bastard or not, I'll probably be comin' outta that camp runnin' like hell. So I'll need ya to have the horses ready and waitin'."

Isabella nodded quickly. "They'll be ready!" she said, a hint of fear in her voice and her pretty peaches-and-cream face suddenly creased with anxiety.

Holten touched her face with a big, rough hand.

"Ya got lots of courage, Isabella," he said in a voice full of sincere admiration for the sumptuous blonde easterner who'd come into his life.

"So do you, Eli!"

The scout nodded. "I'm just doin' what has to be done. Besides riddin' the Territory of a murderin' son of a bitch, I got me some scores to settle."

Isabella smiled. "I know," she said. "Be careful."

"I'm always careful," said the scout.

Then, after quickly checking his Bowie knife and his Remington .44, the buckskin-clad scout slipped away from the rise like a big cougar on the prowl. He padded through the darkening prairie slopes like an Indian hunter approaching a watering herd of skittish pronghorn antelope.

Snaking past clawing plum rose bushes and scraggly sage brush plants, Holten suddenly stopped in his tracks when he spotted a hard-faced Pawnee sentry standing in the shadows a few feet ahead. The bored, shaven-headed Indian was wrapped in a brightly-colored blanket and was watching the happy festivities in the nearby camp.

The scout quietly unsheathed his fearsome ten-inch-long Bowie knife, stepped briskly toward the half-asleep guard, and with a quick, deliberate stroke slit the sentry's throat in a sudden shower of blood. The startled warrior made a couple of gurgling sounds before he fell dead to the buffalo grass at the scout's feet.

Glancing around to see if he'd been spotted, Holten then wrapped the dead Indian's long blanket over his head and around his shoulders. Sheathing his blood-splattered blade, the fully alert scout turned toward the boisterous renegades and began to enter their camp.

With his heart beating wildly against his ribs, Holten padded unnoticed from the shadowy exterior of the camp into the middle of the fire-lit clearing. His piercing eyes were darting from side to side trying to spot trouble before it spotted him. Pulling the scratchy blanket over his head so it covered his hat, the scout walked slowly past the first couple of campfires and the howling, celebrating warriors who were sitting there. Nobody seemed to notice him. The smoky aroma of the broiled mule meat, the acrid stench of the foul-tasting rot-gut whiskey, and the scent of the towering pine trees all assailed the scout's sensitive nostrils. Walking deeper into the noisy encampment, Holten passed a couple of the makeshift buffalo hide lodges and stiffened at the sounds emanating from within them.

"Please don't hurt me again!"

"Oh no, please leave me alone!"

They were the plaintive cries of the settler women.

Holten continued past the lodges until he was smack in the middle of his enemy's camp. Now, thought the scout, all I have to do is find Mole On Face's lodge, rescue Green Moss, and kill the murderous chief.

Suddenly a hand touched his blanket-covered arm.

The scout's heart leapt to his throat.

Turning slowly while making sure his face was still covered by the sentry's blanket, Holten peered into the smiling, painted face of a half-drunk, shaven-headed Pawnee warrior. The staggering brave was holding out a bottle and muttering something in the unintelligible Pawnee tongue.

Then Holten heard a soft voice speaking Lakota.

"I will not dirty myself by sleeping with the crazy chief of the bald-headed Pawnee!"

It was Green Moss, Black Spotted Horse's squaw, and she was speaking from a tepee just a few yards from where the scout was standing with the half-drunk brave. The warrior with the bottle was becoming a pain in the ass, as Holten was trying to listen intently. Suddenly the scout heard the smack of flesh against flesh, followed by the gruff voice of Mole On Face, also speaking Lakota.

"Isn't the slut of the Oglala ready for a real man?"

"I'll never open my legs for you!" spat out Green Moss.

"Then I'll open them for you!"

Green Moss screamed. "Leave me alone!"

Holten decided it was time to take action, but the pesky half-drunk brave wouldn't take no for an answer. Finally the scout smiled and motioned with his head for the warrior to come into the shadows near Mole On Face's tepee. The smiling brave followed dutifully, and was rewarded for his effort with the flashing blade of Holten's Bowie knife being slammed into his gut. The drunken brave's eyes widened with shock, his jaw fell open, and he slumped to the ground like a sack of potatoes. The scout dragged the body further into the shadows and then stepped briskly to the leather entrance flap of Mole On Face's lodge.

Dropping the blanket to the ground, Holten glanced quickly from side to side to make sure he was alone and then burst into the Pawnee chief's lodge. He closed the flap behind him, gripped his Bowie knife, and surveyed the desperate scene in front of him.

"Tall Bear!" blurted out Green Moss.

Holten's revenge-seeking blue eyes quickly scanned the shadowy interior of Mole On Face's fire-lit lodge, taking in the buffalo robes on the ground, the small, smoky cooking fire, and the chief's weapons stacked nearby. Green Moss was cowering on top of the robes, her naked body already covered with ugly looking welts and bruises.

Mole On Face, who was hovering naked over the fallen Oglala squaw, whirled suddenly and glared at the scout, his flashing brown eyes locking with Holten's hateful glare. Mole On Face stood poised for action, his painted chest glistening in the flickering firelight and his broad face twisted into a sudden scowl. The scout saw the brown splotch on the short, muscular chief's face begin to darken with anger.

"Yes, so it is Tall Bear!" said Mole On Face in Lakota.

Like many of the plains Indian chiefs, the half-crazed renegade chief of the rampaging Pawnee was fluent in several of the prairie dialects, including Lakota.

"Tall Bear!" shrieked Green Moss. "Save me!"

Mole On Face laughed. "Yes, Tall Bear, save the little Oglala slut. It was too bad you couldn't save your own little slut back at the fort!"

Holten felt his anger boiling over and he gripped the Bowie knife in his hand until his fingers started to hurt. The scout's steely eyes bore into Mole On Face's smiling, painted countenance.

"You should have killed me, too," said Holten in a voice as hard and cutting as the blade in his hand. "Now you will pay for your mistake, Mole On Face."

"The death of your slut, Tall Bear, was only the beginning. With all the guns my warriors are getting, the peaceful Sioux will be swept off the prairie."

"Those evil whites will be punished, too."

Mole On Face laughed heartily. "By whom, Tall Bear? The army is destroyed! The evil whites, as you call them, are in control of the plains! And soon my warriors and I will drive the Sioux from our rightful hunting grounds."

Suddenly Holten heard footsteps outside the lodge.

A brave spoke in the Pawnee tongue.

The sudden distraction was all that Mole On Face needed to make his break. Before the scout could react, the muscular war chief grabbed a heavy stone war club from his pile of weapons and whirled toward Green Moss. The naked chief raised the club over his head.

"No!" shrieked Green Moss.

But it was too late.

Mole On Face brought the fearsome leather-covered stone club down with amazing speed onto the wide-eyed Oglala squaw's head, smashing her skull with the popping sound of a ripe melon falling to the ground. The twitching woman's head was suddenly reduced to a bloody pulp.

"You bastard!" cried the scout.

Suddenly the front of the chief's tepee was alive with arriving warriors, their excited voices telling Holten that his time was running out.

"Tall Bear is finished!" growled Mole On Face.

From just behind the scout the leather flap of the Pawnee war chief's humble lodge suddenly whooshed open and three shaven-headed, knife-toting warriors began to push their way into the dwelling. The scout reacted with lightning quick reflexes honed from twenty years of survival out on the Dakota plains.

Lashing out with his right foot, Holten connected with the jaw of the first startled Pawnee renegade and snapped the brave's head backwards. The unconscious warrior fell against the incoming braves and blocked the entrance to Mole On Face's smoky lodge.

Holten heard steps from beside him.

Ducking instinctively to the side, the light-footed scout heard the whooshing sound of Mole On Face's heavy war club as it passed within inches of his head. Whirling around with his elbow, Holten then smashed the off-balance chief on the back and sent him sprawling into the other warriors who were trying to enter the lodge.

"It's Tall Bear of the Oglala!" yelled Mole On Face.

Seeing his chance for revenge against the painted

Pawnee chief disappear with the sudden appearance of a dozen or more braves, Holten turned toward the rear of Mole On Face's lodge and slashed a three-foot-long gash in the buffalo hide covering. With a final mournful glance at Black Spotted Horse's mutilated young squaw on the ground beside him, the scout leaped through the sudden opening and sprinted into the dusk.

With the confusion of the half-drunk warriors in the Pawnee camp aiding his escape, Holten quickly retraced his steps to the rise and Isabella.

"Oh, Eli!" gasped the blonde. "What's happening?"

"Time for us to hit the trail!"

As they ran for the nearby tethered horses, the wide-eyed blonde writer turned and glanced at the scout. "Did you kill the chief?" she asked hesitantly.

Holten hauled his lean frame onto the gelding. "Not yet," he said in a tight voice. "But I'll get another chance. That wild bastard'll slip up soon!"

They quickly urged their mounts into a full gallop and headed for the prairie. Holten had some bad news for his long-time Oglala friends.

TEN

The setting mid-summer sun was casting long shadows across the middle of the somber Oglala Sioux camp when Holten and Isabella trotted among the tall, conical dwellings. The two weary travellers had ridden hard for an hour, hoping to arrive at the Sioux camp before sunset.

Now Isabella Cartwright was staring at the gawking Indian children, the ubiquitous short-haired dogs, and the hard-faced warriors on painted ponies. All around the camp angry braves were preparing their weapons for battle.

"I feel as though I've just entered another world," said the wide-eyed blonde in a hushed voice. Holten could see the tired lines on her pretty face.

"Ya have," answered the scout with a smile.

"They're so different from those savage Pawnees we saw back on the prairie."

"Most Indians are warm, gentle people," said Holten. He eased his snorting horse over toward the tall, brightly painted tepee of the tribe's wounded chief. "Them Pawnee were renegades with only killin' on their minds."

As Holten and Isabella were dismounting, Four Bull, the stout warrior who had tracked them down on the prairie, strode over to greet the two tired travellers.

"How," said the broad-faced warrior.

"How, Four Bull," replied Holten. "And what is the condition of Black Spotted Horse? Has he improved since I saw him last at the fort?"

"There has been some improvement in his condition," said Four Bull. "But like all of us, the chief is angry and upset at the loss of our squaws."

Wait until he hears the real bad news, thought Holten.

Holten then reached into his saddle bag and extracted Black Spotted Horse's medicine bundle. Now that the Oglala chief would be out to avenge Green Moss's death, the scout figured the wounded warrior would need it more than he would.

Leaving their tired horse to the able care of a couple of bright-eyed boys, the scout and his shapely blonde companion followed Four Bull into the large tepee belonging to the wounded leader of the Oglala. Stepping to the right as was the accepted custom upon entering a tepee, Holten motioned for Isabella to stay behind him. Four Bull left them alone with the Oglala leader.

Then the scout glanced at the wan, unsmiling chief who was lying on his back with several fluffy buffalo robes covering his large frame. Black Spotted Horse's dark, hawk-nosed face brightened when he caught sight of the scout.

"Tall Bear," said the chief weakly. "I have been waiting for your arrival for a long time. I am glad you have finally arrived."

"I am at your service, my old friend."

Black Spotted Horse glanced at Isabella. "And who is your companion, Tall Bear?"

"Another victim of the Pawnee savagery," said Holten.

The chief just nodded, grimaced with pain, and then motioned for the scout and Isabella to sit near him on the robes.

"My braves have been busy," said Black Spotted Horse. "They have located the main Pawnee camp. That is why you saw them preparing their weapons outside."

Holten perked up at the news. "Where is the camp?"

"In the large canyon where the Gray River runs down

from the hills. It is the hunting ground where Tall Bear and our braves hunted elk and deer in years gone by. Tall Bear must surely remember the site."

The scout nodded. "I remember it well," he said. "It is a natural fortification that will be difficult to attack without a diversion."

Suddenly the tepee's leather flap whooshed open and a wizened old squaw entered carrying a basket full of medicinal herbs and powders.

Black Spotted Horse laughed. "In Green Moss's absence old Crow Foot has been my very capable nurse. That is, if you can stand her foul nature."

The mention of the chief's murdered wife sent a chill of anxiety spreading through the scout's chest. Sometime soon he'd have to tell the wounded Oglala leader the bad news.

Meanwhile, the old squaw cackled. "Keep still and turn over. That wound of yours needs some fresh poultice on it. And if you're nice to me I'll be gentle."

Isabella, while not understanding Lakota, seemed to feel the camaraderie in the tepee and she smiled warmly at the scout. Holten winked at the sumptuous blonde. He was glad that her company had helped to ease the pain of Yellow Feather's loss, and he knew he would be forever grateful to her for sticking with him in his time of need— even though he had tried to give her to the soldiers for safekeeping.

Holten and Isabella watched as the wrinkled old woman expertly spread a paste made of crushed yarrow plants, green skunk cabbage, and a touch of mint into Black Spotted Horse's ugly looking wounds. Then, after quickly changing the weakened chief's foul-smelling bandages, the stooped-over squaw shuffled her way out of the lodge.

Holten returned to the business at hand. "And what about the camp of the evil whites?" he asked, vivid images of Black Bob Callahan's dark-skinned, evil-looking face flashing in front of his mind's eye. "Have your warriors found out where they are hiding?"

"Not yet," said the chief. "But they will soon."

Then the scout extended the chief's medicine bundle and saw the surprise rise in the wounded warrior's flashing brown eyes. Black Spotted Horse accepted the deerskin parcel.

"Does not Tall Bear have need for this?"

The scout looked down at the ground. "I feel maybe Black Spotted Horse will have more need for his medicine bundle after hearing what I have to say."

"You bring bad news, Tall Bear?"

Holten nodded gravely. "The worst kind of news."

Then in a low, somber voice the scout slowly recounted his visit to the Pawnee renegades' prairie campsite, ending with Mole On Face's savage murder of Chief Black Spotted Horse's lovely young squaw. Holten glanced at the stoic leader of the Oglala Sioux and swallowed back his own sadness at having had to tell his friend the bad news. The handsome, hawk-nosed chief just clenched his teeth and nodded at the scout.

"Well, Tall Bear," he said in a surprisingly strong voice, "it seems as though both of us have a good reason to see the Pawnee annihilated."

"There were other Oglala squaws with the Pawnee, too," added Holten, his voice faltering. "I did not recognize all of the women, but I'm sure they were the ones taken from the fort."

Isabella reached out and touched the scout's arm. "Eli, are you all right?" she asked, her pretty face a sudden mask of concern.

"As good as can be expected," replied Holten.

A deathly silence filled the lodge.

"Spend the night with us, Tall Bear. A tepee will be made available for you and your woman friend. In the morning we will prepare to kill the Pawnee."

"But your wounds . . . ?" asked a concerned scout.

The chief held up a big hand. "I will be fine."

The scout nodded at his longtime friend and ushered Isabella out of the tall, conical dwelling. As soon as they had left the tepee, Holten heard Black Spotted Horse's wailing funeral elegy rise into the sultry evening air and drift through the Oglala campsite.

Soon other warriors whose women had been taken by the Pawnee at Fort Rawlins heard their chief and understood what had happened to all the tribe's lost women. The braves began to wail until a chorus of elegies ran throughout the camp.

"What's that?" asked Isabella, her blue eyes widened.

"Funeral songs for the dead squaws."

"They sound so eerie!"

"Ya better get used to 'em," said Holten. "We'll be hearin' 'em all night long."

"You mean we'll be sleeping here?"

The scout nodded toward a tall tepee just ahead. "That's our lodge right there," he said, taking the pretty Bostonian by the arm and escorting her through the mourning Oglala Sioux campsite.

Holten was getting sick of funerals.

Holten and Isabella ate sparingly from the platters of buffalo meat, venison, prairie chicken, and antelope that had been brought to their tepee. Somehow the scout wasn't quite in the mood for eating. He lay back on a downy buffalo robe and began to work on his .44 pistol.

For a couple of hours the two weary travellers settled into their new quarters, Holten cleaning his weapons while Isabella was busy at a mirror provided by Four Bull. All during that time the mournful elegies echoed through the deathly still Oglala camp.

"I can't stand it any more!" said Isabella finally.

"Can't stand what?" asked the scout.

"That horrible moaning!"

"Relax," said Holten as he continued cleaning his long Winchester .44-40. "We got plenty of time. Besides, there ain't nothin' we can do about it."

Suddenly he saw Isabella's face brighten.

"Oh yes there is!" she said.

"What . . . ?" asked the perplexed scout.

Then before the scout could mutter another word, the sumptuous blonde writer began to strip off her tight-fitting riding clothes piece by piece. Her sparkling blue eyes were full of mischief and her pretty peaches-and-cream face was aglow with excitement. Holten watched the shapely honey blonde easterner pull off her soft leather boots, slip out of her hip-hugging dark green pants, and haul her dusty light green blouse over her head until finally she was standing stark naked in front of him. Her curvaceous, creamy white body reflected the shadows cast by the flickering fire in the center of the tepee. Isabella smiled broadly and cupped her big breasts with her hands.

"What do you think, Mr. Eli Holten? Would you like to get your big, rough mitts on these? Or how about this to warm your heart?"

Then with the erotic precision of an experienced striptease, Isabella Cartwright slowly ran her long, tapered fingers down from her breasts to the shiny patch of kinky hair at her crotch where they lingered provocatively in the waxy bush.

Holten felt an erection pressing against his pants.

While the scout's suddenly pounding penis was beginning to throb, Isabella inserted one of her long fingers into her slippery channel and began to masturbate in front of him, her eyes suddenly closing and a strange, dreamy expression spreading over her face.

"Ohhhh," she moaned. "I'm so ready, Eli!"

"I never woulda guessed," said the scout with a smile.

"Take off your clothes!" said Isabella urgently.

Holten chuckled. "What a way to pass the time!"

While the entire Oglala Sioux village was mourning their losses, Isabella Cartwright was trying to make Holten forget about his. Following Isabella's lead, the scout stripped off his buckskins in about one minute flat and was standing ready for action next to the moaning blonde easterner. Isabella stopped masturbating and looked at his penis.

"Oh my God!" she exclaimed, kneeling in front of the scout and planting a big, wet kiss on the tip of his elongated shaft.

"I do like your way of kissin', Isabella!"

The scout's steely blue eyes hungrily roamed the shapely blonde's curvaceous figure, from her round breasts and their rosy red nipples to her glistening bush and its wonderful hidden treasures.

Isabella giggled. "I'm learning more and more about you all the time, Eli Holten. You're making my book writing so easy!"

"Yeah," said Holten, a wry smile playing on his sensuous lips. "You're gettin' an intimate look at a frontier scout, eh Isabella?"

Isabella's melodic laughter filled the lodge. "Come here, you big hunk of western man! I might even write a whole book just about you!"

Isabella pulled him over by his hardened penis.

The two naked lovers slumped to the fluffy buffalo robes and quickly went into each other's arms, the touch of their warm bodies sending a sudden shiver of desire coursing through the scout's fully aroused frame.

Then without any further conversation the panting blonde reached out and began to explore the scout's tingling body with her long, tapered fingers, starting with the tangled mass of hair on his matted chest and working her way across his rippling stomach muscles until she wrapped her hand around Holten's pulsating penis and squeezed it gently.

"Jesus!" breathed the scout.

"Aren't you glad I came out West, Eli?"

"You Boston gals are all right!"

Isabella giggled and quickly mounted the scout, sitting atop his groin and rubbing his enormous shaft in the delicate folds of flesh just inside her glistening opening, the slow, exquisite massage of his sensitive glans nearly causing Holten to explode right then and there.

Taking advantage of Isabella's sudden close proximity, the scout reached out with his big, rough hands and began to knead the supple flesh of her big breasts, slowly massaging each taut nipple in a gentle circle until the writhing blonde easterner was shrieking with delight. Fully aroused now, the wide-eyed sex kitten quickly grabbed the scout's big right hand and guided it to her already dripping vagina, encouraging him to enter her with one of his fingers.

"Enter me, Eli, please!" she gasped, her eyes shut.

Never one to disappoint the ladies, the scout plunged his long forefinger deep into Isabella's warm and wonderful channel, evoking a squeal of delight from the writhing blonde writer. While exploring the deepest regions of Isabella's fully aroused body with his finger, Holten suddenly felt the gasping blonde's hand wrapping around his swollen penis once again.

"Stick this into me, Eli!" pleaded Isabella in a hoarse whisper.

"Whatever ya say!" gasped the scout.

With the writhing sexpot still sitting atop him, Holten maneuvered his elongated shaft into Isabella's fully prepared channel and drove it to the hilt inside of her, causing the blue-eyed hellcat to gasp with ecstasy. For several glorious minutes Holten thrust his incredibly long cock deep into Isabella again and again, the wide-eyed blonde riding his writhing body like a champion bronc buster astride a wild-eyed rodeo stallion.

Finally the scout came in a trembling hot explosion of passion that filled Isabella to overflowing. Holten arched his back and Isabella shrieked. Both of the fully sated lovers gasped with delight and then collapsed in a heap, the panting blonde still on top of the limp and completely exhausted scout.

All Holten heard was the beating of his heart.

Then the familiar mourning elegies of the grieving Oglala warriors drifted into the tepee and swirled around the glistening bodies of the two smiling lovers. Holten lay on his back with his blue eyes shut and his softening penis still inside of Isabella.

"Thank you, Eli," said Isabella softly. "That was the first time I've ever done it in a tepee."

"It was wonderful, Yellow Feather...."

Holten caught himself too late. His eyes snapped open.

"Did I ...?" he asked quickly.

Isabella just nodded, her pretty face a blank.

"I'm ... I'm sorry," said the scout.

An awkward silence filled the dimly lit lodge. Then Isabella Cartwright smiled and reached out with her long, tapered fingers. She stroked his face.

"It's all right, Eli," she said gently. "I know your loss has been great. I understand, and that's why I wanted to help you."

Holten grabbed her hands and kissed them gently. "You're one hell of a woman, Isabella Cartwright," he said, his piercing blue eyes gazing into hers.

Then his penis began to harden inside of her.

"Oh!" said Isabella with a start. "So soon?"

"Ya said ya wanted to help!"

"Any time, scout!"

And then the writhing blonde easterner began to ride her human bucking bronco once again, her erotic gyrations urging the scout's shaft to an even greater length. Holten just closed his eyes and enjoyed the rodeo.

ELEVEN

Holten was standing in front of Black Spotted Horse's tall tepee. He was watching the grimacing Oglala chief step through the passageway of his lodge into the sun-splashed, tepee-dotted Indian camp. Isabella was standing next to the scout holding onto his arm like a small child might cling to its father in the presence of strangers. Slanting orange rays of rising sun streaked the hard-packed Dakota soil.

"You should remain in camp, great Chief," said Holten.

Black Spotted Horse rose to his full height, winced as a sharp lance of pain sliced through his wounds, and smiled at the scout.

"The pain of my loss is much greater than that of my wounds, Tall Bear. Nothing could keep me in camp as long as the murderous Pawnee are free."

"What are your plans?" asked the scout.

The chief glanced around the camp. "Most of our braves are still in mourning. By later today we will be ready to ride to the Pawnee camp."

The scout scanned the still-somber Oglala camp, noticing the deathly silence and the almost tangible feeling of grief that was hanging over the usually boisterous village like a great, black shroud.

Holten nodded. "Then I will plan to meet my Sioux brothers at the canyon by the river some time this afternoon. Then perhaps we can put an end to the Pawnee madness."

"And what about the evil whites?" asked the chief.

Holten grit his teeth. "I'll take care of them," he said in a voice dripping with hatred. "But first we must eliminate the Pawnee. Without Mole On Face and his renegades, the evil whites have nobody to start an uprising for them. And then the army won't buy so many guns, putting the gunrunners out of business for good."

The Oglala camp started to come alive.

"We will meet later then," said the chief.

"I am looking forward to it," replied Holten.

Then after swinging his long, lean frame into his saddle, the scout signalled to Isabella and galloped out of the camp onto the brightening prairie. As they raced past the last of the tepees, Isabella turned toward the scout.

"What was that all about?" she asked.

"The Sioux are fixin' to raid the Pawnee campsite to get their revenge. Black Spotted Horse will be leadin' 'em onto the plains in a little while."

"But he's wounded!"

"In more ways than one, Isabella."

"So where are we going now?" asked the honey blonde.

"To meet Lieutenant James and the troopers. We're goin' to need some help in routing them Pawnee."

The scout and Isabella galloped like the wind across the sun-streaked prairie, racing through shadowy stands of parched cottonwoods and leaping over small clumps of brown, summer-shrivelled sage brush plants.

The brassy Dakota sun was rising in the sky with a promise of more heat still to come. All around the fully refreshed travellers the sultry air carried the sweet fragrance of late-blooming plum rose and the cloying aroma of blossoming purple clover plants.

After an hour of hard riding through the plains, the scout and his pretty travelling companion reined in on the narrow banks of the muddy Gray River that snaked across the Benzman Trail. The summer-parched river had been reduced to nothing more than a three-foot-wide brown stream by the merciless sun.

"Up ahead about a mile or so is where we're supposed to meet the soldiers," said Holten. "The Pawnee camp ain't too far from here, either."

Isabella's eyes widened. "Think we'll see any?"

"If we do," said Holten coldly, "the bastards will be tastin' my lead!"

"Still thinking about Yellow Feather, huh?"

"I'll always remember that day at Fort Rawlins."

"I hope you get your revenge, Eli," said the shapely blonde easterner. "It'll give my book a happy ending."

"Killin' don't make nobody happy," said Holten, wiping the perspiration from his face.

"Then why are you still chasing the Pawnee?"

"Because it's somethin' that has to be done. Out here, Isabella, when somebody kills your own ya gotta make 'em pay for it. That's just the way things are."

Suddenly a volley of shots carried to them on the wind.

Holten's sensitive gelding whinnied sharply.

"Whoa, boy!" said the scout, his own sensitive ears straining to discern the direction of the gunfire. His steely blue eyes scanned the grassy prairie ahead of them.

"What was that?" asked Isabella, controlling her own suddenly panicky horse.

"Sounds like trouble up ahead."

"But that's where the soldiers are supposed to meet us!"

"Exactly!" said the scout.

Then Holten dug his heels into the gelding's gleaming flanks and took off at a gallop toward the sound of a raging gun battle just ahead.

"Eli, wait for me!"

Galloping like hell over undulating sand hills and across summer-dried tributaries of the Gray River, the scout finally reined in his snorting horse on a grassy rise that overlooked the rendezvous point with the soldiers.

Holten peered through the shimmering waves of heat that were rising from the sun-baked plains. What he saw quickened his pulse.

Splashing around in the shallows of the trickling Gray River was the embattled column of troopers from Fort Sampson, their wild-eyed horses huddled among them and their Springfield carbines aimed at a circling band of screaming mounted Pawnee warriors. Several braves were closing in for the kill.

Then the scout saw Mole On Face.

Holten's guts constricted and his jaw hardened.

The short, muscular war chief of the Winchester-toting Pawnee was riding a spirited painted pony and leading the circling braves in their attack on the army.

Suddenly the scout heard the drumming of hoofbeats and whirled around to see Isabella galloping up to his position on the rise. The wide-eyed blonde's hand went to her mouth as she looked at the fighting below.

"Oh my God!" she gasped. "Not again!"

"That's the only fully operational garrison of the 12th Cavalry down there," said the scout, "and it's about to be wiped out!"

"What are you going to do?"

"*We* are going to take some action."

"*We?*" asked Isabella, her eyebrows raised.

"I'll need your help for this," said Holten as he was unsheathing his Winchester .44-40 from its saddle boot. Then the scout unholstered his Remington .44.

"Here, take this," said Holten.

He handed the pistol to Isabella who accepted it as though she wasn't sure which end the bullets came out of. Then Holten handed her some extra cartridges. The shapely blonde glanced at the scout.

"But I've never even fired a gun before!"

"That's all right," said Holten, dismounting. "All ya gotta do is make them Pawnee down there *think* ya know what in hell you're doin'."

"I don't understand, Eli," said Isabella. Her pretty face twisted into a quizzical expression and her sparkling blue eyes clouded with puzzlement.

The scout was busy gathering several parched sage brush plants and bringing them over to his horse. There he took a short length from his lasso and tied the brittle, sun-dried bushes together. Then the scout fastened the scraggly bushes to the saddle horn of Isabella's snickering horse.

"We," said Holten, "are the rest of the 12th Cavalry!"

"But there are only two of us!"

"The Pawnee don't know that."

The scout saw Isabella's pretty face brighten.

"You mean we're going to cause enough of a disturbance that the Pawnee will think it's a whole new force of soldiers coming!"

The scout nodded. "And we better hurry, too."

"What do you want me to do, Eli?"

"When I give the signal, start firing into the air. I wouldn't want ya to shoot down toward the Indians. Ya might accidentally hit a trooper."

"And what are you going to do?"

Holten took out a match, struck it on the side of his holster, and touched the sudden fire to the brittle bundle of parched bushes. The dry sticks burst into flames. Then the scout smacked Isabella's wild-eyed horse on the butt and sent it galloping along the rise but out of sight of the attacking Indians down below. The dust from the dragging bushes and the smoke from the burning sage brush plants sent a thick cloud drifting into the morning sky.

"It looks like a lot of horses are approaching!" exclaimed Isabella, her sparkling blue eyes suddenly full of excitement as she realized what was happening.

"I hope so," said Holten as he swung his tall frame onto

the gelding. "Now start shootin' in the air. I'm goin' to be ridin' along the rise while shootin' down at them Pawnee warriors."

And while Isabella was shooting wildly into the deep blue sky above, her haphazard shots echoing in the sultry air on the rise, Holten took off at a gallop along the ridge with his fire-spitting Winchester sending a sudden hail of bullets at the startled braves below.

A shaven-headed warrior flew from his pony.

Another brave's head disintegrated in a shower of blood.

Still a third warrior tumbled dead from his horse.

Holten saw that the Indians had stopped circling and were gazing up at the suddenly dusty rise, their painted faces slackened with surprise. The scout also noticed that the trapped soldiers were starting to cheer at the sudden turn of events and were beginning to pick off the startled braves.

Then he saw Mole On Face raise his hand.

As though on cue the screaming Pawnee warriors kneed their skittish wild ponies and rode like hell away from the suddenly dangerous river crossing. Mole On Face was riding at the head of the fleeing horde.

Holten stopped shooting. The troopers stood and cheered.

"Look, it's Holten!"

"Why I'll be a son of a bitch! I kinda expected the entire garrison from St. Louis!"

"I'd rather have the scout!"

Turning toward the cheering troopers, Holten saw Isabella standing on the grass along the ridge and waving the Remington pistol in the air like a professional gunman.

The scout smiled. She'd done her part.

"I'm goin' after them Pawnee," said Holten.

"Well," said Lieutenant Bodie James, scanning the regrouping army column all around him, "we lost two men here and got four more wounded. We won't be able to join ya for a while yet, Mr. Holten."

The scout turned to Isabella. "The soldiers need ya to help with the wounded," he said, his steely blue eyes full of new admiration for the sumptuous blonde easterner. "Think ya can handle it all right?"

"Why not?" answered the smiling writer, a mischievous glint in her blue eyes. "So far today I've been an Indian squaw and a gunfighter, so I think I can learn to be an army nurse, too!"

Coyote Jim Stephens and Kansas Joe Adderly strode briskly to where the scout was talking with the lieutenant and Isabella. Wizened old Coyote Jim was stroking his full white beard and shaking his head.

"Thought we was goners for sure, Holten," said the old frontiersman.

"Ain't seen a trick like that for years," said Adderly.

"Now that we got Mole On Face on the run," said Holten, "we gotta keep the pressure on. I'm headin' out after them renegades. I expect ya to fix the wounded as best ya can and join me at the Pawnee camp."

Then the scout gave them directions to the camp.

"That's almost an impregnable canyon!" exclaimed Bodie James.

Coyote Jim's bearded face brightened. "Ya mean you'll be enterin' the camp? Old Mole On Face might not take kindly to havin' ya on the inside!"

"It's the only way. Somebody's got to create a diversion."

"But Eli . . . ?" said Isabella, her pretty face suddenly lined with concern.

Holten grabbed the pretty blonde's arm. "All ya gotta do, Isabella, is stick with the soldiers and help 'em out with the wounded. I'll meet ya at the Pawnee camp."

"Be careful, Eli!"

Holten turned to the lieutenant. "Black Spotted Horse and his Oglala warriors may be headin' for the Pawnee camp, too. Make sure them troopers understand which Indians are on our side."

Bodie James nodded. "Will do, Mr. Holten."

The scout hauled his long body into the saddle and clucked to his big horse. Then with a slight nod of his head toward Isabella, Holten galloped onto the sweltering Dakota prairie in search of his bride's killer.

Holten hunkered in the early afternoon shadows near the hilly entrance of the canyon where the renegades were camped, and scanned the main Pawnee village just ahead. His snorting gelding was tethered to a tall, wavering pine tree nearby.

The scout's piercing blue eyes took in the domed mud dwellings typical of the Pawnee tribe, the dozens of babbling Pawnee squaws mingling among the sun-baked lodges, and the hard-faced sentries who were posted all around the perimeter of the camp at fifty foot intervals.

The multi-family Pawnee dwellings were arranged in a large circle with a wide ceremonial ground in the center. Holten marvelled at the lodges' sturdy construction: a wooden framework of posts and beams covered with layers of willow branches, sod strips, and thick Dakota mud. More than forty feet wide and twenty feet tall, the lodges also served as grandstands for their inhabitants during tribal pow-wows that were held in the wide central ceremonial ground. The sturdy mud dwellings were even large enough to shelter prized war ponies and the tribe's many dogs.

Holten had galloped like hell toward the canyon in the hills, barely glancing at the easy-to-read pony prints dotting the alkaline dust beneath his muscular mount. He'd arrived at the narrow entrance of the canyon, sneaked past a couple of dozing sentries, and edged to within a hundred yards of the bustling Pawnee camp. Now he was ready to enter the enemy village and begin to create a diversion he hoped would allow the soon-to-arrive soldiers a clear entrance to the camp.

Scanning the village even more closely, the scout suddenly sucked in his breath. Seated on the ground in a small circle on the far side of the camp were Black Bob Callahan, Chief Mole On Face, and a couple of fancily dressed dudes who obviously were the gunrunning easterners Lieutenant Bodie James had been talking about. Parked nearby was a stagecoach and a harnessed team of six restless horses.

Holten smiled. All the killers were together.

Suddenly the scout stiffened. He listened intently and heard a woman's soft giggling voice rise from a clump of slightly rustling bushes nearby. Holten's heart began to beat against his ribs. Unsheathing his Bowie knife, the scout padded as stealthily as a stalking prairie predator toward the sudden disturbance in the bushes.

With his palm growing slippery around the cold butt of his fearsome knife, the wary scout peered into the bordering tree-lined clearing and felt a twinge of excitement at what he saw. Rolling around naked atop the cool, shady grass cover were a luscious big-breasted Pawnee woman and her fully aroused lover. The reason for Holten's sudden excitement was his quick identification of the squaw.

It was Spotted Mare, Mole On Face's wife.

The scout knew all about the philandering, sex hungry woman. Her lovemaking escapades were legend among the plains Indians. Only a crazed killer like Mole On Face, with more on his mind than keeping his pretty wife happy, could put up with her many amorous adventures. Now Spotted Mare obviously was enjoying herself with another of her lovers, who happened to be on sentry duty.

Suddenly Holten devised a scheme.

Taking advantage of the two fully engrossed lovers' temporary lack of awareness about their immediate surroundings, the scout burst from the bushes with his Bowie knife held flat and ready for action.

Lying on her back with her panting lover pumping his cock into her shapely, golden-skinned body, Spotted Mare's sparkling brown eyes saucered the moment she saw the scout's glistening blade plunge into the suddenly shocked warrior's fully exposed rib cage.

Holten finished off the wide-eyed brave with a quick slash across the shaven-headed Indian's vulnerable windpipe, a shower of blood spurting onto the cool, green grass in the shady clearing. The gurgling Pawnee warrior rolled onto his back, his still hardened cock extended to its fullest length, and died within seconds.

The scout whirled toward Spotted Mare, grabbed her long lustrous hair, and held the point of his gleaming, blood-stained blade against her throat.

"I know you speak Lakota," snapped Holten in a cold voice. "So listen to me and don't make a sound. Do you understand, Spotted Mare?"

The wide-eyed squaw nodded as best she could.

"I'm goin' to let you get your clothes on, and then we're goin' to walk into the village. Your lover was one of the sentries on this side of the camp, so we should have a clear path to the village."

Holten removed his knife from Spotted Mare's throat.

"If you scream I'll slit your throat," said the scout.

Having been through many difficult times in her life as a renegade, Spotted Mare quickly regained her composure. Then Mole On Face's unfaithful squaw smiled up at Holten.

"I heard that Tall Bear lost his woman," said the big-breasted squaw in Lakota. Her fingers reached out slowly and grabbed the scout's big right hand. "Maybe Tall Bear needs some loving, eh?"

Then the fully aroused nymphomaniac began to rub Holten's hand in her already wet vagina. The scout felt the warmth of her silky folds of flesh on the back of his hand. Spotted Mare's flashing eyes were alive with desire and suddenly the scout was mesmerized by her alluring charms.

Then they hit him with the force of a charging bull.

Two scowling, shaven-headed Pawnee sentries burst from the shadows and smashed into Holten, knocking his Bowie knife into the air and sending the startled scout hurtling to the grassy ground.

Before he could react, Holten was looking into the deadly bore of a shiny, new Winchester .44-40 that was being aimed at his head by a smiling brave.

Spotted Mare reached out and slapped Holten's face.

"You wanted to see the Pawnee village," grated the still naked squaw. "Well now you will. I'm sure Mole On Face will be glad to see Tall Bear!"

Holten felt a jab of fear in his gut.

Then after being hauled unceremoniously to his feet by the two scowling sentries, the scout was pushed toward the bustling Pawnee village up ahead. Spotted Mare quickly hauled on her clothes and followed behind.

Mole On Face shot to his feet.

The scout noticed that the hard-faced chief was wearing his glittering array of silver-adorned weapons: a factory-made dagger and an ivory-handled Colt .45.

"Well, if it isn't Tall Bear!" he said in Lakota.

Spotted Mare ran ahead and planted a kiss on Mole On Face's cheek. "He was sneaking around the edge of our camp," said the philandering wife in Lakota so Holten would understand the trouble she was getting him into. "Then he attacked and tried to rape me before the sentries saved my life."

Black Bob Callahan and the two dude easterners also rose to their feet and were watching the scout with amused smiles on their faces.

"Got yourself in another jam, eh Holten?" growled Black Bob. Suddenly the gunrunning gang leader's flashing eyes narrowed and his voice grew cold. "Maybe I oughtta take ya away from the chief here and kill ya myself for knockin' off my gal!"

"Is this the army scout you were telling me about?" asked Horace Van Nostrand, the bespectacled little gun dealer with the three-piece suit.

"This here is the bastard who's been trackin' us!"

"He'll have to be killed then," said the white-haired dude, pushing his wire-rimmed glasses onto the bridge of his nose. "We can't let anybody in the army know our identities."

Holten saw that the man's hands were trembling.

"Well," chimed in Elliot Brownstone, the fat, blond-haired dude standing beside Van Nostrand, "it looks like them Pawnees will get rid of him for us."

Holten just glared at the evil trio of white men.

Suddenly the scout watched Black Bob turn toward the Pawnee chief and flash some sign language in the short, powerful renegade's dark face. Holten quickly translated and learned that the gunrunners were heading to their hideout in the hills and would meet with the Pawnee later in the day to continue their discussion about getting more weapons.

Callahan turned toward Holten. "So long, scout," he said. "Sorry I can't stick around for your torture session. I understand the Pawnees are masters at that sort of stuff. And this time ya ain't gonna get away!"

The three white men laughed and walked toward the stagecoach and their tethered horses. Within seconds Black Bob and his evil gunrunning dude friends rode out of the Pawnee camp and onto the prairie.

"Now, Tall Bear," grated Mole On Face, "I think I'll turn you over to Spotted Mare. She enjoys making men suffer, isn't that right, wife?"

Spotted Mare held up Holten's knife. "I have just the thing for such a ladies' man as Tall Bear," she said, an evil glint in her flashing brown eyes.

Mole On Face laughed. "He is yours, then. Goodbye, Tall Bear. Now you will be joining your dead squaw in the hereafter in the sky!"

Holten lunged for the chief, but was struck on the head by a nearby sentry. The scout reeled with the sudden sharp blow and watched his bride's killer, who had been within reach of the revenge-seeking Holten twice already, walk across the camp.

"Hold him up," ordered Spotted Mare, gripping the knife.

The two shaven-headed Pawnee sentries propped up the groggy scout by his long arms and held him in front of the smiling Spotted Mare.

Then to Holten's horror, the big-breasted Pawnee woman reached out quickly, unfastened his buckskin pants until they fell to the ground, and grabbed his balls in a painful vise-like grip with her long fingers. The sudden pressure on his balls sent a shaft of pain shooting through his groin.

The gasping scout knew what was coming.

He'd seen squaws emasculate captured warriors before.

Suddenly a crowd of gawking children, giggling Pawnee women, and laughing renegade braves was gathering around the scout and his would-be executioner. Spotted Mare looked around at the familiar faces encircling her, a look of triumph on her pretty face, and squeezed the scout's testicles even harder.

Holten winced with pain.

Then a shot rang out and echoed among the sun-baked mud dwellings. Spotted Mare was jerked off her feet and thrown to the ground, her hand suddenly releasing the scout's balls as she shrieked with pain. Holten looked down at the blossoming circle of crimson around the black bullet hole in the dead squaw's forehead. The gathered Pawnee villagers looked on in stunned silence.

Suddenly the air was alive with bullets.

The Pawnee camp began to panic.

Reacting with the quick reflexes of a frightened cat, the scout suddenly yanked the arms of the two startled warriors who were holding him. The stumbling braves' heads smacked together in front of the scout and the warriors slumped unconscious to the ground.

After bending down to retrieve his Bowie knife, Holten straightened quickly and glanced at the Pawnee warriors who were biting the dust all around him. A wide grin cracked the scout's leathery face when he spotted the charging troopers and the galloping Oglala Sioux—led by the weakened Black Spotted Horse—as they were pouring into the canyon.

The diversion caused by Holten and Spotted Mare had been enough for the soldiers and the Sioux to enter unnoticed. Now the disorganized Pawnee renegades were being shot to pieces in a sudden and bloody surprise attack on their camp.

Holten was looking for Mole On Face.

TWELVE

The battle was short and sweet.

The combined forces of Lieutenant Bodie James' galloping soldiers and Black Spotted Horse's revenge-seeking Oglala warriors easily routed the unprepared Pawnee renegades. Within twenty minutes the Pawnee village was in shambles and the ground was littered with bloodied renegade corpses. Even most of the stolen Winchester repeaters were recovered. The only disappointment for the avenging scout was that a dozen or so of the shaven-headed killers had escaped into the prairie.

Including Mole On Face.

While the soldiers went about the task of securing the canyon and the Oglala braves hopefully searched the mud lodges for their lost squaws, Holten retrieved his hidden gelding and then told Bodie James and the others, including Isabella, about his sudden meeting with Callahan and the dudes. He finished by mentioning the gunrunners' departure in a rented mud wagon stagecoach.

"That must have been the dust swirls we saw on the prairie when we were arriving here!" said Isabella Cartwright, her blue eyes full of excitement.

"That's right," confirmed Coyote Jim. "We was bent on gettin' here, otherwise we woulda stopped and looked into that there dust swirl."

"Maybe it's not too late," said Holten.

"What are ya gonna do, Mr. Holten?" asked the lieutenant.

The scout mounted his gelding.

"I figure Black Spotted Horse's braves and me might be able to teach them eastern dudes a lesson that'll keep 'em away from the plains for good!"

The scout motioned for Four Bull and several other Oglala warriors to come over and join him. Holten knew a small band of Indians would be able to track down the dudes in no time.

"Where will we meet you, Eli?" asked Isabella anxiously.

"Why don't y'all finish up around here and then meet me at the same rendezvous point near the Gray River. Then we'll decide where we'll begin lookin' for that bastard Mole On Face and his survivin' braves."

"Give them dudes my regards!" said Coyote Jim with a big laugh.

Then Holten and a handful of painted Sioux warriors galloped out of the ruined Pawnee camp and headed toward the sun-drenched prairie in search of the easterners.

Following the easy-to-read stagecoach tracks, Holten and his five Oglala friends rode through the sweltering plains for about an hour before they spotted the rented stagecoach stopped near a small copse of cottonwood trees.

From his position on a grassy knoll overlooking the trees, the scout peered through the early afternoon heat and saw three of the Black Bob gang members sipping some coffee around a campfire. Their dark-skinned leader wasn't among them. Seated on specially designed folding wooden chairs beside the stubble-faced gunrunners were the two fancily dressed dudes.

"Those are the fat white men who are responsible for getting the rifles to the Pawnee," said Holten to Four Bull and the other hard-faced warriors around him. "They are just as responsible for the deaths of our women as the men who squeezed the triggers."

"Why do they do such things, Tall Bear?" asked Four Bull.

"For money," replied the scout.

"White men will kill innocent women for money?"

Holten nodded glumly. "I think white men will do most anything for money."

"I will never understand the ways of the whites."

"You're probably better off that way, Four Bull."

Holten studied the white men once again.

"I don't see Black Bob Callahan or Big Nosed John Harper," he said to Four Bull. "I feel the leaders of the evil whites are hiding somewhere."

"We will try and find this hideout for Tall Bear."

Holten nodded. "Right now, let's take care of these fat whites with the rich-looking clothes. They are just as guilty as the others."

"What is your plan, Tall Bear?"

"I want you and your warriors to encircle the copse of trees. Then I'll ride into the white men's campsite with my hands in the air. Maybe I can learn where Black Bob has his hideout."

"Won't the evil whites shoot at you?"

"I think they'll be more curious than anything," said the scout. "But to play safe, I'll blast the first white man who goes for his gun. Then you and your braves can attack at will."

"And if no white man goes for his gun?"

"Then let me ride into the campsite. Once I'm in front of the dudes and draw my gun, I want you and your warriors to take care of the other three gunrunners. But leave the dudes alive for the time being. We're going to teach them a lesson that all their friends back East will respect, too!"

Nodding his understanding of the simple plan, Four Bull had his braves tether their nickering ponies to some nearby sage brush plants. Then the short, muscular Oglala brave explained the plan of attack and watched his copper-skinned, bow-carrying warriors fan out silently into the scorching prairie like shadowy ghosts.

When Four Bull gave Holten the high sign, the scout nodded and started to trot down the grassy slope and into the modest copse of cottonwoods. His heart was beginning to pound like an Indian war drum.

Immediately Holten noticed a couple of the gunrunners put down their coffee cups and point in his direction. The scout slowly raised his hands over his head and eyed the gun hands of the outlaws for the slightest twitch. Holten heard the stubble-faced gunrunners talking to one another and then to the suddenly standing dudes, but he saw no sign of sudden gunplay as he rode into their camp.

"Well, well," said white-haired Horace Van Nostrand, a slight hint of concern in his high-pitched voice. The little man moved backwards half a step. "I thought we left you for dead back at the Pawnee camp, Mr. Holten."

The scout reined in his horse. "There ain't no more Pawnee camp," he said in an even voice, his steely eyes fixed on the nearby killers' gun hands.

Holten picked his targets in case of trouble.

"What do you mean?" asked the fat dude, Elliot Brownstone. Holten saw the fear rise in the blond man's fleshy face.

"It's simple," said Holten. "The soldiers and the Oglala Sioux destroyed the camp an hour ago. The Pawnees are runnin' like scared dogs."

The scout's pulse was racing.

The dudes exchanged glances.

"Then what in hell are ya doin' here, scout?" asked one of the stubble-faced gunrunners in a gruff voice. "Just payin' us a social call?"

"I'm here to offer ya a chance to turn yourselves in."

The gunrunners roared with laughter.

The dudes shuffled their feet nervously.

Horace Van Nostrand cleared his throat. "Do you mean, Mr. Holten, that the army is wise to our involvement in this little escapade? And that if we turn ourselves in, we will escape prosecution?"

The scout shook his head. "Nope," he said simply. "I mean just what I said. I'm givin' ya a chance to come into Fort Sampson real peaceful like."

The gruff-voiced gunrunner exploded. "What kinda deal is that? We turn ourselves in and what in hell do we get in return?"

Holten glared at the man. "Your life," he said coldly.

The three gunrunners flexed their trigger fingers.

Van Nostrand cleared his throat again. "Well, Mr. Holten, if the army doesn't know my identity, or Mr. Brownstone's, then all we have to do is kill you and nobody will know anything at all, will they?"

Suddenly the fat Mr. Brownstone raised his cane and pointed it at the scout. The greasy-skinned, blond greenhorn flicked a switch on the handle of the shiny walking stick and a gleaming six inch blade snapped out of the end.

"I'd like to have a chance at Mr. Holten, Horace," said the unctuous dude in a voice filled with false bravado and unfelt malice.

The gunrunners laughed.

"Old Eli Holten being called down by a dude!" cried the gruff-voiced outlaw who'd spoken before.

"Of course," said Holten, his steely eyes narrowing and fixing on the twitching gun hands of the hard-faced gunrunners in front of him. "I may be kind to ya if ya tell me where Black Bob's hideout is."

Again the gunrunners laughed heartily.

"It's some place you ain't never gonna find, scout!"

"Enough of this!" said white-haired Horace Van Nostrand. The little dude sat in his portable chair. "We're wasting our time talking with this . . . this prairie tramp! Kill him, boys, and let's get on with our business!"

"The business of selling death?" asked Holten.

"Call it what you will, scout," said Van Nostrand. "I'm tired of talking with you. Get rid of him boys, and do it right now!"

Holten glared at the gunrunners, who stared back.

"You heard the man, boys, kill me!" said Holten.

Fat Elliot Brownstone took a step forward, his blade-tipped walking cane held toward the scout and his fleshy face aglow with excitement.

Suddenly the gruff-voiced gunrunner drew his six-shooter. Holten's hands flew down and went to his Bowie knife. Quickly the remaining gunrunners went for their guns.

At the same time the scout heard several whooshing sounds followed immediately by the dull thud of steel-tipped arrows hitting human flesh.

"Christ!" cried the gruff-voiced bandit, his Colt .45 tumbling from his hand and his arms reaching behind him for the feathered shaft that was imbedded in his back.

Again the whooshing and the thudding.

The remaining two gunrunners cried with pain, dropped their six-shooters, and slumped to the ground. Each of them had several Oglala arrows stuck in his body.

"My God!" breathed wide-eyed Horace Van Nostrand.

Holten lashed out suddenly with his fearsome Bowie knife, the gleaming blade striking Elliot Brownstone's nearby walking cane and slicing it in two.

"Jesus!" gasped the fat dude.

Within seconds all the gunrunners were lying dead on the dusty ground and Holten was pointing his long, gleaming blade at the wide-eyed dudes. Horace Van Nostrand quickly drew a tiny Smith and Wesson .32 caliber pocket derringer from the vest of his three-piece suit.

"Drop it or die!" snapped the scout in an icy tone.

The little, white-haired gun dealer from New York let the stubby handgun fall from his trembling fingers. He raised his arms over his head.

Suddenly the surrounding bushes came alive as Four Bull and his bow-carrying braves glided in from the prairie like shadowy brown phantoms. The slashes of white war paint on their broad, dark faces gave the approaching Sioux warriors an even more ferocious appearance.

"Jesus!" gasped Elliot Brownstone. "Injuns!"

"What are you going to do to us, scout?" asked little Horace Van Nostrand in a quavering voice that was filled with fear.

Holten sat back on his saddle and smiled.

"I can't do much," said the scout. "I'm nothin' more than a prairie tramp, remember dude?"

"I'm . . . I'm sorry about that, Mr. Holten," said Van Nostrand in a shaky voice, his narrow gray eyes flitting from Holten to the Oglala warriors.

"We didn't mean any harm," squeaked the fat Mr. Brownstone. "We're just businessmen from back East out here trying to make a few dollars."

"At the expense of innocent women and children!" snapped Holten in a voice so harsh that even the scout's battle-hardened gelding jumped at the sound.

"Show us mercy, scout, I beg you!" cried Van Nostrand.

The scout nodded slowly. "You're lucky, gentlemen," he said. "I'm inclined to be lenient with ya this time."

"Oh, thank you!" said the perspiring Brownstone, the relief evident in the fat blond dude's fleshy facial features.

"But there's a catch."

The dudes' heads swung toward the scout.

"A catch?" asked Van Nostrand, his eyebrows raised.

Holten leaned forward in his saddle, his steely blue eyes boring into the two dudes and making the nervous easterners shuffle their feet.

"Ya ain't never to come back to the Dakota Territory again, is that understood?" asked Holten in a voice as cold and hard as a bullet.

"Yes, yes!" said Van Nostrand quickly.

"Never again!" added Brownstone.

"Good," said Holten leaning back. "Now my Indian friends and me want to send a message to your dude friends back East. Sort of a warning to anybody who has ideas about startin' the same kind of trouble you did."

Van Nostrand stiffened his little body. "A warning?"

"We're goin' to scalp ya!"

Brownstone's fleshy face slackened and his jaw dropped. Van Nostrand took a stumbling step backwards.

Suddenly the scout nodded toward Four Bull. "You and your braves can collect a couple of white men's scalps," he said in Lakota. "But leave the fancy dressers alive. I want them to walk around back East with their little bald patches as a reminder of what can happen out here."

The short, powerful Oglala brave nodded.

Then while Van Nostrand and Brownstone started to squeal like a couple of stuck pigs, the five laughing warriors held the dudes on the ground, reached out with their glistening hunting knives, and deftly removed a four inch square patch of hair from each of the howling dudes' scalps as though they were skinning a jack rabbit. When the Indians had finished their grisly task, both of the gasping easterners were left with shiny, bloodied splotches on the back of their scalps.

"Now get up on the driver's seat of that there mud wagon," said Holten to the stunned dudes, "and get the hell outta here! Do it quickly or I might let the Indians finish their scalping job."

"But I don't know how to drive a six-horse stagecoach!" cried Horace Van Nostrand. "You killed our driver, and I've never driven one of these before!"

"Ya got two choices, dude," said the scout. "Drive that there mud wagon or stick around here and discuss the matter with the Sioux Indians."

"God, no!" gasped the ashen-faced Elliot Brownstone.

The two dudes, their bloody scalps glistening in the early afternoon sunshine, quickly hopped aboard the stagecoach and slapped the reins on the butts of the six nickering horses. The creaking mud wagon rocked and rolled its way onto the sun-drenched prairie in a cloud of dust. The two easterners glanced over their shoulders at the Oglala warriors and the scout saw the fear etched in their ashen faces.

"And don't come back!" cried Holten.

He didn't think they would.

THIRTEEN

Galloping alone across the sun-baked prairie toward his rendezvous with Isabella and the soldiers, Four Bull and his warriors having headed back to their camp, Holten quickly reviewed his quest for revenge.

As the scorching mid-afternoon sun warmed his back, the scout rode through the undulating buffalo grass and thought about Yellow Feather's killers. Twice he'd come close to the bastard Mole On Face and twice he'd been unable to kill his young bride's murderer. He'd also seen Black Bob Callahan a couple of times, but, as with the Pawnee renegade chief, he'd also been unable to gun down the dark-skinned gang leader.

While the powerful gelding was eating up the miles, the scout realized he'd only been able to rid the prairie of big Slim Powell and the fancily dressed dudes from the East. And until he was able to eliminate Callahan, Big Nosed John Harper, and the rest of the gang, as well as make sure Mole On Face and the surviving Pawnee warriors were out of commission for good, then his revenge for the brutal killing of the kind and gentle Yellow Feather would remain incomplete. Holten slapped his mount on its butt and galloped toward the Gray River and his meeting with the troopers.

Adrenaline began to course through his veins.

"Eli!" cried Isabella Cartwright, running into the scout's long arms. Her big breasts bounced under her green blouse and her blue eyes were full of genuine concern. "I've been so worried about you! I'm so glad that you're all right!"

"Welcome back, Mr. Holten," said Lieutenant James.

"Thought maybe ya got lost!" said Coyote Jim Stephens with a cackle. "This here summer heat sometimes drives men so loco they don't know where in hell they're goin'!"

"Holten always knows where he's headin'," said Kansas Joe. The long-haired half-breed stood and watched Holten enter the soldiers' riverside camp. "Did ya find them dudes, scout?"

Holten nodded. "They won't bother us no more."

The scout sat in the shade of a tall, leafy cottonwood that was bordering the narrow Gray River and accepted a cup of cool water from Isabella. Then he explained what had happened to the gun-dealing easterners.

"Ugh!" said Isabella when she heard about the scalping.

"I think it's great!" cried Coyote Jim, his wizened bearded face brightening. "Just think, them two dudes'll be walkin' advertisements for western hospitality!"

The gathered men laughed heartily.

After the laughter died away, Lieutenant Bodie James turned toward the scout. "What's our next move, Mr. Holten?" he asked.

"Track down the remaining Pawnee warriors."

"What about Black Bob Callahan?" asked Coyote Jim.

"The Oglala braves are lookin' for the gunrunners' hideout. They'll let me know as soon as they've found it. Then we'll pay Callahan a visit."

Bodie James rose smoothly. "Do ya want the soldiers to stick with ya?"

Holten shook his head. "You head out along the river and see if ya can find them Pawnee camped out some place near the water. There shouldn't be many of 'em left by now. But remember, Lieutenant, Mole On Face is *mine!*"

Bodie James nodded and strode away toward the soldiers.

"What about us, Holten?" asked Kansas Joe.

"Lieutenant James'll need ya to help track them Pawnee. Why don't both of ya ride with 'em until we finish this here uprisin' once and for all."

The two scouts nodded and went to join Bodie James.

"And what about me, Mr. Holten sir?" asked Isabella in a semi-serious tone. The sumptuous, big-breasted blonde saluted playfully. "I still have a book to finish and I need some final chapters."

Holten shook his head. "No chance," he said. "I gotta find Mole On Face and Black Bob, and when I do it's goin' to be purty dangerous."

"But I can handle it, Eli!" cried Isabella, her big blue eyes pleading with the scout. "I did all right when we helped the soldiers that time!"

"But this is different."

"Please?"

"No, and that's final!"

Then before the scout could get to his feet, the shapely blonde writer quickly reached out with her long, tapered fingers and suddenly unhitched Holten's pants. The scout's hardening penis bobbed free.

"Wait a minute!" cried Holten.

"No," said Isabella. "And *that's* final!"

"But the soldiers?"

"What about them?" asked Isabella, her soft hand wrapping around the scout's now fully grown erection and massaging it slowly.

"They're only a few feet away!"

"That makes it more exciting, don't you think?"

Suddenly the shapely blonde easterner leaned forward and placed the scout's pulsating penis into her mouth, her supple lips quickly moistening the entire length of his fully aroused cock from its hard, hairy base to its pink, sensitive tip. Isabella's tongue gently flicked the now writhing scout's gland, causing him to moan with delight.

"Damn!" he breathed. "You're so persuasive!"

Then while Holten sat writhing in the shade of the towering cottonwood tree and the column of troopers prepared to ride, Isabella Cartwright sucked on the scout's elongated shaft as though it was a candy cane, the only sound reaching Holten's ears was the liquid gurgling of the sumptuous blonde's lips wrapped around his cock.

The scout felt his passion erupting and suddenly he exploded into the pretty blonde's mouth in several shuddering spurts, his entire frame tingling and his sexual needs sated. Isabella's supple lips clung to his shaft until he was completely drained, the luscious blonde swallowing his passion until finally the scout collapsed against the tree and sighed with sexual satisfaction.

Isabella quickly stuffed his penis into his pants.

"Well?" she asked. "Can I go along with you?"

The army column was already mounted and suddenly Lieutenant Bodie James was trotting over to where the scout and Isabella were sitting.

"We're ready to ride, Mr. Holten," said the officer.

The still gasping scout raised a hand. "We'll meet again at the entrance of the canyon where the Pawnee camp was. Let's say at sunrise tomorrow."

"And if we find the Pawnee before then?"

"Finish 'em off," said Holten. "But save Mole On Face for me!"

Bodie James nodded. "And Miss Cartwright?"

Holten glanced at Isabella's pleading blue eyes.

"She'll be ridin' with me, Lieutenant," said Holten with a wry smile. "Miss Cartwright just gave me a real good reason why she should stay alongside me."

"Right," said the dutiful officer, saluting.

The army column disappeared into the sun-drenched plains.

"Thanks, Eli."

"Like I told ya, you're real persuasive when ya put ya mind to it!"

Holten helped Isabella to her feet.

The merciless sun beat down like a hammer.

"I only let ya come with me," said the scout as he and Isabella were riding through the dusty prairie, "because I figured ya might get killed by yourself."

The pretty blonde smiled. "I know," she said.

"If we come across the gunrunners or the Pawnee, I want ya to take care of the horses like ya did before. I don't want ya gettin' involved with any gunplay."

"I won't, Eli," said the sumptuous blonde, her eyes full of admiration for the scout and her long flowing hair streaming behind her as she rode.

"Good," finished Holten. "Let's ride!"

With a resounding slap on the ample butt of his powerful gelding, the scout surged ahead and began to gallop toward the tree-lined hills all around them. He wasn't sure where the gunrunners were hiding, but they couldn't stay hidden from both Holten and the Oglala for very much longer. He pointed his snorting mount toward the traditional hunting grounds of his former Sioux brothers and hoped to hell he'd come across something soon.

About mid-afternoon Holten reined in his horse.

"What's the matter?" asked Isabella as she tried to control her prancing mount.

"Listen!"

From somewhere nearby came the faint sounds of gunfire.

"The gunrunners?" asked the blonde.

"Could be," said the scout. "Or Mole On Face."

The shots echoed through the nearby pine trees.

"Let's go!" said Holten, slapping his horse.

"Wait for me!" cried Isabella.

Galloping up the gentle, tree-lined Black Hills' slope, the scout and his pretty travelling companion quickly crested the shadowy hill and reined in their mounts amidst some clawing shrubs. There they dismounted quickly, hunkered in the shadows, and peered through the shimmering waves of mid-afternoon heat at the slaughter below.

"Oh my God!" gasped Isabella, her eyes saucering.

Down in the small, tree-lined clearing was a small knot of half a dozen white settlers standing beside each other with their hands tied behind their backs. Two other settlers lay dead in pools of blood. On the ground in front of them was a small mound of wallets, watches, and other items of value. Three hard-faced gunrunners were poring over the loot. Standing beside the trembling settlers, his gleaming three-and-a-half-foot-long army saber poised to lop off the head of the first man in line, was Big Nosed John Harper.

"Why the son of a bitch!" murmured Holten.

"Who is it?"

"Black Bob's top executioner!"

Then, while Holten and Isabella watched in horror from their perch on the shadowy slope, Big Nosed John Harper called to his gunrunning cohorts and then reared back with the glistening sword.

"Surely he won't do it, Eli?" said the blonde writer.

With a whistling slash of the gleaming army saber, Big Nosed John sliced cleanly through the first settler's neck bones and cartilage, lopping off his head with a single swipe. The man's head bounced on the ground and the corpse's legs buckled before the body slumped to the ground, blood spurting from the gaping red opening where the head had been.

"I think I'm going to be sick!" said Isabella, turning away from the gruesome scene below and retching in the nearby shrubbery.

"Oh no!" gasped one of the other settlers in disbelief.

Still another fainted at the sight of the headless body.

"Time to put an end to this shit!" said Holten.

Isabella, her eyes clouded and her pretty face ashen, glanced at the scout. "What are you going to do?"

"Give that there gunrunner a taste of his own medicine!"

"But there are four of them!"

Holten unsheathed his Winchester .44-40. "But I got surprise on my side," said the scout. He sat once again on the bushy slope and shouldered his powerful repeater. Holten aimed down the long, cold barrel until he had Big Nosed John's shaggy head in his sights.

Suddenly one of the other gunrunners stood quickly.

Holten squeezed the trigger. The slug hit the other man.

The startled, stubble-faced gunrunner leaped off his feet with the impact of the speeding bullet and slammed dead to the clearing, blood oozing from between his shoulder blades.

"Holy shit!" yelled another of the gunrunners.

Big Nosed John Harper glanced quickly at the hills.

Holten levered and fired again, this time his hot slug barely missing the now running, saber-carrying Harper. The scout fired again and his bullet found its mark in the broad, dumb-looking face of another gunrunner.

"Head for cover!" cried Big Nosed John.

Not wanting to get caught in a crossfire, the frightened settlers, their hands still bound behind them, started to run like hell for the nearby woods.

The final gunslinger looked at the fleeing settlers. "Them sodbusters are gettin' away!" he cried, raising his deadly Colt 145 Peacemaker.

"Get down, you fool!" shouted Harper to his cohort.

But it was too late.

Holten squeezed the trigger again and sent a heavy bullet into the lingering gunrunner's suddenly exposed chest, lifting the wide-eyed killer off his feet and slamming him to the dusty clearing. A widening circle of crimson began to stain the front of the startled gunrunner's dirty white shirt.

Now only Big Nosed John remained.

Holten's shot echoed in the pine trees.

"Take this rifle," said the scout, handing the .44-40 to Isabella Cartwright. "I'm goin' after Harper. If he tries to move away, shoot him!"

"But . . . ?"

"Ya did fine the last time," said Holten with a smile. "Just aim down the barrel and squeeze the trigger real gentle like. Then lever and do it all over again."

Isabella accepted the heavy repeater. "I'll do the best I can, Eli," she said, her apprehension evident in her pretty face.

"When Harper and I start fightin', come down to the clearin' real slow. And when ya do, keep the Winchester in front of ya and ready to fire."

"I'm scared, Eli."

Holten smiled. "Just think of it this way," he said. "Me meetin' Harper down there will give ya one of your book's final chapters!"

Unsheathing his wide-bladed Bowie knife, the scout turned and padded through the clawing brush like an Indian hunter stalking a herd of skittish antelope. Holten's heart was beating a tune against his ribs and his muscles were coiled and ready for action. He reached the edge of the clearing and listened as intently as a predator trying to discern the movements of its prey.

"Who in hell is out there?" shouted Big Nosed John.

The voice came from a row of shrubs ten feet away.

The nervous gunrunner was starting to panic.

"Yellow Feather's husband!" said the scout.

"Who?" came the quick reply.

The sudden rustle of bushes told the scout that Harper had discerned the location of Holten's voice and was on his way to investigate.

"Ya killed my woman at Fort Rawlins, Harper!" yelled

Holten, moving slightly to his left after speaking so as to throw off the approaching gunrunner.

There was a slight pause, then Big Nosed John spoke.

"Eli Holten!" he exclaimed from a row of nearby shrubs. "Kinda figured you'd be lookin' for us. Too bad about your squaw, but I didn't have nothin' to do with it."

"Ya gave rifles to the Pawnee."

Holten slithered through the bushes like a snake.

"I sure did," replied Harper. "Damn good money in stealin' rifles, scout! And this ruckus on the prairie is damn good for rifle sales, too!"

Suddenly the scout spotted the big nosed gunrunner crawling through a row of scraggly plum rose bushes off to the right. Holten stepped to the side and burst into the clearing, but his sudden appearance startled the beak-nosed killer into a crouching position. Before the scout could bring his Bowie knife into play Big Nosed John Harper was standing with his gleaming saber raised and ready to strike.

"Aha!" cried Harper, his scraggly brown hair poking out from under his wide-brimmed hat and his dreamy blue eyes fixed on the scout's glistening blade.

"It don't take much to lop off the heads of a few tied-up settlers, Harper," said Holten. He glanced at the headless corpse lying in a pool of blood, buzzing flies sucking at the gaping neck wound. "Ya always have been a low-down critter, but this is a new low even for somebody as wicked as you!"

"Ya ain't seen nothin' yet, scout!" snarled the beak-nosed killer. "Wait 'til I get through with you!"

And with that final remark the saber-wielding gunrunner lunged forward in a fencing stance and nearly slashed Holten's throat, the whooshing sword missing the scout's windpipe by a matter of inches.

Holten backed up quickly and kept his balance as the now wild-eyed Harper lunged again and again with his razor-sharp army saber, each thrust coming dangerously close to the scout's neck, face, or stomach.

Suddenly there was a crashing sound in the shrubs.

Isabella Cartwright appeared with the rifle.

"Eli!" she cried.

"What the . . . ?" muttered Harper, taking his heavy-lidded blue eyes off the scout for an instant.

It was a fatal mistake.

Lunging forward with his Bowie knife held flat and ready, the scout buried his blade to the hilt in Big Nosed John Harper's suddenly exposed chest. The knife sliced through the wide-eyed gunrunner's heart killing him instantly. Holten extracted the bloodied blade and Big Nosed John slumped dead to the ground.

The panting scout stood hovering over the body.

"Oh, Eli!" said Isabella as she rushed from the brush. "I didn't mean to burst in on you like that, but I was just doing what you told me."

A wide grin cracked Holten's leathery face. "Your timin' was perfect," he said, wrapping a long arm around the sumptuous blonde while double checking Harper's bloodied body.

A rustling sound rose from the bushes.

Holten whirled toward the sound.

"Please!" shouted a bound settler. "It's only us!"

"We saw what ya did, mister," said another tied-up and very frightened sodbuster. "We thought for sure that we was goners!"

"It's all right now," said Holten. He gestured toward Big Nosed John's body. "This here gunrunner finally got what he deserved."

Then Holten and Isabella untied the ashen-faced men.

Another gunrunner had paid the price for the brutal raid on Fort Rawlins, and for the vicious attack in which Yellow Feather had lost her life.

But the scout wasn't finished yet.

FOURTEEN

As the setting sun cast eerie shadows across the withering prairie, Holten and Isabella urged their nickering mounts toward a small gathering of Oglala Sioux warriors who were camped in the middle of the plains. The scout had seen the swirls of dust kicked up by the war ponies of his former Sioux brothers and had steered Isabella toward the painted braves for what he hoped would be a beneficial parlay.

Perhaps the Oglala had some new information.

Chief Black Spotted Horse, looking much healthier than the last time Holten had seen him at the Pawnee camp in the canyon, greeted the scout and his blonde companion. The chief's wounds were still bandaged, but there was no sign of blood seeping from the cuts.

"How, Tall Bear," said the chief, raising his hand.

"How, great Chief," replied Holten. "My spirit soars at seeing the leader of the Oglala looking so fit and ready for battle."

Black Spotted Horse nodded glumly. "Only my heart is still wounded, Tall Bear," he said. "Come and we shall smoke a pipe."

The scout tethered the snorting horses and escorted the wide-eyed Isabella past the two dozen bow-wielding braves who, taking a break from their quest for the Pawnee, were sitting cross-legged in the knee-deep buffalo grass. Most of the surrounding warriors, Holten knew, had lost their squaws in the raid at Fort Rawlins.

Then, while Isabella sat dutifully behind Holten in the accepted Sioux manner for women, the scout and his Oglala friends sat smoking in silence, the sun-scorched prairie all around them seeming to the suddenly relaxed scout to be strangely tranquil. Fleecy white clouds were scudding across the Dakota sky. Holten puffed deeply on the polished, stone pipe several times and waited for Black Spotted Horse to clean out the sizzling dottle, the traditional signal for the conversation to begin.

"I'm hungry, Eli," whispered Isabella.

"All I got is some beef jerky and water in my saddle bag."

"It sounds awful," said the shapely blonde, "but I'm so hungry I could eat almost anything."

"Help yourself," said the scout.

Then he watched Isabella swivel-hip her way to the horses and he felt an involuntary twinge in his loins. Holten was surprised at how much he enjoyed having her along.

"Well," began Black Spotted Horse in Lakota while knocking the pipe against a nearby rock, "what has Tall Bear been up to?"

The scout quickly explained what had happened with the two dudes and Big Nosed John Harper, and then asked the hawk-nosed Oglala chief if the Sioux had uncovered any further information regarding the whereabouts of Black Bob Callahan and his gang.

Black Spotted Horse nodded. "Four Bull and some other warriors have located the evil white men's hideout," said the handsome chief.

Holten's pulse quickened. "Where?" he asked simply.

"I will let Four Bull tell you," said the chief.

Four Bull nodded. "It is a clever spot for a hideout, Tall Bear. And in a place you are very familiar with: the tall waterfall near the canyon of the soaring eagles. There is an old Pawnee ceremonial cave located behind the falls. That is where the evil, dark-skinned white is hiding."

The scout nodded slowly. The waterfall was known to white men throughout the Dakota Territory as Diamond Falls, but Holten hadn't been aware of a cave behind the silvery plume of falling water. And Four Bull was right; it was an ingenious place for a hideout.

"Did Four Bull actually see the white leader?"

"No, but we got as close as possible without getting shot at," replied the short, muscular warrior. "The evil whites have many sentries posted around the waterfall, and it is difficult to get very close."

"That might be a problem," said Holten, rubbing his leathery face.

Black Spotted Horse raised his hands. "It is no problem, Tall Bear, for those who know about the underwater tunnel leading into the caves."

The scout's eyebrows shot up. "Underwater tunnel?"

"Yes," added Four Bull. "We discovered them many years ago while chasing some Pawnee sentries into the pool of water near the falls. All of a sudden the Pawnee disappeared. When we dived into the water to try and find them, we found the tunnel instead."

"And where does the tunnel come out?"

"At the very rear of the cave."

"But won't the white men be expecting something like that? Or maybe they have even followed the opening all the way to the pool of water."

Black Spotted Horse shook his head. "The tunnel's entrance to the cave is covered with small boulders that can be easily tossed aside. Our warriors fixed the tunnel like that anticipating just such a problem."

Holten smiled broadly at the prospect. "It all sounds very interesting, my friends," he said. "I will go there as soon as we finish here."

"It is too heavily guarded for even Tall Bear to attack alone," cautioned the Oglala chief.

"I plan on reconnoitering the hideout first, and then returning with the soldiers later on. Besides, with his top two gunfighters dead, Black Bob Callahan should be kinda jittery and pretty vulnerable right now."

"Very good, Tall Bear," said the chief. "Now if we can only finish off Mole On Face and his braves, the Pawnee uprising will be crushed."

Holten's jaw hardened. His blue eyes narrowed and his fists clenched at the mention of the warrior who had killed Yellow Feather.

"Where is Mole On Face right now?" asked the scout in a voice edged with hatred.

"We followed him and his dozen or so remaining braves to a nearby canyon. Several of the Pawnee renegades are badly wounded. Unless the murdering bastards get some help, we should have them trapped this evening."

Isabella returned to the group, a wide smile parting her pretty face and her sumptuous body pressing against the tight-fitting riding suit she was wearing.

"I think I will go and hunt the evil whites," said the scout. "Our revenge must be complete as soon as possible to avenge the violent deaths of our loved ones."

Black Spotted Horse rose and the other braves stood.

"We will try to rout the Pawnee for you, Tall Bear," said the chief. Then the hawk-nosed Oglala leader looked Holten in the eye. "And we will try to capture Mole On Face alive so Tall Bear can have his revenge."

The scout smiled. "Thank you, great Chief."

Satisfied that he was on the last leg of his revenge-seeking odyssey, Holten turned and began to escort Isabella toward their tethered horses. A warm feeling of confidence was spreading through the scout's chest.

Then the prairie began to vibrate.

The very ground under Holten's feet began to shake.

"Eli?" cried Isabella. "What is that?"

Holten's pulse began to race. He whirled toward the Sioux.

"Buffalo!" he said to the chief in Lakota.

"It's a stampede!" cried Black Spotted Horse.

Suddenly the ear shattering drumming of thousands of hooves rose into the sweltering late afternoon air like a gigantic roll of thunder. Holten turned toward the prairie beyond. His heart leapt to his throat when he saw a cloud of dust, a band of whooping Pawnee warriors, and a herd of wild-eyed buffalo several hundred yards away being stampeded toward the spot where he'd been meeting with the Oglala.

Chief Mole On Face was leading the stampede.

"Oh my God!" gasped Isabella, her hand going to her lips.

"It's a buffalo herd and they're out of control!" cried the scout.

"Mole On Face has found his help!" shouted Black Spotted Horse in Lakota. "His braves have sent the buffalo to kill us where we are standing!"

"Run for your lives!" yelled Holten.

Suddenly the once tranquil prairie was alive with the frantic shouts of rapidly fleeing Oglala braves, the sudden drumming of buffalo hooves, and the frightened whinnying of prancing war ponies.

"Eli, I'm scared!"

"Run for the horses!" shouted the scout above the din of the charging buffalo herd.

Without warning disaster struck the fleeing group.

Frightened into a wild-eyed frenzy by the thunderous buffalo herd, all of the tethered horses suddenly pulled free of their restraints and galloped for safety on the edge of the tree-lined stretch of prairie.

Including Holten's gelding and Isabella's mount.

The Oglala braves tried to give chase, but the instinctive rush for safety by the nickering ponies quickly sent them out of range of the leaping warriors. Holten, Isabella, and all of the Oglala braves suddenly stopped short and glanced in horror at the charging herd of shaggy, two-thousand-pound buffaloes that was bearing down on them. The herd resembled a furry, undulating brown blanket that had suddenly covered the prairie.

"Oh shit!" was all Holten could manage to say.

Then the Oglala warriors screamed and ran for the trees at the edge of the prairie, their flashing brown eyes widened with fear and their copper-skinned legs leaping through the knee-high grass like frightened jack rabbits being chased by a rapidly gaining coyote.

"What are we going to do, Eli?" cried Isabella. Her long fingers gripped the scout's muscled arm like a vise and her pretty face was lined with concern.

Suddenly a hail of bullets zipped through the air.

"The Pawnee are firing at us!" cried Holten.

The scout watched several of his fleeing Oglala blood brothers throw up their hands with the impact of speeding slugs from Pawnee .44-40 rifles. The dead braves sprawled on the dusty ground.

"Let's go!" shouted the scout, pulling Isabella.

"Where to?"

"For the woods on this side of the prairie. From the way the buffalo are comin', this way looks like the shortest route!"

As fast as their legs could carry them the scout and his pretty blonde companion dashed for the safety of the nearby woods that were only a hundred yards away and in the opposite direction from the fleeing Sioux. The thunderous din of the buffalo hooves grew louder until it was useless for Holten to scream any further directions. Bullets were zipping over their heads as they ran.

Finally, with the cries of Oglala braves being trampled to death rising above the drumming of hooves, Holten and Isabella were only twenty feet from the safety of some cottonwood trees. The edge of the wild-eyed buffalo herd was bearing down on the gasping pair until finally, just as Holten dived into the row of trees, the earth-shaking, snorting herd of buffalo thundered past, the closest animal so near that the scout could have reached out and stroked its hide.

Holten and Isabella collapsed on the ground.

The buffalo herd galloped past.

With his heart pounding against his ribs like an Indian war club, the scout waited until the last of the buffaloes had thundered by and then glanced out at where the parlay with the Oglala had taken place. He felt a sudden wave of nausea begin to wash through his stomach as he scanned the death and destruction left behind by the out-of-control buffalo and the rampaging Pawnee who had been driving them.

"Damn!" he breathed, his steely blue eyes quickly surveying the crumpled bodies of more than a dozen Oglala braves that were sprawled on the prairie.

"Oh God!" gasped Isabella, her blue eyes saucering. "Those Indians have been pounded into jelly, Eli! I think I'm going to be sick again!"

"Get sick later!" said Holten suddenly. He shot to his feet and jerked the gasping blonde with him. "We got some visitors comin'!"

"Visitors?"

"Pawnee warriors lookin' for horses and survivors!"

As the scout hauled the wild-eyed honey blonde easterner through the surrounding shrubbery and up toward the shadowy hills, he glanced over his shoulder and watched five Pawnee braves encircling Four Bull and cutting down the short, muscular Oglala warrior with quick swipes of their fearsome stone war clubs. The painted Sioux's head suddenly was a bloody pulp. Other shaven-headed Pawnee braves were gathering the frightened Sioux ponies and hunting down other straggling Sioux warriors. Holten headed for cover and hoped to regroup.

After all, he still had some scores to settle.

* * *

Holten and Isabella were lying in the relatively cool shade of a towering Black Hills pine tree, their bodies exhausted and their clothes drenched with perspiration. They had dashed into the hills and away from the Pawnee.

The late afternoon tranquility had returned to the prairie, but the sudden violence back on the plains had hardened the scout's resolve even more. He grit his teeth and knew that after resting his aching frame a while he'd have to hit the trail again, on foot this time, in his relentless search for the killers of Yellow Feather.

"A penny for your thoughts, Eli," said Isabella softly. The luscious blonde writer was lying with her head on Holten's stomach.

"I don't think ya want to know."

Isabella sat up. "Still thinking about your dead bride?" she asked, her sparkling blue eyes searching the scout's brown, leathery face.

Holten nodded. "And her murderers."

"But what can we do now? Our horses are gone, and you don't have your rifle either!"

"We're still alive," said the scout, his steely eyes looking down where the buffalo had thundered past only moments before. "And that counts for somethin' out on the prairie."

A silence filled the gap between them.

"I've . . . I've learned so much about you, Eli," said Isabella, reaching out and grabbing Holten's big, rough hands. "I feel as though I've known you forever."

The scout smiled. "Don't ever get involved with a frontier scout, Isabella. Ain't goin' to lead to nothin' but heartache for ya."

"I'm writing a book, remember?"

"It should be interestin' readin'."

Again there was silence.

Suddenly the sumptuous blonde rose to her feet and started to undress, her flashing blue eyes fixed on the scout's leathery face.

"I've always been one to take chances," she said.

Holten chuckled. "Tryin' to learn more about the intimate Eli Holten?" he asked, his piercing eyes quickly scanning Isabella's now naked body. His penis was beginning to grow inside of his pants.

Seeing the direction of the scout's wide-eyed gaze, Isabella Cartwright ran her long, tapered fingers over her big breasts, gently massaging the supple flesh and causing the rosy nipples to harden at her very touch. She cupped her breasts in her hands and held them up for the scout, a sensuous smile parting her full, supple lips. Standing naked in the fading sunlight, with her golden tresses falling over her slender shoulders, Isabella looked to the scout like a sumptuous, golden goddess.

Holten's penis now was pounding against his pants in its effort to be free, and his hungry gaze quickly scanned the luscious blonde's voluptuous beauty; her round breasts, flat stomach, shiny pubic bush, and shapely hips. The sight of her firm, round buttocks sent a shiver of sudden desire rippling through the scout's trembling body.

"But I can make you forget your troubles!" challenged the naked blonde as she continued to knead her billowy breasts in front of the near-panting scout.

"Let's see!" countered Holten.

And without further ado the fully aroused scout quickly stripped off his sweat-clogged buckskin clothes and stood next to Isabella, his elongated penis sticking out like an army flagpole. The scout's tall, lean body trembled with pent-up sexual energy and he felt a tremor of desire coursing through his loins when Isabella glanced quickly at his cock. Holten reached out and brought the shapely blonde up against his body.

"Oh!" said Isabella sharply as the scout's hardened cock jabbed her in her stomach.

"See!" said Holten with a wry smile. "I've just about forgotten my troubles already!"

Isabella Cartwright reached down and grasped Holten's pulsating penis with her long, tapered fingers, her velvet touch making the scout flinch, and guided his rock-hard shaft to her fully aroused vagina, gently rubbing his sensitive tip in the delicate folds of flesh there until both of them were moaning with delight.

"Ya got good hands, Isabella!" gasped Holten.

"That's because you're so well hung!"

Then Isabella knelt on the dusty ground, placed Holten's penis in her mouth, and began to suck on him as though his enormous cock was sugar-coated, her fingers gently fondling his balls at the same time.

"Damn!" gasped the scout.

"Let's do it!" said the blonde in a hoarse whisper that was heavy with desire.

Without a wasted motion the panting blonde easterner pulled the worked-up scout down on top of her, his enormous penis finding her already wet channel like an accurately shot arrow hitting its mark.

"Ooooo," moaned Isabella, writhing. "Make it good!"

Then with the fading sunlight slanting across his bare body, Holten began to pump his shaft in and out of the gasping honey blonde writer again and again, until finally Isabella shrieked with ecstasy and arched her back to meet the scout thrust for thrust, Holten finally groaning, shuddering, and exploding into the sumptuous easterner and filling her to the brim with his hot, milky fluid.

They remained locked together, exhausted and sweating.

Only the sighing of the breeze broke the silence.

"Damn, Isabella," gasped Holten, his long frame atop the soft, sumptuous writer. "You're somethin'!"

"You're not bad yourself, Eli Holten!"

The shapely blonde kissed him on the lips.

Then the two lovers, remaining clasped together like a couple of spoons in a drawer, rested for a few minutes in the shade of the towering pine trees, their minds clear and their bodies fully refreshed.

Finally the scout's active mind began to dwell once again on the problems at hand, namely Black Bob Callahan and Mole On Face. The buffalo stampede had changed everything; now the scout was on the defensive. He gently extricated his now flaccid penis from Isabella's body and started to dress, his mind trying to devise a plan to get them some horses.

It was a long walk to the Gray River.

Heading on foot through the tree-lined Black Hills, hoping to reach the rendezvous point by early morning, Holten and Isabella suddenly heard voices.

Voices speaking the Pawnee tongue.

The scout pulled the blonde easterner into the shrubs.

"Who is it?" asked the wide-eyed writer.

"A couple of Pawnee warriors just up ahead," replied Holten, his heart pounding like a war drum and his steely blue eyes scanning the terrain.

"What are we going to do, Eli?"

"Pay 'em a visit."

Before the slack-faced blonde could reply, the scout had already jerked her to her feet and was leading them both on the run toward the rocky ridge just ahead. Reaching the boulder-strewn crest, Holten hunkered in the shadows of the rocks and pulled Isabella close to him. Together they peered through the shadowy late afternoon sunlight at the clearing below.

"Look!" whispered Isabella. "Your horse!"

The scout quickly scanned the two shaven-headed Pawnee warriors, the pile of Oglala Sioux weapons they were divvying up, and the scout's snorting gelding tethered with three other ponies to a cottonwood at the edge of the clearing.

The braves obviously were part of Mole On Face's remaining raiding party and were on their knees poring over the spoils of their victory at the buffalo stampede. Holten's guts constricted when he saw a couple of fresh, bloodied Oglala scalps hanging from the belts of the jabbering Pawnees. Was one of them Chief Black Spotted Horse's? In any event, the sudden meeting with the Pawnee renegades gave the scout a chance to obtain a couple of mounts—and to reclaim his gelding.

"We're goin' to get them horses," whispered Holten.

"*We* are?" asked Isabella, her blue eyes as big as silver dollars and full of apprehension.

"Take off your blouse," said the scout.

"How can you think of sex at a time like this?"

"You're goin' to be what is commonly known as a diversion, Isabella. I want ya to walk to the edge of the clearing without your blouse. Give them braves a good look at your big, beautiful tits!"

"I will not!" snapped the blonde. "Why I never . . . !"

"Ya will if it means gettin' some horses. It's a long walk across some purty rough terrain 'til ya reach Fort Sampson to the south."

Isabella pursed her lips. "What are you going to be doing while I'm exposing myself to those . . . those savages down there?"

"I'll be killin' 'em!" replied Holten simply.

Isabella paused, then started to unbutton her blouse.

"The things you make me do, Eli Holten!"

"Consider it research for your book," said the scout, unsheathing his Bowie knife. "I'll be usin' my blade. It's more quiet, and if some of these warriors' Pawnee friends are still hangin' around, we don't want 'em to come runnin' at the sound of gunshots."

Finally Isabella was topless, her big breasts looking like

fresh, ripe melons in the late afternoon shadows. Holten nodded his approval.

"That oughtta get 'em horny," he said with a smile.

"Just don't wait too long before you kill them, Eli."

The scout chuckled. "Go do your stuff."

With a disgusted glance at the scout, Isabella Cartwright, distinguished eastern writer from a proper Boston family, strode topless toward the clearing below and the two unsuspecting Pawnee warriors, her rosy-tipped breasts jouncing as she stepped out of the bushes.

The Pawnee renegades shot to their feet.

At the same time, Holten padded as stealthily as a stalking coyote through the clawing brush that surrounded the clearing and suddenly burst from the shrubs, his gleaming blade raised and ready to toss at the Indians.

The Pawnees talked excitedly and started toward Isabella.

"Eli!" shrieked the blonde.

The warriors froze in their tracks.

Holten whistled. The Indians whirled.

Without a wasted motion, the scout lunged toward one of the wide-eyed warriors, quickly slashing the brave's throat with a swipe of the knife. A shower of blood splattered on the ground. Before the other startled warrior had a chance to react, Holten completed the attack by jabbing the Bowie knife into the shaven-headed Indian's exposed painted chest. The slumping warrior died with a scream caught in the back of his throat.

In the best Oglala tradition the attack had been swift and silent. The scout cleaned the blood off his blade, smiled at Isabella, and strode purposefully toward his gelding.

After all, he still had some scores to settle.

FIFTEEN

The feel of the gelding's familiar bulk beneath him sent a warm rush of happiness through Holten's chest as he and Isabella galloped away from the scene of the buffalo stampede disaster and headed toward the Gray River for their morning rendezvous with the soldiers.

But now that he and the shapely blonde were once again in the saddle rather than walking, the scout had decided after leaving the dead Pawnee warriors back in the clearing that he'd try to find the nearby hideout of Black Bob Callahan and the remaining gunrunners.

The famous waterfall that Four Bull and the Oglala warriors had told Holten about, known as Diamond Falls, was only a few miles from the scout's present location. A quick look around to reconnoiter the place would definitely help him to prepare his attack with the soldiers in the morning. So with Isabella galloping alongside him, the scout dug his heels into the gelding's flanks and headed for the cave behind the waterfall.

And for Black Bob Callahan.

They arrived at the shimmering pool of water that fronted the tall, silvery waterfall just as the orange sun was dipping below the western horizon. Isabella's blue eyes widened at the picturesque, five-foot-wide wall of falling water that was cascading from the side of a rocky cliff about fifty feet off the ground.

"It's so beautiful!" gasped the pretty blonde.

"And so misleadin'," said the scout, shaking his head in

disbelief. "For all these years I never knew that a cave was behind that there waterfall."

Suddenly a flash of movement from the rocks.

A gunrunner sentry was making his rounds.

The scout pulled the gasping blonde easterner into the shadows and quickly surveyed the flat-faced cliff, the narrow waterfall, and the shimmering lake in front of them. Holten quickly noticed some steps cut into the face of the cliff and several hard-faced sentries on guard duty at various points along the route leading to the cave behind the falling water.

"I'm goin' into the cave," said Holten.

Isabella's eyes widened. "And what about me?"

"You stay here and take care of the horses," said the scout, his eyes still fixed on the gunrunner sentries. "If I get into any trouble up there, I'll need to know for sure that the horses are all right."

"What if the sentries find me? Won't they take the horses, too?"

"That's why I want ya to tether the mounts in the woods and wait for me at the edge of the little lake. That way we'll always have the horses if we need 'em."

"What if you don't come back, Eli?" asked the shapely blonde, her sparkling blue eyes full of concern as they searched the scout's leathery face.

Holten smiled. "I'll be back."

Then the scout handed Isabella his Remington .44.

"Do you think I'll need this?"

"Better to be safe than sorry," said Holten. "Besides, you're an old hand at it by now."

Then the scout turned his attention to the waterfall and the cave that was supposed to be behind it. He didn't want to use the secret underwater entrance just yet; he might need it in the morning should he return with the soldiers. For now, Holten decided to enter the cave in the conventional way—through the front door.

But how?

The scout racked his brain for an answer.

Holten looked at Isabella Cartwright, recalled her bare-breasted diversion at the clearing, and suddenly he had his answer to getting into the gunrunners' cave.

He'd create a diversion!

"What are you thinking about, Eli?"

"Fire," replied the scout.

"What fire?"

"I'm goin' to set fire to them parched bushes up there near the waterfall. That oughtta bring most of them sentries runnin'!"

Checking to make sure he still had some matches in his buckskin shirt, the scout then hauled his Winchester .44-40 from its saddle boot and turned toward the waterfall. Then Holten looked at Isabella.

"Remember," he said, "stay out of sight."

"I will, Eli."

"And take care of the horses."

"You can count on me," said the shapely blonde from Boston. "I've learned all about being a frontier scout the past couple of days!"

"I think your book is comin' to an end," said Holten. "At least I hope it is. And it should be a tragic endin' for Callahan and his boys."

Isabella smiled. "Good luck, Eli."

Leaving the smiling honey blonde easterner holding the reins of their mounts at the edge of the shimmering lake, the scout padded through the surrounding grass and headed toward the rocky cliff just ahead.

Holten's plan was simple: sneak through the gathering dusk until he was within striking distance of the first gunrunner sentry, knock out the unsuspecting guard, and work his way halfway up the rocky steps until he was abreast of the dry shrubs growing from fissures in the rocks. Then he'd light a fire, wait for the resulting commotion, and enter the cave.

Everything was working right until he was seen.

A dozing sentry whom the scout had not noticed was standing among some leafy box elder trees, his Winchester repeater cradled in his arms and his heavy-lidded eyes closing and opening as sleep threatened to overtake him. Suddenly Holten stumbled into the sleepy sentry.

The stubble-faced outlaw's eyes snapped open.

"Holy shit!" he cried. "It's the scout!"

Not wanting to alarm the other nearby guards, Holten stabbed the barrel of his Winchester toward the sentry with the same deadly speed a fencer would use to thrust with his rapier. The cold barrel caught the startled gunrunner in the solar plexus and dropped him like a felled ox.

Standing just twenty yards from the face of the cliff, his pulse racing, Holten quickly scanned the surrounding area to see if he'd been spotted. Apparently the other sentries were just as casual in their approach to their duty as the fallen guard at the scout's feet. Nobody had seen him. Holten dragged the unconscious sentry further into the bushes and then continued his trek toward the waterfall.

Approaching the tall, silvery plume of falling water, the scout noticed that the noisy splash of the cascading water into the lake helped to drown out any noise his footfalls might be making on the ground. The falling water also sent a fine spray into the air that clung to the scout's eyelashes and touched his leathery face.

With his heart pounding and his palms growing slippery, the scout flattened himself against the jagged face of the rocky cliff, sharp edges of rocks jabbing into his back, and peered up toward the source of the waterfall. To his amazement he could see the beginnings of a large cave just behind the tall, narrow sheet of falling water. The scout started to mount the slippery steps.

Suddenly a couple of rifle-toting sentries came into view

up near the cave's opening, followed by a dark-skinned gunrunner with a lean, chiseled face and deep-set eyes.

Black Bob Callahan. Holten's jaw hardened.

The scout strained to hear their conversation.

"Are ya sure it was Big Nosed John?" asked Callahan.

"Hell, yes!" replied a sentry. "The boys found the body in a clearing on the prairie. He'd been stuck with a knife and left to rot!"

"Well, that makes Slim and Harper gone. We better make our next move before them Pawnee are wiped out by the goddamn scout and his Sioux friends! Let's go inside and talk about this Fort Sampson thing."

Then the three gunrunners disappeared from view.

Next move? Holten had to investigate.

Gripping his Winchester .44-40 with both hands, the scout mounted one rocky step at a time until he was up on the man-made staircase about twenty feet off the ground. Then he spotted the first of the two sentries he figured he would encounter before reaching the mouth of the hidden cave.

The dumb-looking, stubble-faced guard was looking out at the shimmering lake and hadn't glanced toward the scout yet. Holten noticed the drowsy sentry was perched on a small ledge. The scout knew he would have to strike with the speed of a rattlesnake and the stealth of a coyote.

Slowly unsheathing his fearsome Bowie knife, the scout drew back his right hand and sent the glistening blade flying through the gathering dusk. The razor-sharp knife slammed into the unsuspecting sentry's chest and buried itself to the hilt, slicing the guard's heart in two. The stunned gunrunner died almost instantly with his mouth open in a silent scream and his eyes widened with shock. The guard slumped on the small rocky ledge.

Glancing around to see if any of the other sentries had noticed the death of their cohort, Holten then took the rocky steps two at a time until he was standing beside the guard's bloodied corpse. Retrieving his knife, the scout then proceeded to mount the remaining few steps to the cave.

To Holten's surprise, there was no other sentry waiting at the cave's opening. Apparently one of the rifle-toting guards who went with Callahan was supposed to be on duty at the mouth of the shadowy gunrunner hideout. The nearby waterfall, with its roaring silvery plume, hid the scout from any sentries down below. Holten smiled, extracted his matches, and went to work.

Knowing it wouldn't be long before somebody spotted him, the scout struck a couple of wooden matches and tossed the flaming little sticks into the nearby sun-parched shrubbery. The dry bushes burst into flames and quickly spread to the surrounding desiccated plants. Suddenly Holten heard a commotion from inside the cave.

"Christ, a fire!"
"The cave's fillin' up with smoke!"
"Get some water, quick!"
"What in hell?"

The screams were followed by the sudden clump of heavy leather cowboy boots on the ancient stone floor of the former Pawnee ceremonial cave. Holten clung to the shadows of the hideout's opening and waited for the commotion to center its attention on the smoky blaze in front of him.

As half a dozen wide-eyed gunrunners, including Black Bob Callahan, raced past him, the scout slipped unnoticed into the gang's hidden hideout. The loud rush of the falling water lessened as Holten clung to the walls and edged his way into the recesses of the cave.

The scout pressed up against several crates marked DYNAMITE and listened intently. No wonder the gang was so nervous about fire with all these explosives around, thought Holten. With his heart beating a tune against his ribs, the scout scanned the former ceremonial cave's shadowy interior.

The torch-lit cave was about the size of a small saloon, with a few chairs and a table off to one side. On the other side of the gunrunners' clever hideout, separated from the rest of the cave by a six-foot-high stone wall, was a row of double-decker bunk beds that could sleep about twenty men. Food and whiskey enough for several weeks was stacked near the bunks and a black, sooty cooking stove was nestled against the rocky rear wall of the cave.

The rear wall! And the secret entrance.

With his pulse racing, Holten checked the commotion at the smoky front of the hideout and noticed that the gunrunners were almost finished battling the small blazes in the bushes. Then the scout pushed away from the wall and strode purposefully toward the rear of the cave. Reaching the darkened part of the hideout, Holten strained his eyes and quickly checked for the Indian-made stone wall that Black Spotted Horse had mentioned—the wall that was supposed to cover the secret entrance from the underwater tunnel.

Running his fingers along the shadowy rear of the cave, the scout suddenly found what he was looking for. A five-foot-in-diameter section of the rocky wall was obviously loosely packed and could be pushed away easily from the other side. Holten felt a warm wave of confidence wash through his chest. The gunrunners could be attacked by using the secret underwater tunnel.

Suddenly the scout heard approaching voices.

He hunkered in the shadows, his pulse quickening again.

"How in hell could fires start up here?" asked Black Bob Callahan.

A heavy-set gunrunner shrugger. "I seen fires start out on the prairie all by themselves, boss," he growled. "Same thing coulda happened up here."

Holten's route of escape was suddenly cut off as the

entire gunrunner gang began to trickle back into the ceremonial cave. The scout licked his parched lips and gripped his Winchester .44-40. The confirmation of the secret entrance wouldn't do him any good if he couldn't tell the soldiers about it. Feeling a cold tremor of anxiety rippling through his gut, Holten racked his brain trying to think of a way to get the hell out of the gang's hideout.

Then he heard Isabella's shrieking voice.

His heart sank.

"What the hell?' snarled Black Bob.

"Let me go!" cried Isabella Cartwright.

Peering cautiously from his position at the rear of the shadowy cave, Holten saw a couple of the laughing rifle-toting sentries roughly shoving the wide-eyed blonde writer into the cave. The stubble-faced guards pushed Isabella the final few yards, and she sprawled on the cave's dusty stone floor at Black Bob Callahan's feet.

"We caught the bitch spyin' on us near the lake," said one of the sentries.

"Well, well," said Black Bob with an evil smile spread across his dark-skinned face. The gunrunner gang's ruthless leader's deep-set brown eyes flashed with excitement and his lean, chiseled face brightened.

"Hey!" said a nearby gunrunner. "Ain't this the scout's woman?"

Callahan nodded slowly. "She's the same good-lookin' bitch we've seen ridin' with the scout." Suddenly Black Bob's expression grew serious, clouding his once flashing eyes. "And if this here whore is around the hideout, then sure as shit the scout is, too!"

"And maybe that explains the fire!" said a guard.

A couple of other gunrunners exchanged glances.

"Search the entire area!" ordered Black Bob.

"Right, boss!"

And to his dismay the scout watched most of the gang rush out of the shadowy cave in search of him. He knew that from now on the killers would be extra alert. Then Holten smiled to himself as a sudden idea struck him like a quick right jab to the jaw. If most of the gunrunners were out looking for him around the waterfall, then it meant almost nobody was left to keep him penned up in the cave. He checked and saw that only three of the gang, plus Callahan, remained.

Isabella's appearance may have been a blessing.

"Now as for you, sweetheart," growled Black Bob, reaching down, grabbing Isabella by her big breasts, and yanking her painfully to her feet. "You and me are gonna spend some time together, eh?"

Isabella shrieked with pain.

"Leave me alone!" she cried, apprehension etched in her pretty face and her voice edged with fear.

Holten couldn't wait any longer.

Gripping his rifle, he burst from the shadows.

The scout stepped into the flickering torch light and held his Winchester repeater at hip level, the long barrel pointed at the three smiling gunrunners who were standing beside Isabella and Black Bob.

"Isabella, get down!" cried the scout.

"Christ, it's Holten!"

The gunrunners slapped their leather holsters.

The scout squeezed the trigger.

Suddenly the cave was alive with ricocheting bullets, cries of pain, and the stench of spent gunpowder. Two of the startled gang members caught speeding slugs from Holten's .44-40 in their chests and went sprawling onto the cave's hard stone floor, blood spurting from their wounds.

"Eli!" shouted Isabella.

"Run for it!" cried the scout, racing for the waterfall-covered front of the hideout.

Isabella stood quickly, Callahan smashed her on the head.

The pretty blonde went down like a log.

"You bastard!" yelled Holten.

The scout whirled, aimed his rifle at Black Bob's scowling, dark-skinned face, and squeezed the trigger. The quick-moving gang leader leaped for cover behind the nearby iron stove and Holten's bullets whined harmlessly against the ceremonial cave's ancient stone walls.

Suddenly the scout heard voices near the waterfall.

Realizing there was no time to retrieve Isabella and still escape in time to help lead the soldiers back to the hideout, Holten turned and strode briskly from the cave, leaving the unconscious blonde writer from Boston temporarily in the evil hands of Black Bob and his cut-throats.

"It's the scout!" cried a returning gunrunner.

The gunman fired wildly, his ricocheting slug nicking the front wall of the waterfall-covered cave and sending a shower of rock fragments into the scout's face.

Holten screamed with sudden pain.

Trying to blink the painful rock dust from his burning eyes, the scout suddenly realized his time was growing short. The remainder of the gang, alerted by the sound of gunfire, was returning to the cave. Bullets started to ricochet all around the half-blind, stumbling scout.

Knowing approximately where the edge of the rocky cliff was, and trying to remember how far away from the rocks to leap to assure not getting smashed on the jagged boulders below, Holten threw all caution to the wind and ran toward the waterfall and the edge of the rocky precipice.

He flew into the air and floated toward the lake below.

The scout landed with a big splash.

"Shoot the son of a bitch!" cried Black Bob.

"Where in hell did he go?"

"Who cares? Just fill the lake with lead!"

As the scout sunk like a rock to the bottom of the shallow, waterfall-fed lake, he quickly began to swim underwater toward the far shore and the tethered horses, his Winchester still gripped in his big right hand. A shower of bullets zipped through the water all around him.

The sudden contact with the cool, mountain water quickly cleared the scout's eyes, and before long, with his lungs about to burst, he surfaced with a gasp in the growing evening darkness and quickly located the trees where the horses were waiting. Swimming rapidly through the welcome cover of darkness, Holten noticed that the gunrunners had lost sight of him and were starting to give chase.

"Don't let him get away!" shouted Callahan.

Heading for the horses, Holten suddenly stumbled on his Remington .44 pistol on the grass beside the gelding. Isabella hadn't even tried to defend herself before she was captured by the sentries.

The scout headed for his saddle and didn't look back.

SIXTEEN

The scout had ridden like the wind all during the night, galloping through the prairie while also leading Isabella's riderless horse away from the danger at the hideout cave. Now as a glorious sunrise was bathing the shadowy prairie in an orange glow, Holten had come across Lieutenant Bodie James and the small column of troopers at the agreed upon rendezvous spot.

The scout's burning eyes were better now, but the pain he felt for having lost Isabella was as bothersome as a fresh bullet wound. Every woman who touched his life, it seemed, was doomed to a violent death.

Telling himself over and over that he didn't have any choice but to leave the pretty blonde easterner at the mercy of Black Bob and his gang, Holten was burning with anger and impatience as he tethered his gelding and strode over to the awakening troopers on the banks of the narrow Gray River.

"Mornin', Holten," said Coyote Jim Stephens. The white-bearded frontiersman narrowed his blue eyes and studied the scout's face. "Ya sure look terrible! What in hell happened out there, scout?"

"Did ya get Callahan?" asked Kansas Joe.

"Ya, Mister Holten," said Lieutenant Bodie James as he strode over to the campfire. "And how did ya make out with your Oglala friends?"

"Give me some coffee," said Holten.

Then the bone weary scout slumped on the grassy river

bank and quickly recounted the details of the information he'd received from the Sioux, the buffalo stampede, and the reconnoitering trip to the gunrunners' hideout cave.

"Holy shit!" was all Kansas Joe Adderly could manage to say. The young half-breed stroked his high-cheekboned face in thought.

"Well," said Bodie James. "It's too bad about the Oglala and Miss Cartwright. But it seems as though we're close to puttin' an end to this here uprisin' once and for all."

Holten's eyebrows shot up. "What about Mole On Face?"

"We got him pegged in a narrow ravine a few miles from here. A couple of the men are watchin' him and his dozen or so renegades. Seems like them Pawnee are sorta gettin' tired of fightin'. Been drinkin' pretty heavy."

Holten drained his coffee cup with a quick backward jerk of his head. "Mole On Face never gets tired of fightin', Lieutenant," said the scout matter-of-factly. "He was born to raise hell!"

The entire column was awake now and ready to ride.

"What's the plan?" asked Coyote Jim.

"First we hit the Pawnee," said Holten. "I got a feelin' Black Bob and his boys won't be leavin' that there hideout 'til they pull off whatever job it is they've been plannin' at Fort Sampson. They think that there cave is soldier-proof."

"So we hit Mole On Face right now?" asked Bodie James.

Holten nodded. "Then after takin' care of the Pawnee, we ride to the cave. This'll show any outlaws around the territory that they can't expect to mess with the army and get away with it for long."

"What about Miss Cartwright?" asked the lieutenant.

Holten just shrugged his shoulders, but he felt a pang of sadness for the luscious blonde from Boston. "All we can do is hope that we get there soon. We all know how

Callahan and his boys'll treat the lady."

Silence descended upon the river bank.

Cut-throat gunrunners didn't treat their women very kindly and the scout was fully aware of it. Isabella Cartwright would have to hold on until help arrived.

The column headed after the Pawnee renegades.

It was the third day after the brutal massacre at Fort Rawlins and now the scout felt he finally was about to get his full measure of revenge for the savage murder of his luscious bride-to-be.

"There's the canyon!" said Bodie James, pointing.

Bouncing atop the galloping gelding's broad back, Holten glanced at the tree-lined, narrow ravine where a couple of nervous troopers who had been left behind to keep an eye on the Pawnee began to wave frantically.

"What's wrong with them sentries, Lieutenant?"

"Maybe Mole On Face and his braves are fixin' to hightail it outta that there ravine!"

"Let's hit 'em!" shouted the scout.

"Column ho!" cried Lieutenant Bodie James.

Riding with their army issue Colt .45 revolvers held at the ready, the small column of eight troopers, two scraggly frontiersmen, Lieutenant James, and Holten raced toward the remaining band of Pawnee warriors.

And toward Mole On Face, Yellow Feather's killer.

Almost immediately the echoing sound of gunfire rose inot the previously calm and peaceful early morning prairie air. One of the two army sentries fell from his perch high atop a large boulder, a gaping bullet wound in his chest. Then the scout saw Mole On Face and his surviving ten warriors burst from the narrow entrance of the tree-lined ravine and gallop toward the open prairie.

"The Pawnee are gettin' away!" shouted Coyote Jim.

"Keep after 'em, boys!" yelled Holten. "I'm headin' after Mole On Face!"

Obviously spooked by the sudden appearance of the entire heavily armed army column, Chief Mole On Face suddenly had led his warriors out of their apparent trap and out onto the wide, sun-drenched plains.

The fleeing braves fanned out and went in different directions. Only Mole On Face had company in the form of two hard-faced friends. Holten gave pursuit.

While the soldiers branched out and picked their individual targets to pursue, Holten hunkered down in his saddle like a jockey and raced after the fleeing Pawnee chief and his two hard-riding companions. Glancing around to get his bearings, the scout noticed that the galloping Indian trio was heading for one of the most inhospitable territories in the entire American West.

The fearsome Bad Lands!

Holten knew once the fleeing Indians reached the cave-filled, rock-strewn Bad Lands his task of tracking them would be nearly impossible. A wily, stealthy plains Indian could survive for weeks in the arid Dakota Territory landscape that was simply, but accurately, named.

Realizing this, the scout quickly hauled his Winchester .44-40 from its saddle sheath, released the reins, and shouldered the heavy rifle. Holten squeezed the trigger and sent a speeding bullet into the copper-skinned shoulder of the trailing warrior. The brave fell forward on his pony but kept on riding with the others.

Holten aimed again at the bouncing backs of the three galloping Indians up ahead, but suddenly Mole On Face and his friends disappeared into a rocky ravine loaded with tiny caves and fissures.

Suddenly Holten heard hoofbeats to his left.

A shaven-headed Pawnee warrior being pursued by Coyote Jim came galloping into the same clearing where Holten was reining in his gelding to get a better look at the fleeing Mole On Face.

"Look out, Holten!" cried the white-bearded frontiersman from twenty yards away.

The scout turned in his saddle just in time to raise his Winchester and deflect the whooshing swipe of the war-club-swinging warrior. The charging brave's stone-headed club caught the barrel of Holten's repeating rifle with a ringing clang and sent the weapon flying from the scout's hands. Holten was pushed from his saddle with the impact of the club and landed in a cloud of alkaline dust in the clearing. The scout's wild-eyed gelding whinnied sharply and galloped out of the clearing.

The shaven-headed warrior, sensing a chance to finish off the famous Tall Bear of the hated Oglala Sioux, quickly turned the head of his spirited painted war pony, howled a bloodcurdling war cry, and raced toward the fallen scout.

"I'll help ya, Holten!"

The stumbling scout, trying vainly to regain his feet, suddenly saw Coyote Jim Stephens galloping into the clearing with his Sharps .50 caliber rifle shouldered and ready to send a heavy slug into the Pawnee brave.

But the Pawnee warrior saw him, too.

Quickly changing direction the charging brave lunged toward the suddenly startled frontiersman and bashed Coyote Jim Stephens on the side of his head with the heavy stone war club, the resulting thud reminding Holten of a watermelon popping open after being dropped on the ground.

Coyote Jim's head flew apart in a bloody shower.

The old-timer fell to the ground.

"Ya dirty son of a bitch!" murmured the scout.

Leaping to his feet with the speed of a frightened wildcat, Holten hurtled his body the few remaining feet that separated him from the mounted Pawnee warrior, unsheathed his gleaming Bowie knife, and plunged the blade into the wide-eyed brave's chest. The startled warrior cried out in pain and then tumbled head over heels off the rump of his prancing pony. Holten stood hovering over the bloodied body and tried to catch his breath.

Seeing that Coyote Jim Stephens was beyond help, the scout quickly located his nickering gelding, swung into the saddle, and headed after Mole On Face once again. This time all the scout had to do was follow the bloody spoor of one of the wounded warriors who was accompanying the chief.

The blood led to a small, boulder-strewn cave.

Holten reined in his horse quickly, scanned the surrounding terrain with his steely blue eyes, and then dismounted smoothly. Feeling reasonably sure that he wasn't stepping into a Pawnee death trap, the scout unholstered his Remington .44 pistol and padded as quietly as a stalking mountain lion toward the shadowy cave just ahead.

A hundred yards beyond, Holten noticed as he approached the cave, was the stark beginning of the arid, rocky Bad Lands. The scout noticed the gleaming white rock formations sticking into the sweltering prairie air like natural warning signs telling men to enter at their own risk.

The scout pressed up against the rocky front of the small cave and listened for any signs of the fleeing Pawnee renegades. The glistening drops of fresh blood led into the darkened recesses of the cave. At the same time, a strange aroma tweaked Holten's sensitive nostrils and caused him to grimace at the acrid smell. The scent was familiar but the scout couldn't place it immediately.

Taking a deep breath, Holten gripped his .44 and stepped into the cave. He pressed against the inner wall to wait for his eyes to adjust to the dark. He was nearly blind after moving into the darkness from the bright early morning prairie.

Soon the scout's eyes adjusted sufficiently for him to notice a gray form on the floor of the cave about five feet away.

Holten's pulse quickened. His palms grew slippery.

Stepping cautiously to where the crumpled form was lying, the scout stiffened when he saw that it was the body of the Pawnee brave he had shot back on the trail. Looking even more closely, Holten realized that the brave's throat had been slashed from ear to ear. Obviously Mole On Face didn't want to be slowed by a wounded warrior so the ruthless chief had butchered his own brave and left him behind to throw off the scout.

Then Holten saw the moving fur.

It was a tiny, innocent-looking grizzly bear cub.

But the scout's pounding heart leapt to his throat when he heard the deep, guttural growl of the cub's enraged mother from somewhere just inside the cave. Suddenly Holten remembered where he'd smelled the strange aroma before.

While hunting grizzlies with the Oglala Sioux!

A sudden crash of branches from somewhere in the cave followed by the heavy footfalls of the mother grizzly's mammoth feet sent a wave of anxiety washing through the scout's suddenly queasy stomach. Another roar filled the cave.

Then he saw the gleaming eyes and bared fangs.

Thinking quickly, Holten reached down, picked up the dead Pawnee warrior's bloodied corpse, and tossed it into the path of the rampaging mother bear. The trick worked, and the snarling grizzly suddenly began to tear the fallen Pawnee's torso into bloody little pieces.

Holten dashed out of the cave.

With his heart still beating a tune against his ribs, the scout quickly located his tethered gelding and swung his tall, lean frame onto the nickering mount's wide back. Holten clucked to his horse and started after Mole On Face, the bloodthirsty killer of his young bride.

The scout plunged into the fearsome Bad Lands.

SEVENTEEN

The merciless sun beat down on Holten.

Within half an hour after trotting into the jagged, rock-strewn landscape called the Dakota Bad Lands, Holten's buckskin clothing was saturated with perspiration and his mouth was as parched as shrivelled rawhide. Even his trustworthy gelding, usually able to travel for days on just a few swallows of water, was starting to wilt.

Keeping his burning eyes glued to the dusty alkaline trail, the scout followed the relatively easy-to-read tracks of Mole On Face and his one remaining travelling companion. From all indications, like the freshness of horse dung along the trail, Holten figured the bloodthirsty Pawnee war chief was about ten minutes ahead of him.

But the scout still kept his eyes peeled for an ambush.

Glancing up from time to time at the sun-baked, jagged rock formations all around him, Holten realized the Bad Lands, with all its caves and fissures, was a perfect spot for an ambush. The wary scout kept his muscles tensed just in case.

In addition to the danger posed by the fleeing renegades, the scout knew, too, that rattlesnakes and packs of marauding timber wolves were also a threat in the Bad Lands. In the past he'd been cornered on more than one occasion out on the inhospitable terrain by either a nest of summer-active rattlers or a pack of hungry wolves with pups to feed.

Suddenly Holten reined in the gelding.

The scout's animal-like sixth sense, his inner survival instinct that he'd developed after twenty years on the treacherous plains, was speaking to him once again.

It warned of trouble just ahead.

With his pulse quickening and his muscles tensing for action, the eagle-eyed scout quickly scanned the surrounding terrain for anything unusual.

He spotted it almost at once.

To the average prairie traveller, or the typical hapless greenhorn, the slight scratch marks in the trail just ahead wouldn't mean anything. To Holten the ruffled sand signalled one of the deadliest traps the plains Indians could rig.

It was a shallow pit filled with rattlesnakes.

Once a traveller's horse accidentally stepped into the hole, the angry snakes would nip its ankles and send a stream of deadly poison circulating through the unlucky mount's bloodstream. The horse would die almost immediately. And without a reliable mount in the Bad Lands, even the most experienced prairie veteran was a goner.

The perspiring scout dismounted slowly and scanned the surrounding parched terrain with his steely blue eyes. His heart began to beat like an Oglala war drum. Since the trap was planted a few yards ahead of him, Holten figured Mole On Face and his Pawnee companion, hidden behind some nearby rocks, were watching him at that very moment.

And they were waiting to pick him off.

The scout licked his parched lips and decided to fight the Pawnee dirty trick with one of his own—a trick he'd used many times in the past. Holten swung his long, lean frame onto the gelding's broad back and dug his heels into the nickering mount's gleaming flanks. Steering wide of the rattlesnake pit, the scout galloped along the trail, the gelding's hoofbeats echoing among the jagged rocks.

Quickly unsheathing his Winchester .44-40, Holten then leaned out of his saddle to the right so the bulky body of his galloping horse shielded him from any shots by an Indian to his left. Then holding onto the gelding's thick, flowing mane with his left hand, the scout held the Winchester in his right and aimed at the rocks along the side of the trail.

He saw a sudden flash of movement to his right.

As soon as the scout had galloped past the spot in the trail where the rattlesnake pit was lying in wait for an unsuspecting visitor, the broad-faced, shaven-headed Pawnee warrior who had accompanied Mole On Face into the Bad Lands shot to his feet and was aiming a gleaming army Winchester rifle at the passing scout.

The scout was ready for the attacker, however, and quickly sent a hot slug slamming into the broad, painted chest of the suddenly startled warrior before the Pawnee brave could even get off a shot. The report from Holten's Winchester roared in the confines of the jagged rock formations. The dead warrior was lifted off his feet with the impact of the .44-40's heavy bullet and went sprawling on the sun-baked ground.

Suddenly a couple of bullets zipped over Holten's head from the other side of the trail. It had to be Mole On Face, thought Holten. The still galloping scout remained hidden by the gelding's bulk until the big horse had raced behind a couple of nearby boulders. Then Holten dismounted quickly and ran to a position beside the trail and behind one of the large boulders.

If he knew renegades, then the chief would be running.

And he was.

Almost before the scout had taken up his position behind the boulder, Mole On Face, astride a wild-eyed painted pony, burst from behind some jagged rocks and headed along the trail toward the scout's present location. Holten saw the maniacal look on the Pawnee chief's twisted face. The shaven-headed warrior's Winchester repeater was gripped in his hands and aimed at the scout.

Holten waited a few seconds until finally, just before Mole On Face's galloping pony reached the deadly rattlesnake trap in the trail, the scout shot to his feet and sent a hail of hot lead toward the charging renegade chief.

The chief's pony reared with surprise and fear.

Then while Mole On Face was trying desperately to control his skittish horse, the pony's rear hooves stumbled into the shallow rattlesnake pit. The spirited paint whinnied sharply and kicked up its hind legs, its widened eyes filled with pain and fear.

Then the pony fell dead to the ground.

Mole On Face tumbled to the trail.

The short, broad-faced chief rolled a few times, his rifle still gripped in his muscular arms, and tried desperately to locate the scout.

Without wasting a second the scout quickly drew a bead on the rolling Pawnee chief, the bloodthirsty killer who had murdered Yellow Feather, and squeezed the trigger. The hot slug from the scout's smoking Winchester slammed into Mole On Face's left leg and exited on the other side in a spray of blood.

"Ayyyy!" cried the chief, gritting his teeth.

"Damn!" said Holten.

Quickly levering and firing again the scout watched another of his bullets slam into the ever-moving Pawnee warrior's left shoulder. Again Mole On Face cried out in pain and blood spurted, but again the tough, persevering renegade continued to scramble for the safety of the rocks alongside the trail. Within seconds the wounded killer had made the rocks.

"Goddamn it!" swore the scout.

Suddenly Holten saw a couple of buzzards in the sky.

"Ya can have the bastard in a few minutes!" yelled Holten skyward.

205

Then the scout returned his smoking Winchester to its saddle boot and unsheathed his fearsome Bowie knife. Now was the time for the coup de grace, the final few minutes of Mole On Face's evil life.

Padding toward the rocks across from his with all the stealth of a stalking cougar, Holten kept his steely eyes peeled for the wounded killer. As with wild animals, a wounded plains Indian could be more dangerous than he normally would be otherwise.

Suddenly the scout heard the scrape of moccasins.

"Tall Bear!" yelled Mole On Face in Lakota from behind some nearby rocks. "Your bullets bit me twice. I am making a bloody mess all over the place!"

The scout ducked behind a boulder.

"That's only the beginning!" replied Holten.

The Pawnee war chief laughed harshly. "All this trouble, Tall Bear, for a woman! There are many Indian squaws. Why can't you just forget this one?"

"Somebody like you wouldn't understand, Mole On Face."

"I understand that Tall Bear is going to die here this afternoon for something so silly as a woman! Why don't you go back to your white brothers and let me die in peace?"

"Like you let all the settlers die in peace? Or the Oglala braves you slaughtered with the buffalo herd down in the valley?"

"They all deserved to die!" snapped the chief.

While the strained conversation continued the scout was trying to figure out how to circle around the wounded Pawnee warrior.

"But now your uprising is finished!" said Holten.

"It is finished because we joined forces with the evil whites! We never should have listened to that dark-skinned leader of theirs!"

"Now it's too late for anything, Mole On Face. Now you

are going to die here in the Bad Lands. I think it is a good place for someone like you to die."

Mole On Face cackled. Then there was silence.

Holten's pulse quickened.

His grip tightened on his Bowie knife.

The scout padded cautiously to a neighboring boulder and waited in the hot sun, his heart pounding against his ribs like a hammer and sweat trickling down the inside of his buckskin shirt.

Seconds passed like hours.

Suddenly Holten heard the scrape of moccasin leather a fraction of a second before the unbelievably tough and badly wounded Pawnee chief leaped upon him from a nearby rock. The force of the bleeding warrior's body smashing into him knocked the scout off his feet and onto the dusty ground.

Quickly regaining his feet, Holten held his wide-bladed Bowie knife flat and ready for action. The scout turned and stared into the broad, dark face of the wounded renegade war chief, his muscles tensed for battle. Mole On Face was standing with a gleaming hunting knife in his hand.

"This is the way it should end, Tall Bear!" snarled Mole On Face in Lakota. The large brown mole on the chief's left cheek was darkened with anger. "The hunter and the hunted squaring off in a life or death struggle!"

Holten saw that the chief's two wounds, in his leg and shoulder, were bleeding badly and that the staggering Pawnee warrior was functioning more on pure animal instinct than anything else.

And pure ruthlessness, too!

Holten knew this warrior liked only to kill!

"You look in pretty bad shape, Mole On Face!"

"Good enough to kill you, Tall Bear!" rasped the chief in a hoarse whisper. The scout noticed that the Pawnee warrior's facial mole was almost the color of coal.

Holten lashed out quickly and struck Mole On Face's left arm with the flashing Bowie knife, opening a new wound that spurted blood onto the ground. Mole On Face cried out in pain and danced backwards.

"I should carve you into pieces for what you did at Fort Rawlins!" grated Holten.

Mole On Face was grimacing with pain.

"I'd do it again if I had the chance," replied the short, broad-faced chief in a weak voice. "All Oglala Sioux are pigs who deserve to die like Tall Bear's woman. And once the Pawnee regain their traditional hunting grounds from the treaty-loving Oglala, they will!"

"Brave words from a dying man!" said Holten as he circled in a crouch, his steely blue eyes fixed on the wounded chief's knife hand.

"Let's see how Tall Bear handles a dying brave!"

Without warning the surprisingly quick Pawnee war chief lunged forward and nicked the scout's buckskin pants just above the right knee. A thin ribbon of blood appeared from the slight cut beneath the material. The scout flinched at the needle-like pain from the wound.

"So Tall Bear does bleed like other men!"

"All Mole On Face did was ruin a good pair of pants."

Suddenly the savage growl of several nearby wolves pierced the sweltering early afternoon air and echoed off the surrounding jagged rock formations. Holten stiffened and listened to a hungry wolf pack starting to devour the fallen Pawnee warrior back in the rocks.

Mole On Face heard the wolves, too.

To the scout's amazement the broad-faced chief straightened at the sound of the feeding wolfpack and seemed to lose his concentration for just a second. Holten took advantage of the mistake.

The scout reared back with his right hand and tossed his gleaming blade through the air. The wide-bladed Bowie knife thudded into the suddenly exposed painted chest of the wide-eyed Pawnee war chief and buried itself to the hilt. Mole On Face cried out with pain and surprise, but to Holten's horror he didn't die.

The amazingly tough Pawnee war chief reached up with a trembling hand and tore Holten's big blade from his bloodied chest, a sudden spurt of fresh red staining the dusty ground at his feet.

"Tall Bear . . . !" gasped the chief.

The defenseless scout was standing wide-eyed.

Then Mole On Face looked at the blood-stained Bowie knife, examining the wide blade as though he'd never seen one before, until finally the dying chief's flashing brown eyes rolled toward the heavens and he pitched forward onto his face.

Holten's pulse was returning to normal.

"That's for Yellow Feather," murmured the scout.

Then, while the feeding wolves were busy devouring the dead warrior behind the rocks and the wheeling buzzards waited for the scraps, Holten picked up his knife and strode purposefully toward the gelding. His revenge-seeking journey had almost ended.

Only Black Bob Callahan remained.

EIGHTEEN

Holten hunkered in the bushes and looked at the shimmering lake in front of him. The silvery waterfall was falling in a foamy cascade from out of the rocky cliff. Somewhere in the face of the steep escarpment was a cave hiding the gunrunners, Black Bob Callahan, and Isabella Cartwright.

"I don't see no cave!" said Kansas Joe, his high-cheekboned face half hidden in the shadows. "All I see is that there waterfall!"

"The cave's behind the waterfall," said the scout.

"I see a sentry!" said Lieutenant Bodie James. "Up there near the cliff."

Holten nodded. "They'll have about half a dozen guards all around the place. Maybe more now that they know we're on our way."

"Them bastards are still in there, Mr. Holten," said the young lieutenant. "We've had a couple of the boys sittin' near this here lake since we saw ya last. Seems like Black Bob figures the army ain't gonna try and scale that there cliff, so he's stickin' around!"

The scout had ridden out of the parched, sun-baked Bad Lands as soon as possible after killing Mole On Face and headed for Diamond Falls, and the gunrunners' hideout. There, as previously arranged, he met up with Lieutenant James and the surviving troopers from Fort Sampson who had done a fine job quelling the Pawnee uprising under very trying circumstances. Now they were about to finish off the bastard Callahan and his money-grabbing cutthroats—and rescue Isabella Cartwright.

If they could get to the cave!

"What's the plan, Mr. Holten?" asked Bodie James.

"I'm headin' for that underwater tunnel I told ya about before," said Holten, his piercing eyes scanning the lake and the waterfall. "It's supposed to be located about twenty feet from this here bank."

"And then what?"

"I want ya to wait five minutes, or until I get through the tunnel and up into the back of the cave. Then give 'em hell with all the firepower ya got!"

Kansas Joe Adderly stroked his copper-skinned, halfbreed face. "Won't that kinda leave ya outnumbered up there, Holten? I mean, a couple of us could maybe come with ya."

The scout shook his head. "You'll all be needed down here to pump a helluva lot of lead into that there cave opening. For my surprise attack from the rear to work, I'll need ya to really keep the gunrunners busy."

"Then we charge 'em?" asked Lieutenant James.

"I hope so," said the scout with a smile. "I'll be able to hold 'em off for only so long. I'd hate to try and hightail it back through that underwater tunnel hauling Miss Cartwright along with me!"

"Look!" shouted Kansas Joe suddenly.

All heads whirled toward the cascading water and the shadowy cave hidden behind it. Holten's guts constricted as he saw Black Bob Callahan, Isabella Cartwright, and a handful of heavily armed gunrunners emerge from behind the curtain of falling water and begin to descend the steps on the cliff.

"Damn, them gunrunners are headin' out!" said Lieutenant Bodie James. "And they're armed to the teeth. Looks like they're fixin' to raid again."

The scout's jaw hardened. "Probably Fort Sampson!"

he said through clenched teeth. "We gotta hit 'em now! Get your men ready, Lieutenant!"

"Yessir!" snapped James.

"Where you goin', Holten?" asked Kansas Joe Adderly.

Holten rose swiftly. "Swimmin'!" he said over his shoulder as he strode briskly toward the shimmering, mountain-fed lake in front of him.

"We're ready, Mr. Holten!"

"Then open fire!"

"Yessir!" replied Bodie James. "Column, pick your targets, but be careful of Miss Cartwright. Ready, fire at will!"

Suddenly the late afternoon stillness was pierced by the thunderous volley of gunfire directed at the line of gunrunners who were picking their way down the steep front of the rocky cliff.

"Holy shit!" cried Black Bob.

"It's an attack!" cried a gunrunner.

"Get back to the cave!"

"Ayyyy, I'm hit!"

At the same time, with army bullets zipping over his head, the scout dived into the chilly lake and quickly ducked below the glassy surface. Holten's powerful arms pulled him through the crystal clear depths until his wide-open blue eyes finally spotted the secret tunnel's three-foot-wide circular opening.

Feeling his air-starved lungs already beginning to ache, the scout kicked with his long legs and knifed into the darkened tunnel entrance like a fish swimming upstream. The sudden darkness momentarily blinding him, Holten felt his way along the rough sides of the twenty-foot-long rocky tunnel until finally he saw a brightened opening just ahead.

With a final strong leg kick, the scout propelled himself through the remaining several feet of chilly mountain water and burst from the water with a gasp, his aching lungs finally getting some relief and his tired muscles relaxing at last. The gasping Holten held onto the edge of the tunnel opening for several moments and let his hungry lungs get their fill of fresh air.

Finally, hauling his long, lean frame from the narrow tunnel, the scout rose to his full height and found that he was standing in a shadowy passageway somewhere inside the steep cliff near the waterfall. Several shafts of sunlight streaked into the underground tunnel from tiny cracks in the rocks above.

Holten unsheathed his Bowie knife and strode cautiously up the steeply inclined tunnel. His steely eyes pierced the semi-darkness looking for signs of trouble. Somewhere just ahead, he knew, was the rock-covered rear wall of the hidden Pawnee hideout cave. The scout padded along the surprisingly large passageway until finally he heard the staccato sound of gunfire from the other side of a nearby wall. Holten froze in his tracks.

He had reached the gunrunners' cave.

Hearing the gruff voices of the suddenly embattled outlaws on the other side of the wall, the scout started to dig at the rocky partition as quietly as possible with the wide blade of his knife.

Within a few minutes he had broken through.

Peering into the torch-lit cave through the two-inch hole he'd dug with his knife, the scout quickly saw the gunrunners firing back at the soldiers below, Black Bob Callahan directing their attack, and Isabella Cartwright close to the scout at the rear of the cave.

Holten continued to dig quickly until the hole in the rear wall of the cave had widened to about a foot in diameter. Gripping his Bowie knife and tensing his muscles, the scout called softly to Isabella.

"Pssst!" he hissed. "Isabella!"

The blonde from Boston whirled around, her sparkling blue eyes saucering and her pretty face slackening with surprise.

"Who . . . who is it?" she asked in a quavering voice.

"It's me, Holten!"

"Eli!" shrieked the blonde writer.

"Shhh!" cautioned Holten. "They'll hear ya!"

Isabella finally located the scout's small hole in the back of the stone-strewn rear wall of the hideout and slowly edged over to him.

"Are ya all right?" asked the scout, his steely blue eyes quickly scanning Isabella's shapely figure, trying to discern if she'd been harmed.

Gunshots echoed all around them.

"Oh, Eli!" gasped Isabella. "It was terrible! These men are animals!"

"Did they . . . ?" asked the scout quietly.

Isabella lowered her head. "I . . . I didn't have any choice, Eli. They said they were going to . . . to . . ." The luscious honey blonde broke into tears.

Holten grit his teeth. "It's all right," he said, knowing nothing could ever make a gang rape seem all right no matter how much sympathy was given.

Suddenly the cave was alive with bullets.

"The soldiers are chargin'!" yelled a gunrunner.

"Let's get the hell outta here!" cried another.

Black Bob Callahan's gruff voice filled the shadowy hideout. "Get back and fight, you yeller bastards! We ain't finished yet! Hell, we got the woman here. If worse comes to worse, we'll use her to get us free!"

Holten's heart leapt to his throat. Time was running out.

"We gotta get ya outta here!" said Holten quickly.

Holten quickly slipped his Bowie knife back into its sheath and drew his Remington .44 revolver. Then pushing through the rocky wall with all his strength, the water-logged scout burst into the gunrunners' hideout in a sudden cloud of dust.

"Christ, it's the scout!" snapped a gunrunner.

"Shoot the bastard!" cried Black Bob Callahan.

Holten grabbed Isabella's arm. "Get down!" he shouted.

Suddenly the rear wall of the shadowy hideout cave was being peppered with a hail of hot lead from the gang's flaming guns. The scout and Isabella ducked quickly behind the heavy iron stove near some nearby stacks of grub. The huddling duo was suddenly showered with misty rock dust and tiny stone fragments caused by the errant shots that were striking the stone wall above their heads.

Holten waited until there was a lull in the shooting and then shot to his feet. He peered through the thin veil of acrid gunsmoke that was hanging in the air. Then the scout brought his Remington .44 to waist level and squeezed off five quick shots, three of the bullets finding their marks in the chests of three wide-eyed gunrunners who were starting to charge the scout's position near the blackened stove. The screaming gunmen slammed dead to the hard rock floor of the ceremonial cave.

Holten ducked again and started to feed cartridges into his smoking .44. Suddenly a shadow was cast across the huddling scout and his cowering blonde companion. The scout looked up quickly and his heart skipped a beat.

Black Bob was standing nearby aiming a pistol.

"Eli!" cried Isabella Cartwright.

"Duck!" yelled Holten.

But it was too late. Callahan fired his gun.

The speeding .45 slug tore into the scout's left shoulder and spun him around, causing the Remington .44 to fly from his right hand with the impact. Holten sprawled on the floor, his bloody wound feeling as though an Oglala buffalo lance was slicing through his arm. He gazed with a sudden feeling of horror into the gunrunner gang leader's dark-skinned, smiling face.

"Goodbye, scout!" growled Black Bob Callahan.

Suddenly the scout reached into the bottom of the iron stove, grabbed a handful of powdery ashes, and tossed the sooty mess up into the hovering gunrunner's suddenly startled face. Black Bob's dark-skinned countenance was suddenly a gagging ash-covered mask of agony as the stumbling outlaw tried to clear his eyes.

But Black Bob Callahan was a survivor.

While Holten was reaching for his nearby .44 revolver, the bleary-eyed gunrunner was stumbling toward the front of the cave, his Colt .45 Peacemaker spitting fire and lead in the general direction of the scout.

"Get down!" shouted the scout to Isabella. "That son of a bitch is still dangerous!"

"Eli, your arm!" cried the blonde easterner.

"I'm all right for now," said Holten, blinking back the stabbing pain in his shoulder that was threatening to overtake him and blur his vision. "We gotta get the hell outta of this here cave!"

Finally Black Bob's pistol ran out of bullets and the staggering, dark-skinned gang leader ducked near the cave's entrance and tried to wipe his eyes. Suddenly the scout watched the half-blind gunrunner's hands touch the wooden boxes marked DYNAMITE that were stacked in the front of the cave. Callahan suddenly yanked open one of the crates and took out a bundle of dynamite.

Holten felt a sudden jab of anxiety in his gut.

While the scout and Isabella were preparing to dash into the secret passageway at the rear of the cave, Black Bob took a match from his pocket, struck it on the rough-hewn side of one of the dynamite crates, and lit the fuses of the explosives in his hand.

"Eli, that's dynamite!" cried Isabella, her blue eyes saucering.

"Get into the cave!" ordered Holten.

"But what about you?"

"I'll be right on your tail!"

While Isabella Cartwright was stepping through the secret passageway's rocky entrance, Kansas Joe Adderly and Lieutenant Bodie James suddenly appeared at the mouth of the cave, their smoking pistols gripped in their hands and looks of concern etched on their weary faces.

"Holy shit!" cried Kansas Joe when he spotted Black Bob and the sticks of dynamite.

"This is the end, scout!" growled Black Bob. The dark-skinned gunrunner, and the architect of the current Indian uprising that had killed Holten's young bride, suddenly reared back and prepared to toss the flaming sticks of dynamite at the wounded scout.

Holten's .44 spat fire and sent a speeding slug into Black Bob's suddenly exposed chest, the impact of the slug knocking the wide-eyed killer back against the stone side wall of the shadowy cave.

The dynamite fell to the floor.

"Jump into the lake!" cried Holten to the two slack-jawed army men who were standing ten feet away from the ready-to-explode sticks of dynamite.

Then as Bodie James and Kansas Joe Adderly turned on their heels and leaped from the cave toward the shimmering, mountain-fed lake below, the bleeding scout whirled and followed Isabella Cartwright through the narrow passageway that led to the underwater tunnel below.

A deafening explosion rocked the cave.

Holten was nearly knocked off his feet.

"Eli!" cried Isabella, reaching for his hand.

"Keep movin'!" shouted Holten. "Then dive into the water before this here tunnel comes down on top of us!"

With the entire passageway trembling and the very ground beneath their feet quaking from the blast of the dynamite, Holten and the pretty blonde from Boston reached the end of the darkened passageway and slipped into the chilly water. As soon as they splashed into the lake, the passageway behind them collapsed with an ear-shattering roar. Taking deep breaths, the fleeing couple plunged into the water.

Emerging from the secret tunnel with a gasping splash, Holten and Isabella Cartwright quickly began to swim toward the nearby shore. The scout's wounded arm throbbed. Beyond them the ancient Pawnee ceremonial cave located behind the still beautiful waterfall had disappeared beneath tons of falling rock. Several yards away, Bodie James and Kansas Joe Adderly were hauling their water-logged bodies out of the shimmering lake.

Holten stood finally on the shore and helped the exhausted blonde out of the water. The scout nodded slowly and looked toward the heavens.

"That's for you, Yellow Feather," he said in a soft voice, his emotions tightening the back of his throat. "Now ya can rest in peace."

NINETEEN

"Give me some damn chewin' tobacco, Mr. Holten!" said General Frank Corrington from his bed in the infirmary at Fort Sampson.

Holten smiled. "The doc says no tobacco, sir."

"Hell, Holten!" snapped the General. "I'm your commanding officer and I tell ya I need a chaw of tobacco in the worst way!"

The chuckling scout relented and tossed a pouch to his gray-bearded boss, a slight twinge of pain rippling through his bullet wound. The scout's flesh wound in his shoulder had been bloody but not serious. Holten glanced at the wiry officer and was glad Frank Corrington was recovering so rapidly from the ugly war hatchet wound he had received at Fort Rawlins.

Fort Rawlins! And Yellow Feather!

So much had happened since that fateful day when the Pawnee renegades had stormed out of the prairie and attacked the suddenly vulnerable Army outpost. Holten sighed, satisfied now that he had avenged the savage death of his smiling, gentle bride-to-be who had died so young. But he knew, too, that no measure of revenge would bring her back to him.

"So give me the re-cap," said General Corrington, sending an amber stream of fresh tobacco juice ringing into a nearby brass spittoon.

"Well," began the scout, "it seems that Chief Black Spotted Horse survived the Pawnee buffalo stampede and is now back at his camp proudly wearing the peace medal he received, although he's still grieving the loss of his squaw."

The General shook his head. "Those Pawnee sure as hell raised a lot of cain this past week, eh?"

Holten just nodded and continued. "The peace treaty with the Sioux is working well, and I don't think we'll have any problems with renegades breakin' it."

"We all need some peace around here about now," said Frank Corrington, spitting some more tobacco juice into the shiny spittoon.

"And Fort Rawlins should be re-built in a couple of weeks. Lieutenant Bodie James, who did a fine job by the way, is leadin' the column in charge of fixin' the Fort."

"What about the eastern dudes?" asked the General.

Holten smiled. "I don't think we'll have any trouble from the likes of them again. I got a hunch them dudes don't think too much of the prairie!"

"And what about Miss Cartwright?"

The scout chuckled. "She's finishin' some notes about that there book I was tellin' ya about. Seems she feels her stay out here was really worth the trouble she had."

General Corrington shifted his wiry frame atop the creaking Army bed. "Seems like quite a woman, eh Holten?" said the smiling General.

"I'll tell her ya said that, sir," replied Holten as he headed for the infirmary door. "I'm supposed to say goodbye to her in a few minutes. She's headin' for Boston."

"So soon?"

"Says her book is overdue."

"Make sure Miss Cartwright spells my name right in her book, will ya scout?"

Holten smiled and stepped out of the room.

When the scout opened the door to the Fort Sampson

guest quarters, he noticed Isabella Cartwright hunched over the room's modest writing table. The shapely blonde, dressed in a long dress for her trip back East, glanced up quickly and her pretty face brightened.

"Oh, Eli!" she said, her blue eyes sparkling with admiration for the scout. "I'm just finishing up my notes. I'm all packed for my trip, and I can't wait to get home to complete my book!"

The scout closed the door. "I dropped by to say so long," said Holten.

Isabella put down her pen and looked up quickly.

She glanced at the scout.

"Oh, Eli!" she said, getting up and rushing into Holten's strong arms. "I owe you so much! And I'm really going to miss you in Boston!"

"Ya kinda found a spot in my heart, too, Isabella."

The luscious blonde writer looked up into the scout's blue eyes, her admiring gaze searching his leathery face and her long fingers gripping him like a vise.

"I still need a final chapter for my book," she said in a hoarse whisper that was heavy with desire.

"What . . . ?" asked the puzzled scout.

Then Isabella reached out with her long, tapered fingers and quickly started to massage Holten's growing penis through the material of his buckskin pants. The scout flinched at her velvet touch.

"Give me something to remember you by, Eli!"

Holten smiled. "Are ya gonna take notes?"

"I've memorized your body already!"

"And I'll never forget yours, either," said Holten.

"Then take me, Eli, for old times sake!"

Never one to disappoint the ladies, the scout quickly hauled off his sweat-soaked buckskins and in a few moments was standing naked alongside Isabella, who had also peeled off her elaborate travelling dress. Holten's steely eyes quickly scanned the curvaceous blonde's billowy breasts, glistening pubic bush, and bouncing buttocks.

His erection was suddenly enormous.

"Oh, Eli!" gasped Isabella, reaching out for his rock-hard shaft. "I'm going to miss my long, hard friend!" The wide-eyed blonde knelt down and planted a big, wet kiss on the tip of Holten's penis.

Then without warning the panting blonde from Boston escorted the fully aroused scout over to the big brass bed near her writing desk and pulled his lean, naked frame down on top of her soft, supple body. Isabella's big breasts flattened against the scout's matted chest and her warm thighs pressed against his fully grown penis.

"I'm ready, Eli, please!"

Holten touched her waxy bush. "You're already wet!"

"I know!" gasped Isabella.

Without wasting another second the worked-up scout entered the now writhing eastern sexpot and plunged his incredibly long cock deep into her innermost regions, causing the blonde writer to suck in her breath and arch her back to meet his every thrust.

"Fill me to the brim, Eli!"

It was easy for the scout to comply.

After several incredible minutes of plunging again and again into the shrieking blonde's writhing body, the scout finally exploded into her with several shuddering spurts of white hot passion, his fully aroused body finally coming to rest with his wildly beating heart threatening to pound out of his matted chest.

The two lovers lay quiet for several glorious minutes.

Then Holten rose and started to dress.

Finally strapping his weapons to his side, the fully satisfied scout glanced at the smiling blonde who was looking at him from the bed. She was lying naked atop the crumpled sheets, her long legs spread and a dreamy look etched on her pretty face. Holten smiled, walked over to the shapely writer, and kissed her on the forehead.

"Goodbye, Eli," said Isabella Cartwright softly.

"Bye, Isabella," replied Holten.

Then the scout strode purposefully toward the door without looking back. He would never forget Yellow Feather and the life they would have spent together. But Holten was glad Isabella had come into his life when she did. The spirited blonde had helped ease the pain of his loss.

"I'll send you a copy of my book," called the blonde in a voice heavy with emotion.

"Thanks," said the scout over his shoulder.

Then after pausing a moment in the open doorway, the scout closed the pine slab door gently behind him and started to walk toward the livery stable and his gelding. He peered through the gathering dusk, breathed deeply, and thought what a beautiful night it was going to be out on the prairie.

THE SURVIVALIST SERIES
by Jerry Ahern

#1: TOTAL WAR   (768, $2.25)
The first in the shocking series that follows the unrelenting search for ex-CIA covert operations officer John Thomas Rourke to locate his missing famly—after the button is pressed, the missiles launched and the multimegaton bombs unleashed . . .

#2: THE NIGHTMARE BEGINS   (810, $2.50)
After WW III, the United States is just a memory. But ex-CIA covert operations officer Rourke hasn't forgotten his family. While hiding from the Soviet occupation forces, he adheres to his search!

#3: THE QUEST   (851, $2.50)
Not even a deadly game of intrigue within the Soviet High Command, the formation of the American "resistance" and a highly placed traitor in the new U.S. government can deter Rourke from continuing his desperate search for his family.

#4: THE DOOMSAYER   (893, $2.50)
The most massive earthquake in history is only hours away, and Communist-Cuban troops, Soviet-Cuban rivalry, and a traitor in the inner circle of U.S. II block Rourke's path. But he must go on—he is THE SURVIVALIST.

#5: THE WEB   (1145, $2.50)
Blizzards rage around Rourke as he picks up the trail of his family and is forced to take shelter in a strangely quiet Tennessee valley town. Things seem too normal here, as if no one has heard of the War; but the quiet isn't going to last for long!

Available wherever paperbacks are sold, or order direct from the Publisher. Send cover price plus 50¢ per copy for mailing and handling to Zebra Books, 475 Park Avenue South, New York, N.Y. 10016. DO NOT SEND CASH.